Jack Curry

Two and Out

By

John A. Curry

© 2001 by John A. Curry. All rights reserved.

No part of this book may be reproduced, stored in a retrieval system, or transmitted by any means, electronic, mechanical, photocopying, recording, or otherwise, without written permission from the author.

ISBN: 0-7596-6965-1

This book is printed on acid free paper.

Acknowledgments

First thanks to Marcia, Susan, and Sue for their love and encouragement with this book.

My very special thanks to my friend Charles Coffin for his time spent advising and editing.

My gratitude to all who read the manuscript in different incarnations.

Particular thanks to my daughter-in-law Sue Curry for her strong technical assistance with the manuscript. She offered critical advice at critical moments.

Author's Note

Parts of this work are drawn from actual incidents yet <u>Two and Out</u> is a work of fiction.

1

Brian Hughes pushed the blackboard along its track and then timed his turn toward his captive audience for maximum effect. Whirling quickly, he asked his question simultaneously.

"So if you were the investigator, the detective lieutenant in charge of the case, what would you have looked for? Patrice?"

An empty-faced ash blonde looked down on him from halfway up the amphitheater as most of the one hundred university students in attendance looked relieved to have escaped interrogation, if only temporarily.

"I'm sorry, Professor Hughes, but I'm not sure if I understand the question," the petite athletically built sophomore stammered through thin lips.

Brian Hughes paused and grimaced and then ran his hand through his brilliantined hair, acting now to the hilt, assuring that the class members were riveted on him. Acting was an important component of good teaching, he felt. It was the truly disconnected faculty, the pompous asses, who didn't appreciate its value to the learning process.

He smiled at his student. "Ah, Patrice, I'm a bit confused, too. Are you saying you don't understand the question? Or you don't have an answer to my focused query?" He paused, allowing the ripple of laughter to cross the room.

"I guess I just don't have an opinion, Dr. Hughes," Patrice replied softly.

Hughes decided to move on. "Well, do any of you so-called criminal justice majors know where to begin?"

The fat dork in the first row - the one who raised his hand whatever the topic - blurted a response before Hughes could call on any one of the ten or so arms in the air. "I'd look to see if an insider were involved."

Hughes nodded. "Pretty good, Vernon. Not bad. A good investigator always looks first to the inside. Who knows whom?

John A. Curry

Who had a reason? What we're talking about here is motivation. Motivation. And what else?"

He scanned his audience, his eyes jumping about, his enthusiasm evident, his connection with his students complete. "And what else?" he repeated, his left hand circling the air. "And no matter what the motivation, what else could you look for, you investigators of the future!" he implored.

From the second row a bright-eyed, well-dressed yuppie raised his hand. When he was recognized, he grinned at Hughes and said, "Opportunity."

"Very good, Keith. Opportunity is correct. Who had opportunity?" Hughes asked rhetorically as he walked to the podium. "Let me summarize," he said, looking down at his notes and up at the clock. He paused a moment for effect as one hundred future law enforcement professionals shifted their attention to their notebooks.

"We're talking here today about the most critical points I can make regarding a major felony, particularly a high profile robbery. First, the people who pulled off the Brinks heist - Joe McGinnis, Mike Geagan, all of them - were smart. They killed no one back there in 1950. And that was critical because the authorities then faced a statute of limitations. With a murder, as I said earlier, there would have been no statute of limitations. They don't receive enough credit for being intelligent. Second, as they planned the job, they thought like the investigators. They anticipated. And third, you as an investigator-to-be have to always put yourself into that thinking man's realm. Always, and I mean always, begin with those two words - motivation and opportunity - imbedded in your brain cells.

"The Brinks job here in Boston in the '50s and the Brinks Depot heist in Rochester, New York, in the '90s are great case studies for us. We'll continue our discussion on Thursday, but in the meantime re-read that November 14, 1993, <u>New York Times</u> article on the Rochester case and be ready to discuss why in both cases the perpetrators were caught."

Two and Out

In the distance the bell rang and like track sprinters they flew out of their seats before any second bell might ring, declaring them guilty of a false start.

Brian Hughes collected his notes and stepped away from the podium, his crystal blue eyes warmly surfing the departing crowd, returning their nods of approval with a relaxed smile. But he felt something different as he mingled with them as they descended the steps from Shillman Hall to the Centennial Common. He loved imparting his knowledge of the criminal justice system, his years of study coming to the fore, controlling the classroom situation where he was master; but he hated the life itself, the idiot students, the long hours and the short pay. Turning to the south behind Northeastern University, he headed for the Leon Street parking lot and his 1993 Ford Taurus. Glancing at his watch, he thought he could make it to Lynn in half an hour at this time of day.

At 2:00 PM Johnny Casey climbed the steps to the Church of the Sacred Heart on Boston Street in Lynn. He pulled open the huge oaken door and walked lethargically to a bench halfway down the center aisle, genuflecting before entering the pew and then sitting ever so briefly before he knelt on the maroon pad. He was the only parishioner in the church.

He had a face like an Irish wolfhound, angular and homely with a neatly trimmed gray mustache above a crooked nose. He looked about him as if discovering the church for the first time, although, since he had lost his public school teaching job, he came here every day to sit and to contemplate, ever in search of answers. He loved to stare at the luminous windows made of expensive stained glass and at the depictions of the Stations of the Cross, which reminded him of his own suffering, and of his having disappointed God so often over the years.

Sighing, he found himself wishing for a drink, but he knew it was too early to start. Yet, he could almost taste it now, the Jack

Daniels biting his tongue, swirling in his mouth, before it hit his head, allowing him to forget today and yesterday as well. He had shamed the priesthood, had failed his God, had lost his wife and daughter and was now virtually friendless, a disgrace both as a man of God and as a man. Absorbed in himself, he scarcely heard the sound of approaching footsteps before Brian Hughes tapped his shoulder, motioning him to move over.

"How goes the battle, Johnny?" Hughes asked, studying his face for signs of the real answer.

"We can't talk in here, Brian. Not in the House of God. Let's go," he responded, standing in place.

Hughes shrugged his shoulders. "Then why did you ask me to meet you here?"

"We can walk across the street to Barry Park," he whispered. "I only meant for us to meet here, not to discuss this awful business in God's presence. Shit!"

Hughes laughed, almost too loudly. "Not very good language for a former servant of God," he said as they moved to the aisle.

Descending the steps they crossed Boston Street and walked into the deserted park, the grass just now beginning to overrun the baseball diamond, the hundred-yard-long concrete stands still wet from the past evening's rain.

"We can sit over here," Johnny gestured, pointing to the stands. "No one comes here in the fall. We'll be alone."

Brian breathed deeply, inhaling the smells of early fall - the clear, cool air and the pungent scent of apples from the trees in surrounding yards. They sat in the third row.

"Every fall reminds me of our years at the Heights," Hughes smiled, stretching his legs. "And of you especially, Johnny, and the football season. You were something else."

Casey grimaced. "That was a long time ago. I don't think much on it anymore."

"Not so long, Johnny. 1984. And you were superb. The best tackle the Eagles ever had," Brian replied, smiling.

"Fifteen years is long ago," Casey muttered. "At least to me it is."

His eyes scanning the horizon, Brian thought back to their years at Boston College. He had first met the big tackle from Lynn in the Western Civilization course they had taken together as freshmen. Father Maxwell's staggered seating plan found him beside the jovial all-scholastic athlete who befriended him almost immediately. As an honors graduate of the Bronx High School of Science with a full academic freshman scholarship, Brian's natural arrogance was tempered by a desire to be accepted, to be apart but also to be a part of some group. And decidedly Johnny Casey needed help academically. Despite the outward veneer, he felt inadequate, hiding his self-doubt about his ability to handle the college work. And so, over a short time, out of an unexpressed mutual need, they became friends.

Fascinated by the world of athletics, Brian attended every BC football game over his four years. Because of Johnny's status with the team, Brian became accepted as an unofficial member. In his junior year he roomed on campus with Johnny because Casey had insisted on it and the coaches - no fools - recognized the positive influence Brian already had on Johnny's classroom performance. Ever since that first year he had helped Johnny organize himself, taught him short cuts to academic understanding, looked at his key papers before Johnny submitted them, generally leading him to a performance that he probably otherwise was incapable of. Brian coasted through the four years himself, always positioned in the top ten percent of their class, engaging the faculty in sharp, crisp exchanges, his haughtiness lessened along the way thanks to Johnny's ability to soften him socially, to teach him to relax with people, to bury somewhat that superior self lurking beneath the surface.

And in particular, their senior year was the most glorious of all. In the fall Brian traveled with the team to the Orange Bowl in Miami where Doug Flutie threw the "Miracle in Miami" pass to upset the great Bernie Kosar and the University of Miami in a game that will always live in the annals of Eagle football. And on their return Brian learned of his acceptance to the master's degree law enforcement program at John Jay College in New York City, a full tuition ride complete with an assistantship for the two years. Then, within a month, Johnny made the choice between a possible professional football career and the priesthood.

Casey bent down to the bleacher step, picked up a loose rock, and scaled it across the brown grass. He sighed and turned to look at his friend. "I'm not sure of this, Brian. Not sure at all."

Brian Hughes threw a playful right hand to Johnny's jaw and embraced him. "Hey, boyo. Relax. I've got it all planned. In and out in five minutes. Minimum exposure. A breeze."

"A breeze up my ass is more likely, Brian. It's just not me. What do I know about a fuckin' armed robbery? And how much time are we talkin' about if we're caught?"

"First of all, we won't be caught. I'm telling you this is fuckin' foolproof. Look, let's go over it again."

"Go over my ass with a lawnmower, Brian, if you like, but I still don't like anything to do with it."

"Johnny, I'm telling you the Brinks people are asleep at the throttle. Listen to me, my friend. Can we at least go over it one time?" Brian pleaded.

Casey offered sleepy eyes, as he looked back toward the church, extending his view above Brian's head, refusing to look him in the eye. "All right," he conceded. "One more time and that's it."

Brian smiled in his direction while simultaneously rolling his hand through his hair. "Good. Then listen carefully, Johnny, and process the information and make the right decision. I need you, and you need this."

He shifted his position, sitting a bit more erect, the idea of the caper again overwhelming him, causing his adrenaline to flow, his attention riveted on the moment.

"What's the date, Johnny? The third of September right? Autumn's in New York and it's here, too, Johnny. A chance for rejuvenation, renewal for you and a chance for a big lifetime score for both of us. Think of that, will you? Two heists within two weeks, and we'll both have enough money to retire - to start something new in life. To start a new life, for Christ's sake, buddy."

Casey shook his head, slowly back and forth. "I'm not a thief, Brian. Whatever else I am."

Brian sighed audibly and pounded his right hand with his left. "And what the hell are you, Johnny? Look at yourself will you? No job. A big problem with the hard stuff and with gambling. No family now. What the hell are you, Johnny, and where are you going?"

Casey stared hard at him, his eyes narrowing, his lips thinning. "I have my memories, Brian, and I have my pride," he responded, his voice reedy and weak.

"Screw the past, Johnny. Think about the future. Think about what you can become." He paused, seeking the right words.

"We've been friends for fifteen years, and you know I care for you, Johnny. I'm telling you this whole thing is going to go perfectly. I've planned it so. You have confidence in me, don't you?"

Johnny Casey nodded slowly. Today he felt more depressed than manic. "Go on, I'm listening."

"I was saying, it's early September and the slow-witted adolescents are back in class. Now the tuition payments have been made, and there's not much straight cash in all of that anyway - what with checks and all-year friggin' payment plans. There's no one dealing in much cash up in the cashier's cage.

"But the ATMs in the student center - now that's another story. Every day, for the first two weeks of the quarter, they are loaded with cash. Cash from mama and papa to buy food, books, for living expenses, to buy the booze that the parents swear the kid never drank until he arrived at the university two weeks ago. Did I tell you how much cash we're talking about on a daily basis?"

Johnny nodded. "You said something about three ATMs inside the student center, each containing maybe $100,000 late in the afternoon. Brought in by Brinks every day."

"That's right. $300,000 altogether this time of the term. Plus at least another million in the Brinks truck itself."

"But what about security?"

Brian leaned forward. "And that's the beauty of the whole plan, my friend. There's no way that you can easily get to the tuition cash. They take it out to Fleet Bank via hourly pick-ups so that at any one time there's little cash exposure - if there's much cash at all, as I said earlier.

"But with the ATMs the Brinks guards come in once a day laden down with cash, bringing it into us like gifts from the Magi. We just take it from them. I've watched them over four different terms now, and everyday their procedure is the same. They..."

Casey interrupted him by placing his hand on Brian's knee. "I'm no professional, and neither are you. Even if we possibly pull it off, how can we get away with it?"

Hughes narrowed his eyes. Pausing for effect, he replied. "Because we will never be suspected - no motivation, no opportunity, therefore, no suspicion."

Johnny Casey regarded his friend closely. He still looked good. He had all his hair - the black cover hiding the gray that was only just beginning to appear around the temples, the skin as unlined as it had been in college.

"And what about the second job?" he finally said.

Brian shook his head. "Let's not get into that at all until after the first one. The fewer people who know, the less chance for a major fuck-up. No one knows anything about the second one but me, and let's leave it like that for now, Johnny."

The afternoon sun attempted a last golden burst through the clouds as they were quiet a long moment, both thinking through the conversation. Casey first broke the silence. "I need more details on the Brinks hit."

"And I need an answer, Johnny, before you, me, some others talk more about details." He spoke quietly but forcefully.

"Can you give me one more day, Brian?"

"Then, that's it," Brian nodded. "One more day, Johnny. And let's set the place and time."

"I'll meet you at the Kernwood over in Lynnfield tomorrow night at 7 PM."

Hughes stood, his back to the ball field. "Be with me, boy. I need you on this one, and we'll both end up on the fuckin' beach in Aruba, all worries behind us."

Casey ran his tongue along his lower lip. He needed a beer, a Pellegrino, a Jack Daniels, anything that would calm him down. Something to allow the depression to set in, to overwhelm the mania.

"See you tomorrow," he said, stepping down from the bleachers.

2

Mike Fallon's eyes opened to blackness, but he was quickly all the way awake, catapulted by some kind of jack-in-the-box mechanism that had taken over his body this past half year, ever since Rita had been diagnosed. But yet he didn't move. He lay there, listening for his wife's sound. He heard the regularity of her even breathing as she slept on.

He lay there thinking about getting through another day. As an FBI agent, he needed not only to get through the days but also to contribute to their passing, to do more than take up oxygen, which was all he felt he was accomplishing lately. When the long nightmare began, when he felt he still possessed some analytical ability, he had tried to get through the days by sheer willpower. But little by little, his focus had splintered, the base of his life disconnecting, separating.

Now, six months later, he could concentrate for five minutes. If he could function and focus for that, and then a few minutes later focus again for another five minutes, he was pleased. Recently he had stopped the jogging in order to have more time with Rita, switching to sit-ups, driving himself hard, and trying to tire himself physically and shake the mental doldrums. And yet, even when so very tired, he could never really sleep.

He sat erect, and as quietly as possible swung his legs from the bed.

The Fallons lived in a duplex on St. Botolph Street in Boston, and as Mike threw handfuls of water to his face he witnessed the thin veneer of pink hanging in the eastern sky out the window over the sink.

His job now was to start the family moving, get the breakfast going, but he felt now as he had every morning for months. He really couldn't move himself. He couldn't face what had to be done. And yet he couldn't remain paralyzed for long. He just had to stop thinking so much.

Two and Out

Long ago he and Rita had decided on a split of domestic chores. He had always helped with heavy cleaning; he'd fixed things; he lifted. In turn, Rita took care of the three girls from their birth - Jessica, Nicole, and Melissa.

But now it was all on him. And how could he do it all? As the flow of self-pity consumed him, he braced his arms and hands on either side of the sink, trying to fight the feeling. How could he balance a job, the need to care for Rita and the three kids when it had taken both of them every bit of energy to accomplish chores together?

He raised his head and looked at the ribbon of pink once again. It had not grown appreciably wider.

For the next half-hour he busied himself making ham and cheese sandwiches, his every-other-day chore. The only item the kids would eat at school was pizza, and Rita had insisted on some nutritional balance.

"What are you doing, Dad?" a blue-eyed blond fifteen-year-old asked from the pantry entrance, her posture erect, her antennae on alert.

"What's it look like I'm doing, sweetie, wrestling with alligators?"

She folded her arms across her chest. "Mom puts mustard on the sandwich, not butter you know? It's the way I like it."

"I stand corrected. How you doing?"

She marched confidently toward him. "Good. Let me help you, Dad. You get the breakfast, and I'll finish the sandwiches."

"Sounds like a good deal. How's oatmeal sound for today?"

"If we must," she sighed.

"That's what I like - a little enthusiasm," he said, tugging at her long ponytail.

She turned and reached her arms around his neck, a forlorn look crossing her face. "How's Mom today?" she asked.

"Sleeping right now. Can you go upstairs for me and ask the two little ones to be quiet so she can sleep more?"

"Sure, Dad. Only they aren't so little, at 12 and 10," she retorted, today as on every day, doing her best to play lady of the house while hurting like the little girl she still was.

Having just gotten them off to school, he closed the door and closed his eyes, fighting off the tired feeling he felt almost twenty-four hours a day now. He thought of the workday ahead, both here and downtown. He had three robberies under investigation and no thoughts on any of them, something he was sure had also been noted by his superiors.
"Mike, have they gone?" Rita, suddenly awake, called from the bedroom.
"Gone, but not forgotten," he yelled, as he ascended the staircase.
From the doorway he noted his wife had already propped herself up and was smiling at him.
"Have a good night?" he asked.
"Best night in the last few weeks," she replied, eyes searching his face as he sat on the bed.
"You look like shit, though," she said, a delicate finger working over his beard. "Your bags have bags."
"Actually I'm trying to fool the crooks by not appearing like my usual warm and fuzzy self."
She laughed. "Well, I think you're succeeding."
He touched her hair. "So how about some tea? Coffee? Sex?"
"H'm. Don't tempt me. Maybe first I should just get up."
"You sure?"
"Mike, I had a really good night. I want to try walking around more today."
"Then maybe sex later?" he teased.
"Much later," she laughed. "You don't mind do you, Mike?" she asked placing one hand in his.
He smiled at her. "Rita," he began squeezing her hand firmly into his, "you're my life. The only true one in the world.

I want to do only what you want to do. And I'm never disappointed, never, ever. You understand me?"

A small tear formed in her eye and slowly ran down her cheek. "Just hug me, honey."

He looked out the window, noticing the ribbon had now broadened considerably, the thin sliver now covering the entire East Coast with new life. At least he and Rita had this morning. He would try to keep cheerful for the next few minutes, which then would become a half-hour, then an hour, and later an afternoon. And maybe tomorrow morning would find her as well as this morning. And maybe God in His wisdom would find some way to keep every morning the same.

3

Tony Amonti opened up his Mustang on the Nahant Causeway. The 5.0 liter engine pushed the 1990 maroon vehicle up to 75. At this nine o'clock hour traffic was flowing toward Lynn in the opposite direction. There was no sign of the law, and he felt exhilarated what with the chance to push the Mustang.

He slowed at the end of the Causeway and pulled into a parking space, facing Lynn Beach. Killing the engine, he scanned the area, concentrating on the curving stretch of sand leading back to Lynn. In the long distance a length of walled stone thirty feet high prevented the waves from crashing into the circuitous boulevard which led drivers into Swampscott and on to Marblehead.

When he saw the solitary figure walking close to the shoreline, now about a half mile away, he got out of the car and descended to the sandy beach, walking directly to the water fifty yards ahead. Once there, he turned toward Lynn and the man coming his way.

Hungry gulls swept over the beach, peeling in squadrons of four or five as they zeroed in on the largely forsaken beach hopeful that remnants of summer were still obtainable. Ahead of him an unleashed cocker spaniel ran frantically toward the water, bounded into the sea, scooped up a tennis ball, and ran quickly back to its master.

Tony bent down, selected a flat, glossy rock and scaled it toward the waves. Turning, he observed the man walking confidently toward him. He looked unhealthy, maybe in his sixties. His complexion was the color of modeling clay; his facial skin pulled down, exposing deep crevices in his cheeks. He had the look of a man who had seen much of life, and who wouldn't be seeing much more of it. He pulled at the belt of a

Two and Out

charcoal gray trench coat and then nodded at Tony as he closed to his side.

"Tony Amonti?" he asked, looking directly into the younger man's eyes.

"You got it, sport. In the flesh."

The gray man put on his don't-fuck-with-me face. "In or out?"

Tony pulled open his sport jacket and found the Newports. He searched his side pocket for the Bic lighter, in the process exhibiting a solid and rangy build. He stared back at the man, pausing deliberately, giving as hard a time as he felt he was getting. "I need to know some more about both heists. Right now I know shit about the second one and only a little more than that about the first."

"You know all you're going to know for now, pal. In or out? Right now I need to know," the gray man replied.

"Fuck you, sport. Go for another wheel man if that's your attitude."

The gray man stared at him for a long time. "Then it's out and thank you for your time." He pivoted and walked briskly away.

Tony started after him. "Hey! Wait up a fuckin' minute, will you? I was just lookin' for some info, that's all. Count me in."

The gray man turned around, a self-satisfied smile running across his heavy wrinkles. "Good. That's good, son. So now listen up because I'm going to say this only once."

Tony averted his eyes and bent for another rock. He turned toward the charging waves and flung it, hopefully demonstrating his disdain silently.

"Today's Tuesday. They'll be a meeting on Thursday where you'll learn the full details. The first job's going down this Friday at 2 P.M. So make no plans for either day. You know where Hood Park is in Lynn?"

"I can find it," Tony replied, bending in search of another missile.

"Then be there at 1 P.M. Thursday."

As he watched the gray man move away, he thought back to this early morning before the drive up from the Cape. Over a year ago he had rented the trailer in Dennisport for Sandy and for Doug. But now it was all falling apart. This morning had proved it anyway, what with the shouting and bickering all over again.

"What am I supposed to do with this check? Use it to wipe my ass?" Sandy had snapped at him. "Big fuckin' race track driver you are," she chided. "Never in the money and now driving taxis all over Cape Cod for piss."

He had glared at her. "Stow it, Sandy. Not in front of the kid. How many times I got to tell you?"

Fuming, she stood up at the tiny table and moved to the sink. "He doesn't know his own fuckin' name, never mind what I'm talking about."

From the rectangular table the seven-year-old stared without expression at the thin auburn-haired woman.

He had tried to stay calm, for the boy's sake. "Jesus, Sandy. You never used to talk like this when we started out."

"When we started out, Tone? I didn't figure the race would be over just after we started, y' know? A few laps around the track, and we're dead last. Look at this shithouse, will you? The summer's over, you're not making any money, and I'm supposed to care for a retarded kid."

He had met the track groupie up at Loudon last racing season. A drink or three had led to her bed, and from there to what he thought was mutual attraction and admiration. She had moved in with him and Doug, initially showing interest in the boy, with even some small demonstrations of her having accepted him.

He flinched and stole a glance at Doug. Dressed in a soiled sports shirt and blue jeans, the blond boy looked to Tony, his

Two and Out

eyes now a bit more alert, a smile touching the corners of his mouth.

Standing, Tony tousled his son's hair, memories of his wife's death in childbirth returning as they so often did when he looked at Doug. "It's almost time for the school bus man. Go on out to the street now, son," he had directed.

The boy nodded, stood, and offered his face to his father. Tony had embraced and kissed him, then gently pushed him toward the door.

And now, as he left Lynn Beach, he knew it would not work with Sandy. He had to get away, take the boy with him, leave her behind, and somehow start a new life - maybe in California. Find a school, a good private school for Doug. But he would need money for all that. The two heists would provide it.

4

The gray man decided to cross Boylston Street in front of the Four Seasons Hotel. As he waited, he stood for a minute watching the well-dressed and the self-indulgent drive up to the entrance, disengage themselves from their Mercedeses and Lexuses and stroll arrogantly and confidently toward lunches that most of them could stand to forsake.

When the light changed at Arlington and Boylston, he moved toward the Public Gardens, entering through a side entrance, strolling leisurely to the park benches on the edge of the swan boat lagoon. The sun peeked through the trees, its strong light rushing diagonally toward the grassy areas. Near the benches young guides gathered large groups of meandering students together, urging hand holding as they prepared to move toward the swan boat boarding area.

Up twenty yards or so, Phil Hanrahan, the gray man, spotted Vic Fleming feeding the pigeons as he shelled peanuts and then sent both peanuts and shells onto the pavement five yards in front of him. Without a greeting, the gray man sat down next to the retired Boston police captain.

"How did it go, Phil?" the captain asked, his eyes riveted on the dirty birds devouring their newly found fortune.

"A little bullshit, but he's in," the gray man replied.

Fleming threw him a quick look. "Bullshit about what?"

"Him not knowing much about job one or job two."

"Fuck him. You told him he doesn't need to know?"

"It's okay, Vic. All taken care of."

Fleming turned toward him, as if looking at him for the first time. At sixty-seven Fleming's silver gray hair was still all there. A tanned and angular face featured hollow cheekbones and a nose broken more than once. His piercing blue eyes sought the gray man's and locked in.

"I'm depending on you, Phil. We okay with this?"

"Captain, after what you did for my family and me? No one's ever going to know anything from me."

Fleming nodded. Back in 1982, Phil Hanrahan had been robbed and pistol-whipped one snowy January night at his Park Drive liquor store just behind Fenway Park. Two men, Black pros from Mattapan, had taken over $25,000 from a safe and left Hanrahan, an ex-boxer, badly hurt. Through careful work Vic Fleming had turned one suspect against the other within a day and recovered the $25,000 in its entirety.

From the perpetrators, Fleming had also found the source of Hanrahan's money—the illicit preparation of fake passports for favored customers. He had visited the badly beaten proprietor in the hospital and suggested an arrangement. For a $5,000 cut of the $25,000 and a similar percentage from future illicit business, Fleming would bury the truth from his superiors. Because Hanrahan had no police record, no one would believe the Black pros if they caused a problem. Just destroy any evidence regarding the counterfeits now before the Black guys went to trial, Fleming had cautioned. From that night a working partnership and a friendship had evolved.

"Thanks, Phil. Remember, whatever happens in the future you never met this driver guy. Right?"

"No problem, captain," he said, always being sure half the time to pay the retired policeman respect by addressing him with his old title while the other half utilizing his first name.

"You know the next step, Phil. I'll see you over the weekend then," he said as he stood and threw the empty peanut bag toward the receptacle. He grabbed Hanrahan's hand, pumped it vigorously, and walked briskly in the direction of Beacon Street.

5

Brian Hughes spent the wait staring at the blond secretary in the main office of the College of Criminal Justice. She knew he was observing her so she posed - first looking out the first story window at the students changing classes and then at her computer. And then a few strokes to show him she knew her business. Next she templed her hands under her chin - contemplative, he thought, again for his sake.

Suddenly the door swung open and Dean Perry Johnson moved to greet him. He was a middle-aged, mid-sized man carrying too much weight, draped in the poor fit of a double-breasted vested black suit. He wore small round glasses that only accentuated his general flabbiness.

"Brian, please come in," he said cheerfully, waving his faculty member forward with his left hand.

Once in his well-appointed office, he made sure to position himself behind the desk, indicating that Brian should sit in one of the two straightbacks fronting him.

"I appreciate your stopping by what with the opening of school and all that," the dean began.

As if he had any choice, Brian thought.

"I need to speak to you about a delicate matter, Brian, one we've talked about before unfortunately," he continued. He opened a manila file centered on his desk and began reading.

"You graduated from Boston College in 1985, fifteen years ago. Went on to John Jay for your master's and to NYU for your doctorate. All completed on time, all completed with distinction and with great promise. You attained full-time faculty status at John Jay, but, as you know, failed to gain tenure at the end of your six-year probationary period.

"We, too, felt you had promise. Your teaching record is simply superb with outstanding evaluations from fellow faculty and from our students. You've now been here five years, and we, like John Jay, face the tenure decision this coming spring."

Brian sat erect, assuring his body language connoted his concern, knowing what was coming, and caring less. Was there a more cutthroat business than academia? With his plans now set, with the team practically set, with only three days before the heist, he felt relaxed, exhilarated, in command. Who cared about this recitation of the obvious when in just three weeks he would be a multi-millionaire? But for now, he awaited the other shoe, the infamous "but" word. His teaching might be superior, but he hadn't published. He could say the words for the dean, if the dean allowed. Pay attention, he commanded himself.

"We'll go through the full process this fall, Brian," Dean Johnson continued, "but your record of scholarship is decidedly wanting. There's your dissertation, a few articles in less than prestigious journals, but no book, no major contribution to the field of criminal justice."

Give me the next three weeks and I'll make a contribution to the field that will make all of you forget the Brinks job, Brian mused.

"But I want to be fair with you, Brian. You've been good for the College and for our students. Anticipate a negative vote from the tenure committee, from me, from the provost and the trustees. Start looking for another position so that come next September you have something."

Come next September, I'll be sitting on the beach in Aruba, or down at Lido Beach in Sarasota, or enjoying the Las Vegas good life, Brian reflected.

But it was critically important that he play the game. "Perry, I thank you for the advice. And I know you people will treat me fairly. Look, I should finish the book this winter, and I have two or three articles awaiting review in the Journal of Criminology. I'm optimistic, Perry. I really am. I feel I've earned tenure."

He observed the older man shifting his position, discomforted, and knew it was time to excuse himself. He stood and extended his hand. "Whatever the outcome, Perry, thanks for your advice throughout all this."

Pompous ass, he almost said aloud, as he turned to take one more look at the blond. She would look good on the beach in Aruba.

6

Vic Fleming lived in a small house in Revere that screamed of yellow clapboard siding and maroon asphalt shingles. The houses on Sargent Road were crunched together so closely that you had better not have drunk too much on the way back to the old homestead at night.

At three o'clock in the afternoon, he sat by himself in the living room sipping Dewar's on the rocks, gaining that heady feeling that only the good hard stuff provided. He smirked, reflecting on the new age pansy men who favored wine, engaging themselves in the elaborate ritual of inspecting, sniffing, and sipping before nodding at a waiter as if accepting the keys to the kingdom.

His home was appointed to match his tastes and because he hardly ever invited company his library was devoted strictly to her. She really wasn't a real beauty what with the high forehead, the upturned nose, the almost too plump cheeks, but those eyes - no one had eyes like Alice Faye's. Vividly blue, they expressed the integrity of their owner. It was, indeed, the Faye eyes that moviegoers of the 30's and 40's loved and that he, a real fan, couldn't resist to this day.

On each wall he had hung posters. On the left wall the placard from Irving Berlin's "Alexander's Ragtime Band" with the stunningly handsome Tyrone Power embracing her; and on the opposite wall the poster featuring Alice's rendition of the 1944 academy award winner "You'll Never Know" from "Hello Frisco, Hello," in his mind the best love song ever written.

He sat simply enjoying the moment as he played the CD from that movie, the wistfully plaintive Faye voice tugging away at him as she sang of misplaced love.

He loved things of the past, enjoyable caught memories from his youth, because, in reflection, what did he have of the present to inspire him? Widowed for three years now, he lived alone, almost seventy years old, waiting for death, put out to pasture with a pension - enough to live comfortably in Revere, but not enough to live the life he desired. He wanted Los Angeles, preferably, with side trips to San Francisco. A new life in the Golden State.

When last he had visited the City of Angels, he had treated himself, staying at the Plaza in Century City, just a short walk to the intersection with Pico Boulevard and the home studios of 20th Century Fox. Just think, he had contemplated, looking down from a pedestrian bridge above at the old western towns, the storefronts, New York Avenue - this is precisely where Alice Faye had made "Tin Pan Alley" with Betty Grable in 1940.

With the upcoming scores, he would be self-sufficient at last, able finally to move to the Coast, lose himself in a great climate, maybe even meet some show people. With real money to supplement his pension, he could even attract some starlet, a girl on the make who valued a man like him - a man with money, a connected ex-cop who, if things went right, could open doors for her. If that fuckin' deviant Anthony Quinn could find a 30-year-old at 85, then he had a chance as well.

When his cell phone rang, he was pulled back to the present, a place where he was beginning to feel increasingly comfortable now because soon, with the two heists, he would be securing the future and moving away from the fuckin' cold. This just had to be his last season in the freezer.

"Yeah?" he answered.

"Victor, my main man. It's your favorite felon."

"Convict is the better word."

"Now, now, Captain. Let's not get nasty," Wayne Greer laughed.

"What have you got for me, Wayne?"

"Got the shit you wanted, Captain. Two Glock 9's, a 357 Mag, the automatic machine pistol - all present and accounted for."

"Wayne, did you do what I asked?"

"Captain, you think Wayne Greer got shit for brains or somethin'? Now maybe I didn't get to go to Latin School, but livin' over in Southie with those Irish fuckers caused me to do some serious thinking. Like so I could survive."

Fleming yelled into the phone. "Wayne, cut the Black crap. Are the fuckin' guns traceable or aren't they?"

"Captain, what's that Fed Express ad say - 'Absolutely, positively guaranteed to get there the next day'? Well Wayne Greer's here today with the shit in hand and the same guarantee. When do you take delivery?"

"I'll call you tomorrow, convict."

Greer laughed. "We niggers don't like to be dis'd, Captain. What's that fuckin' dead man's music in the background anyway?"

"You wouldn't understand," Fleming replied.

"Thank Christ for that," Greer said before hanging up.

7

Johnny Casey had always felt there was no drink as good as the first one. He let the VO and water ease into him. There was nothing in the whole world as perfect, as beautiful as that first drink - not sex, not friends, not drugs, no other form of ecstasy.

Before calling Donna he needed the drink and later, before he even reached the Kernwood, he would have had one or two more until his mind clouded over and he could forget to think about any decisions that needed to be made. He looked forward to that feeling of numbness, that descent into depression as it won its forever battle with his manic side.

For a moment, trying to gather courage from the amber, he just sat in the living room looking around at his circumstances. The silence pressed in on him from all around the three-room apartment on Lewis Street in Lynn. The walls were painted white and were basically bare except for a huge crucifix on the left and a painting of the Last Supper on the opposite wall. He sat on a purple-colored couch with oak arms and across from him were two matching easy chairs. Outdated newspapers were strewn around the room.

Standing slowly, he walked to the kitchen where yesterday's dishes lay stacked on the counter. Sighing, he dialed her number and tried to rehearse his words, fearful that the one shot might already have had an effect on him.

"Hello," a pleasant male voice answered.

"Steve, this is Johnny. How are you doing?"

"Fine, Johnny, just fine. You want to speak to Donna?" Steve asked in his usual friendly manner.

"She there?"

"Hold on. Just a minute."

He sipped his drink while he waited, the cubes clanking a bit too loudly.

"What do you want, Johnny?" his ex-wife asked in that tone which only meant she didn't care what he wanted.

"And good evening to you too, Donna! I was hoping I could speak to Laura."

A loud sigh came through the instrument. "Johnny, how many times do I have to tell you. She doesn't want to talk to you. Now you can go to court, get some judge to grant you visitation rights again, but she doesn't want to see you or talk to you. What can I do?"

"You could try to explain to her, Donna. You could try to influence her decision," he replied evenly.

Donna gave out another sigh and then paused before responding. "Johnny, don't you think I've tried to influence her? God knows I've tried, Johnny. But how do you explain to a twelve-year-old that since her parents divorced six years ago her father, with full visitation rights, living in the same city, couldn't see her more than two times a year, and even then would fall asleep on her more than half that time?"

"I know, I know, Donna. But I've been feeling better lately and..."

"What's the clinking sound, Johnny? You at the stuff already?" she interrupted.

"Just the one, Donna. Just one."

"And what was it the psychiatrist told you? No drinking. Not with your depression problem, and not mixed with Prozac."

"Those psychiatrist assholes are sicker than I am," he replied.

Her voice softened. "Look, Johnny, Steve and I were just getting ready to go out. I need to cut this short."

"Will you let her know I called?" he pleaded.

"She's not here right now, but I will tell her, Johnny. All right?"

"Donna, one other thing. I'm not angry. I hope you know that. And I appreciate your trying with her, you know?"

"I understand, Johnny. I have to go now."

"Okay. I'll call you soon."

With the click, the silence swept in even stronger. He stood there for a long moment. What decision did he really need to make? What more would be lost that already hadn't been lost?

Two hours and three drinks later he drove his green '95 Grand Marquis onto Walnut Street in Lynnfield and turned into the vast parking lot of the Kernwood Restaurant. At least once a month he met Brian at their favorite restaurant, at the elongated bar across from the fireplace with the piano accompaniment in the background.

He slid onto the barstool next to Brian who was busily engaged in conversation with Ray, the affable bartender who was as much a draw as the wonderfully consistent food provided by the Konaris family.

"Gilkey couldn't hit the water if he fell out of a boat," Brian was saying.

"Yeah, the Yankees pick up guys like David Justice, Glenallen Hall, Denny Neagle, all guys to contribute in the stretch run and we bring on lightweights like Gilkey and the San Diego guy - what's his name?" Ray asked, setting a glass in front of Johnny.

"Ed Sprague," Brian volunteered. "Fuckin' Duquette brings back Saberhagen from the dead and thinks that means every National Leaguer who was ever injured belongs with the Red Sox."

"What you guys know about baseball couldn't fill a Topps card," Johnny said, pointing to the long line of bottles behind Ray.

"My. Aren't we in a pleasant mood," Brian rejoined.

To their right two noisy well-dressed businessmen were debating the merits of the two presidential candidates.

"Bush's an asshole," said the taller man.

"Well the other guy walks like a robot. Looks like he's got a pole up his ass. Next he'll be saying he invented Trojans. He takes credit for everything else."

Brain waited until Johnny had his VO. "Let's get something to eat," he said, sliding off the stool and pointing to a vacant table for two next to the fireplace.

They ordered from a waitress who wore so many earrings and bracelets, she sounded like a wind chime. When she left, Brian leaned forward. "And so?" he asked.

Johnny more gulped than sipped the VO. "I tried calling Laura again earlier tonight," he said.

"I gather it didn't go well," Brian replied.

Johnny's eyes were filmy. "Donna's no problem. She really tries I think, but the kid won't see me, call me, nothing."

"How's the stepfather been acting?"

"Huh. There's the rub. Steve's a good guy; everything I'm not to Laura. Nobody says anything - him or Donna - but they have a new life and I'm no part of it. End of subject."

Brian tented his fingers under his chin and waited until he had Johnny's full attention. "Johnny, I hope you thought long and hard about Friday. We're only three days away now. I need to know now if you're in or out."

Johnny finished the last of his drink. "I'm in, Brian. I need something different in my life. I need to get away from Lynn. Begin again somewhere. Maybe try teaching somewhere close to the sea -Sarasota or Naples. There's nothing much for me here anymore. I'm in, but I'm still worried. I'm no fuckin' pro."

Brian remembered a time when Johnny Casey would never swear. When he finished his senior year at BC and chose to enter the seminary, he was committed to God. It had never been clear to Brian what had happened within those walls, but a few years later, Johnny had come out a changed man. And a year after his ordination he left the priesthood. There had been his own explanation of a less than full commitment to God and the Church, and then the beginnings of heavy drinking. In time, he had met and eventually married Donna Jordan, who became a real stabilizing influence in his life. Laura had come along, and for an ever so brief period Johnny had seemed at peace. But the heavy drinking had resumed, and with it diagnosis of his manic-depressive condition and in quick order Donna's request for a divorce.

"I told you before, Johnny. You don't need to be a pro. The plan is foolproof," Brian replied.

Johnny fidgeted with his glass. "Who else is in this with us?"

Brian shook his head quickly. "I'll only tell you there's two others. Remember what I said about this being foolproof? It's that because I'm the only one who knows the whole set-up. You'll meet the other two on Thursday, but you'll never know who they are. But I can tell you one thing - they have, like us, no record. Clean as a baby's ass after his bath.

"We'll be in and out quickly, Johnny. Like I told you, they'll be at least $1,000,000 to $2,000,000 on that truck on Friday afternoon. Then, about ten days later, we'll score even more with the second heist. Two heists and out. Then, we wait around here a while, cause no suspicion, and eventually move out to a new life."

He lifted his Canadian Club and ginger ale. "To success," he toasted.

Johnny slowly lifted his glass. "Let's hope so."

8

Mike Fallon sauntered into the FBI building at 1 Center Plaza in Boston. Forsaking the elevator, he walked up the stairwell just off the main lobby to the FBI's sixth floor offices.

"Hey, Mikey!" A stick-thin older man, perhaps in his late fifties, yelled the greeting as Fallon walked through a large room that was partitioned into smaller workstations by chest-high dividers. Dozens of agents were busy in their pods, working on files, tapping away at computer terminals, or talking on phones. "How are things at home, Tiger?"

Paul Harper looked like Drew Bledsoe after the Buccaneers were through sacking his ass six times last Sunday, Fallon thought.

He paused at the opening for a moment. "Not bad, Paul. We're getting by," he lied. "And thanks for asking," he stated dismissively. He had learned over the last few months to conclude personal inquiries about Rita quickly with his standard "Thank you for asking," a device meant to end the conversation almost before it began. He didn't want to talk about what was on his mind every minute of every day.

From his office at the end of the corridor Sam Morris waved to him and then beckoned him forward. For months now he had dreaded every such invitation, sensing that the director of the Boston office might openly state what Mike knew everyone knew - despite vacation time, an extended leave, his leaving early on many days - he was no longer carrying his share of the workload.

"Good morning, Mike," Morris said. He was, as usual, impeccably well dressed in a cashmere sport jacket, Sansabelt slacks, and Gucci loafers. He had a lean face, sandy-colored hair, with deep-set eyes, the feature that one noticed above all others. There was that serious look about him, something that implied a no- nonsense demeanor. He wore an expensive wristwatch and a glowing tan, giving clear indication that he had recently returned from the tropics.

"How are things at home, Mikey?" he asked, motioning Fallon to the maroon easy chair in front of his overloaded desk.

"Okay, Chief, and thank you for asking."

Morris sat down and shifted some papers from one large pile to another. "Mike, I was hoping we didn't have to get into this subject now what with Rita not well and all..."

"We can get into any subject you want at any time," Fallon interrupted.

Morris stared at him for a moment, and Mike held his eye. "Well, good, Mike. Good. Mikey, let me be blunt then. For a year now ever since The Photographer case you've..."

The Photographer. Jonathan Ordway. Mike went back into the recesses of his mind to bring out The Photographer once again, a rich, handsome playboy from San Francisco, and a serial killer who had terrorized the nation a year ago. Born in Liverpool, England, Jonathan Ordway had come to America in 1998. A young investment banker, he had a penchant for things beautiful - fast cars and women.

In 1998 three attractive "10" types in the Bay area were declared as missing persons by worried parents who were never to see them again. In December of that year came the first connection to Ordway. Judith Hadley's parents reported that she had been dating Ordway recently and when she had not come home one evening they had suggested the investigators question him. He had denied any knowledge of Judith's disappearance, but days later made some comment to them about her car having been found at the San Francisco International Airport, a fact that the police had not conveyed to him or anyone else publicly.

With the investigation continuing, he suddenly disappeared. And thus began a series of killings across America: a nurse in Denver, a real estate agent in Chicago, a swimming champion in Philadelphia. He met the women at dances, at the beach, at bars. They were always "10s", really beautiful women who were flattered to have their pictures taken. They would disappear with no trace. But friends would mention the handsome, cultured man who took picture after picture of the beautiful women who were fascinated by both him and his camera.

As he moved to the top of the FBI's Most Wanted list, the profilers labeled him "The Photographer." Noting his tendency to frequent major urban centers, they had placed all East Coast cities on alert. Studying the wire reports, Mike Fallon followed Ordway's path across the United States. He decided to take the consolidated sketches provided by Washington and visit the upper class bars in the downtown Boston area. For over a month he wandered from the Ritz Bar to the Four Seasons, over to Zachary's and Biba, all around the town, night after night, asking the bartenders whether they had seen a beautiful woman accompanied by a handsome Englishman who might just be taking pictures of her in public.

One night, while he sat in the bar at Legal Sea Foods at the Prudential Center, his beeper sounded. Excusing himself from continuing a discussion regarding the downfall of the once proud Celtics with a traveling salesman, he punched in the Ritz Bar on his cell phone.

"Mike Fallon here."

"Mr. Fallon, Freddie at the Ritz. Thought you might want to know. You remember that sketch you showed me a couple of months ago?"

Mike remembered clearing his head, templing his nose, focusing intently on each word as the bartender spoke.

"Yeah. Sure I do, Freddie."

"Well, for the last two nights a guy who looks like him has come in. About eight o'clock. I was going to call you last night, but I wasn't sure. But tonight he's got a camera and is taking pictures of this doll and..."

He came alive with excitement. "Freddie. Is he still there?"

"Yes. If last night's any indicator, he'll be here another hour."

"I'm on my way. Do whatever you can to detain him, Freddie. I'll be there in ten minutes."

And in fewer than ten minutes he had walked into the bar and arrested, without incident, the most wanted man in America. It had made his career, the culminating event of a truly distinguished career. But then Rita had become ill.

Morris's ardent vocal tone brought him back to the present. "Mike, you with me?" He waited until he had caught Fallon's eye before proceeding.

"Like I was saying, you aren't producing results, Mikey. Zero. Nada, since The Photographer case. One grand slam can't make a season, Mike. I have to keep reassigning your cases. You want an indefinite leave?"

Mike shook his head vigorously. "Just give me a bit more time, Sam." In truth, he didn't know what he needed, but deep down he knew that he wasn't going to improve much with Rita failing. Stall. That was all he could do.

He didn't want their sympathy, and he didn't want conversation. He just wanted to be left alone. No one could help him. And they could all go fuck themselves. He would focus as best he could, and if that wasn't satisfactory, he'd take early retirement. Only Rita mattered. Whatever happened, he would take care of her.

"I don't want to put you into a fuckin' desk job, Mikey. But I will if I have to. We clear on this?"

"Crystal," Fallon replied too quickly.

Softening, Sam nodded to him. "Hang in there, Mikey. I'll help all I can."

Standing, Fallon moved to the doorway. "Thanks, Chief. I appreciate that," he replied, moving quickly through the door.

9

"When you leavin' and why, big shot?" Sandy demanded as Doug raced ahead of them on Glendon Beach. In early September the crowds had left with Labor Day having marked the start of the Oklahoma land rush back over the Sagamore Bridge to Boston. Now only a few couples without children sat in the warm sun while two or three older men, complete with headgear, swam rhythmically through the flat, blue surface trying to hold on to summer for a while longer.

Tony ignored her question, instead looking out to the sea, happy for the first time in months, seeing a new life over the horizon, a new beginning in a new land.

"Well?" she persisted.

"I'm going to see a man about a racing contract. Should take me this afternoon and all of tomorrow. I'll be back Friday night around seven."

"A contract, huh? With the wins you've been piling up at Loudon, he should spend ten fuckin' minutes with you. He must be some kind of owner. What's his record, 0 and 365 for the year?" She laughed at her own joke.

"You're a riot, Sandy. Why don't you go over to Yarmouth up on 28 there and join one of them comedy club shows. Make us some money instead of sitting on your sit-down watching that guy on 'The Young and the Restless' screwin' every broad he meets."

She smirked and threw him a disdainful look. "I might just do that, Tony. I might just find some life beyond you and the retard, y' know."

Ahead of them Doug ran toward the jetty dividing the public beach from private property and started to climb onto the huge boulders.

Tony started to run slowly and yelled, "Doug, get down from there!" But he stopped after three or four steps, wheeled and pointed his right hand at her. "You call him a retard one more time, and I'll fuckin' kill you, Sandy. Keep it up!"

He ran to the rocks scooping up his son and lifting him, kissing him on the forehead, yanking him to his shoulder tops. Turning to the ocean, he thought of its vastness, of another ocean on another coast, and of being with his son living a storybook new beginning somewhere beyond this sea.

10

Why not a public park? Brian Hughes thought as he gazed out his bow-shaped front window at the traffic slowing down on Joy Street at its intersection with Beacon. He lived in a four-story townhouse right at the corner. Looking diagonally, he could observe the to-and-fro skate boarders transversing the long set of steps leading down to the Park Street Station.

Yes, why not? Who would ever think that a group of thieves would plot a heist at a playground! For months he had planned the whole operation meticulously, leaving nothing to chance. He prided himself on his intelligence, on his possessing superior mental faculties that allowed him to plan with a vision and still pay attention to every detail, every possible eventuality. He knew that people liked him and yet found him arrogant. So be it, if having confidence in one's own ability gave that impression. No one simply gave you credit for being vastly more intelligent. They had to add the knock—arrogant.

He glanced at his desk, at the four rubber masks. Moving away from the window, he checked his Rolex. 12:30 P.M. Time to head to Lynn.

Descending Beacon Hill, he turned his Taurus right on Berkeley Street and then right again onto Storrow Drive. As he drove over the Tobin Bridge, he unzipped the large gym bag on the front seat and fingered the masks as well as the soccer ball and the tape measures. He glanced over to Admiral's Hill on his left and thought back to his first meeting with retired Boston police captain Victor Fleming—that time when Fleming had guest lectured to one of his graduate seminars.

During the two-hour discussion, he grew to like the edginess, the toughness of the detective. He gave succinct, straight answers to the onslaught of questions from the small and largely inexperienced group. The detective had allowed Brian to make the opening and closing comments regarding the proper interrogation of suspects, but throughout his presentation, he had enthralled them all as he emphasized the importance of a multi-faceted approach.

"It's like good teaching," he had said. "For some students, a soft approach inspires them, gets them stimulated, engaged, involved as the doors of knowledge open. For others, fear motivates. They respond to outright fear—a fear of failure, a fear of the instructor, a fear of appearing stupid. For still others, a moderate approach wins the day. They respond to the instructor who can be soft and kind and yet hard when hardness is required. We all respond differently to each of these teachers. But with interrogation, you can't afford to utilize one approach—whether it be soft, hard, or moderate—because if you choose the wrong one, there's no comeback with the alleged perpetrator. He's read you. You've tried, say the hard approach, and he's a tough enough case to withstand whatever you toss at him. Then where do you go from there? Nowhere is where.

"Therefore, absolutely never utilize one interrogator on one suspect. The methods may be similar to the principles of teaching and learning, but you need both a "good cop" and a "bad cop" approach. You need at least two going at the guy. I'm Mr. Hard; you're Mr. Soft. Between us we get him spinning. We see how he reacts and we take advantage of him and his weaknesses. It's even better to throw in a third, Mr. Moderate, as well. In any event, we won't fail. We'll break him over a period of time."

Brian smiled as he recalled the class response to the veteran. Although largely idealists, they understood and accepted him, and they inculcated his message. Following that class, they had gone to dinner—Brian's treat—at Brasserie Jo's, at the Colonnade Hotel. Over drinks and a leisurely meal, they had agreed to make the classroom visit a part of Brian's Procedures course each semester.

And so, over a two-year period, their friendship had grown. In time, Vic Fleming had described his frustrations with retirement, his basic boredom and loneliness since his wife had died, his desire to move on to California, a dream that his pension couldn't support. In turn, Brian related his growing aversion to the basic dullness of academic life. He was an excellent classroom teacher, caught in the "publish or perish" dilemma, which all academics faced. And he resented it. He wasn't disciplined enough to play the required game, but all in all, he saw it largely as an unfulfilling game anyway. He needed something else in his life, something where risk would lead to reward.

Over many nights and over many drinks, they shared both frustrations and dreams. Both of them needed money to move toward a new life. And then one night, at the bar at the Hardcover in Danvers, Brian broached his idea.

"I think I know how we can make a $1 million-$2 million score," he had begun.

"Yeah, you and a few other lottery nitwits," Vic laughed.

And yet while Brian explained the plan step by step, Vic sat erect in his seat, nodding, interested.

"Maybe, just maybe, it could work," Vic finally said. "But you have to have real balls to pull this kind of caper off. You got those kind of balls, kid?" he asked.

Brian smiled at him. "Yeah, I think so, Vic. Especially if I have you as my on-site supervisor. There's a big risk here, but if we pull it off, I've go an idea for a second heist, and then that's it. We back out completely and get on with a new life. Two and out."

Vic Fleming stared at his companion. "It is a good plan. It could work," he finally said. "Let me think on it some more."

11

As he turned from Boston Street in Lynn on to Holyoke Street, Brian looked out to his right toward the massive playing fields of Hood Park. He noted only a single woman leading her young charge toward the swing set in the playground to the left of the soccer areas. In front of him, three cars were parked. Pulling in behind them, he stopped directly across the street from the newly constructed Lynn Classical High School.

When he exited the car, carrying the gym bag, he moved with purpose toward the center of the soccer field directly in front of him. Behind him three men, dressed in work clothes just like him, stepped out of their vehicles, almost in unison and followed Brian to mid-field. He waited for them to surround him.

"Good morning," he began. "First of all, thanks for being here on time and for making the commitment to this project and the one to follow. Let me assure you that if you follow my plan, in fewer than three weeks you'll have more money than you ever could imagine. You'll be set for life."

He knelt down, unzipped the gym bag, and took out the soccer ball, rolling it a bit away from them. He then handed each of them a tape measure from the bag.

"We're out in the open here for a reason. It's much safer. While I'm talking with you, we'll occasionally walk away a few yards, two by two. Act like you're measuring the areas from here to the sidelines. We shouldn't be interrupted at all out in the public eye like this. But if we are, we're surveying the field for proper drainage because we're putting in a new field over in Beverly. Got it?"

He waited for them to nod in agreement. "My strong guess is no one will bother us," Brian said as he stood and looked around. "I've been here four or five times, and no one's here until after school ends at three o'clock. So let's get to it. We'll be here for thirty minutes tops. Time enough for you to understand the plan and to ask questions."

Vic Fleming scanned the area as Johnny Casey and Tony Amonti riveted their attention on Brian.

"Now look into the gym bag while I show you something. There's four rubber masks in here—Bush, Gore, Lieberman and Cheney. From this time on, that's us. I'm Bush, you're Gore," he said, pointing to Fleming, "you're Lieberman," he indicated to Johnny, and "you're Cheney," he motioned to Tony.

"Now you don't know who I am, and I don't know you," he continued, emphasizing the half-truth. "Part of my plan is to maximize our protection as individuals. None of you has a police record, and no one of you has ever been involved in armed robbery before. We're amateurs, technically, and so there's no reason unless we really fuck up for any of us to draw suspicion. And the less we know about one another, the better for all of us.

"Right now, you each know only a little bit about the plan and I'm going to put the pieces together. Mr. Cheney here is our wheels. He's found us a van, which will be awaiting you outside Fenway Park at 1:00 P.M. tomorrow afternoon. You get there on your own. He'll drive Mr. Gore and Mr. Lieberman to Northeastern University and get there before two o'clock."

"What about you, Mr. Bush? Where will you be?" asked Tony evenly.

Brian glared at him. "I'll be around. Where I'll be exactly, you really don't need to know. Okay?"

"Okay with me," Tony shrugged.

Brian watched the lady pushing the swing about a hundred yards away from them. She seemed to pay them scant attention, only occasionally glancing their way.

"Let's Mr. Lieberman and I go across the field, and you two hold the tape. A little three-minute break. We'll reconvene then. Give me an occasional wave."

Along Holyoke Street cars, few in number at this time of day, proceeded to the lights at O'Callaghan Way with no one paying any attention to the workmen measuring the well-groomed field.

When they met again at mid-field, Brian studied his watch. "All right then. You all arrive in the van at exactly 1:50 P.M. The Brinks truck will arrive at the west side of the student center at two o'clock. Almost always, it's right on time.

"Mr. Cheney, when you leave here today, park near the old Boston Arena. It's now called the Matthews Arena. You know where it is?" Tony nodded. "Walk back along St. Botolph Street west, past the Uptown Garage, and you'll see the roadway to your left leading into a parking lot. The road leads you right to the student center. There's a ramp there which also serves as a passageway leading directly into the center, with the cafeteria about twenty-five yards off to the left once you're inside." He passed each of them a detailed map of the approach and of the center itself.

"Mr. Cheney, get familiar today with the road in, the entrance, the same route back out. You'll have only two minutes tops to get them out.

"Mr. Gore here will be in charge of relieving our friends of what we anticipate will be more than a million dollars, maybe as much as two million. He knows he also has only two minutes to accomplish that, preferably without any violence. Mr. Gore?"

"Mr. Bush knows I'll be armed with a machine pistol tomorrow, and I'll have two Glock Nines for you two tomorrow when we meet. Anybody know anything about weapons?"

"I did some shooting as a kid back home," Tony said.

Johnny shook his head. "Never."

"Well, I like that answer better. If there's any shooting to do, I'll do it. Clear?" He waited for a long moment. "There should be no reason for violence. If Mr. Bush is right, they'll all be in the open together for a brief moment. And that's when we strike."

"The security men will be half asleep," Brian interrupted. "First of all, they're not the brightest light bulbs on the lamppost, and second, they will regard this as a regular, easy assignment.

They're at a university surrounded by preppy, good-looking students. They're simply placing cash in ATM machines for the kids to pay for the booze and whatever else. They'll violate Brinks' policy of the driver staying inside the vehicle because the driver will want to get a look at the young ladies."

"We'll take them on the ramp as they start to enter the center," Vic continued. "There won't be many people on that side of the building so we'll have a definite advantage. Mr. Lieberman here and I will disarm them as soon as the driver opens the rear of the truck. Then Mr. Cheney will enter the truck and fill the duffel bags I'll provide."

"What about the van then?" Tony asked. "I leave it alone?"

"You keep it running. Once you're out of the truck, go straight to it. We'll cover the guards and any others," Vic replied.

"Take a pair of these latex gloves," Brian directed. "Put them on before you enter the van at Fenway Park. And wear sweatsuits, something very common and difficult to trace. Each of you bring a large gym bag to the van."

Brian glanced at his watch. "Questions?"

"What happens to the money once we're out of there?" Tony asked.

"Mr. Gore will cover that tomorrow, but we'll meet at the Hilltop Steak House parking lot at seven o'clock to divide it up," Brian responded.

"Long as I don't lose sight of it. And how about the drop points?" Tony asked.

"You'll drop me in Copley Square, and Lieberman in Cambridge," Gore replied.

Brian moved toward the soccer ball and collected the tape measures and then handed the gloves to each man. "No other questions? Then let's leave together and gentlemen, as that wired guy on TV says, 'Let's get ready to rumble.'"

12

Johnny Casey drove past Flax Pond and pulled into the parking lot of the Cuffe—McGinn funeral home on Maple Street in Lynn. In the early twilight, hot winds, remnants of summer, yanked loose paper about the road as he walked to the front door.

Paying his final respects to Al Doyle was important to him, although he hadn't seen his former high school classmate since their days together at St. Mary's. He smiled to himself as he thought of the day Al had been caught smoking by their baseball coach while he was warming up to pitch against Lynn English. Warming up was as far as Al got.

Entering the big room, he shyly introduced himself to members of the Doyle clan and proceeded to kneel in front of the bier. Al really didn't look much different, Johnny was thinking—pock marks all over his face and all—when a cell phone rang. At first, he wasn't sure whether the sharp ring came from his own person or from that of dear old Al, but then it was highly unlikely anyone was calling the dead body, even in this age of instant gratification and lack of privacy.

As he stood, he faced the angry glares of ten or so pairs of eyes. He nodded contritely and then walked quickly to the hallway.

"Fuckin' cell phones," he muttered. But then, again, he should have shut it down. But what if Brian were trying to reach him? Looking down, he recognized the number and punched it in.

"Yeah?" came an unfriendly voice from seemingly half a continent away.

"Sonny, what the fuck do you want calling me at a fuckin' funeral home!" Johnny fumed.

"What now I'm a mind reader, too? I'm one of those what do you call 'em—psychos?"

"Psychics, you dumb shit," Johnny replied.

"Well, wherever you are, the man wants to talk to you and he wants his money, Johnny. What do you have to say about that, Alky?"

Johnny tried to calm himself. "Put him on," he replied.

After a moment the raspy voice of one of the North Shore's leading Mafia figures cut through the air. "How are you, priest?"

Johnny pictured the short man with the leathery face, sitting in his office on Route One in Saugus, his iron-gray hair slicked back perfectly above his impeccable Armani suit.

"Fine, Paulie. I'm just fine."

"That's good, priest. That's good. Now what about my $15,000?"

"You'll have it day after tomorrow."

"Is that right—day after tomorrow? If that's so, priest, we won't charge you the vig for Saturday. Just to show you what a good guy I am."

Paulie Ayala, the intimidator, Johnny thought. Taunting him. Loving to repeat the word "priest" to remind him of his falling, of his failure to measure up.

"You'll have it just like I said," he finally responded.

"Who do you like in the Notre Dame game Saturday, John? Want to roll it all over? The Irish are getting twelve against Nebraska. What do you think?"

Johnny Casey, right at that moment, didn't want to think at all. He had enough on his mind for the next day or three. "I'll pass, Paulie," he said.

"Suit yourself, priest. Then I'll see you on Saturday. I'll be in all day."

Hanging up, Johnny reluctantly thought of the game, of placing a bet, a well of dryness moving into his throat followed quickly, as it was invariably, by a strong desire for a drink. To calm himself for tomorrow's action, he would need a bite of the dog, maybe just one boilermaker over at the Kernwood and then he would be ready.

13

Vic Fleming watched the famous "Sheik of Araby" number from "Tin Pan Alley" as Alice Faye and Betty Grable, in two piece harem sarongs, sang and danced around the overweight sheik, Billy Gilbert. When the scene ended, he rewound the tape back to the beginning of the scene and watched the big production number once again.

He sat with his Jack, sipping it slowly, relaxing now. He had to give the professor credit. He had found a great mark—a Brinks truck in a college setting, loose security, a big prize, clear roadways in and out—and had formed a solid plan.

They were amateurs, the whole lot of them, but he could see them through. About that, he was positive. The action beckoned him, and he couldn't wait for tomorrow. California was only a few weeks away now.

As Alice Faye sang "You Say the Sweetest Things, Baby" to John Payne, he downed his second Jack and eased back into the couch.

———

"When the fuck you coming back?" Sandy yelled so that half of the people in the Copley Hotel on Huntington Avenue could hear.

"Quiet your piss, Sandy," Tony Amonti replied calmly. "I'll be there tomorrow about 7 p.m."

"What are you doing in Boston anyway? Getting it off with some motorcycle mama?"

Calm her down, he thought. Tomorrow, if all went well, he would collect Doug, move him in with his sister in Framingham for just a week or two, until the second score went down. Then they would be off to a new life. How had he ever gotten involved with Sandy in the first place?

"Look, be patient, will you? The contract talks are going good. Watch the boy for me, and tomorrow night we'll hit Michael Patrick's, have some fun, a few pops. What do you say?"

"Well, all right," she muttered. "I could stand a good time for a change."

"Then you got it. See you then, Babe."

For the last fuckin time, he should have added.

Brian Hughes crossed Joy Street and descended into the Boston Common, running downhill parallel to Beacon Street, his pace quickened by the excitement he felt. Just hours away now, he thought, as he flew by those ascending the hill—young lovers from the offices surrounding the area, a guitarist left over from the hippie generation with a container for dollars at his feet, a group of French sailors ready together to explore the wonders of Boston, or at least its female population.

He ran directly toward Commonwealth Avenue, his arms pumping, and his head full of tomorrow. He centered on his crew, and on their ability to perform. Fleming was a pro, retired but aching for action, lonely and ready to be back in the saddle again. He would be fine. And the kid driver whose name he didn't know—a bit sullen, seemingly weighed down with problems, whatever they were, but a wheel man with a brain if Brian was right.

Of them all, he worried most about the one he knew best. Along with the booze problem and the gambling habit, Johnny Casey was an in-and-out personality. Very close to being unreliable, especially for this caper. But again, he knew him better than anyone, and he was gambling that he had him motivated, that Johnny knew there weren't many more chances left.

Turning onto Beacon Street, he climbed toward his home and a long shower, a sandwich, and then a good night's sleep.

John A. Curry

He was as ready as ever, confident of success. And afterward, the real fun would begin as whoever the law planned to pit against him tried to outwit him. Motivation and opportunity, he reminded himself. He had no motivation, and as for opportunity, he planned to be sitting with Dean Johnson, his chief witness, right smack in the middle of the student center when the crime went down. No opportunity, either.

14

"Can you take care of breakfast for the girls?" Mike Fallon asked his oldest daughter.

Jessica stirred in her bed and came alert quickly. "Is she all right, Dad?"

Mike stroked her hair as he sat on the bed. "It's been a bad night, honey. A real bad night, but she's resting now. I should be with her, though. Can you -"

Jessica sprung from the bed, nodding. "I'll get them up."

"I'll be down in a while, sweetie," he said, standing to embrace her.

"Can I go see her now?"

"Maybe a little later. Let me see how she's doing first."

She slid into her slippers and padded away toward the bathroom. Now alone, he punched in his office number on his cell phone.

"Paul Harper here."

"Paul, Mikey. She's had a bad night. I'll be in later. Maybe close to 9:00 A.M."

"Sure, Mikey, I can cover. Nothing that can't wait."

"Anything new on the Rinaldi deal?" Mike asked.

"He's due in with his fuckin' sleaze lawyer, Minton. Claims he knows nothin' about the bearer bonds being taken on the interstate."

"Who—him or Minton?"

Harper laughed. "Good question. Two fuckin' thieves. Take your pick."

"I got to go, Paul. You start the interrogation, but stall a bit. The nurse is due at eight o'clock. I'll stay a while, and be with you as soon as I can."

Ending the call, he walked toward their bedroom, the sounds of the children arguing about who had the right to boss whom reaching him from the kitchen.

Rita sat upright in bed, her once beautiful face now jaundiced, the sallow complexion presenting evidence of a hard battle fought through another night.

"Cancer sucks," she smiled as he sat on the bed.

"Big time," he grinned, reaching for her hand.

"That was the worst in a long time," she grunted.

"You take the pills?"

She rolled her eyes. "For all the good they do."

"You want me to get Dr. Hazlitt?"

She shook her head. "We'll wait until the regular date on Monday."

He walked to the window and opened it an inch or two. "We need a little more air in here," he said.

"Yeah, and it also helps cut down on the stench of vomit, don't you think?"

He sat back down on the bed. "There's no fooling my girl, is there?"

"No," she spanked his hand. "And don't you even try." She stared at him for a moment. "Mike, promise me something?"

"I promise them anything, but I give 'em Arpage," he joked.

She frowned at him. "I'm being serious, Mikey. When this is over, you find someone. I want you to promise me you'll find someone. For you and the girls."

He winced and shook his head from side to side.

"Rita, stop talking like that. You're going to beat this fuckin' thing. I—"

"Stop it, Mikey. You heard the doctor. Just months, that's all. There's not too many winners with pancreatic cancer. Promise me," she pleaded.

"Rita, you know I'll do whatever you want me to."

"I know you will, Mikey. You just take care of my girls and take care of you."

"You up to seeing them before they go to school?" he asked, choking back a tear.

She perked up, pushed herself up on the pillow and winked at him. "Ready when they are, Mr. DeMille," she said.

15

"You know how much those fuckin' Celtics charge for a ticket now?" Walt Cochran asked his partners as the gray Brinks armored truck pulled away from the curb at Boston University and headed north on Commonwealth Avenue.

"Look at that fuckin' bicyclist!" Joe Dunn yelled as he swerved to avoid a young man dressed like a bank vice president pedaling parallel to the passenger side.

"Fuckers have no sense of the traffic," he snarled. "They'll barrel into some old crow and not even stop to see if she's got a pulse," he continued. "This goddamn city ought to ban those bike messengers from the downtown streets."

"Jesus, at least in my day they had a light on the contraption," Walt Cochran replied. "You know when I was in school back in the 50's a policeman would flag you down if you didn't have a light on your tricycle."

Joe Dunn looked across at the well-groomed old-timer. "Yeah? Well now, the fuckin' city cops more likely will wave them on with a go-flag. What were you saying about the Celtics?"

"Two dollars. That's what I paid back in the 50's and 60's. Now they want $75.00 plus another half million for a popcorn and a Coke."

"Ain't that the truth?" Cal Morgan joined in through the small, open sliding window as he squatted on a small seat inside the truck.

"And in those days, you saw an NBA doubleheader for your $2.00. Did you guys know that?" Walt asked.

"No shit," Cal Morgan said.

"I'm not kidding you," Walt continued, turning to look at Cal. "I'd see the Celtics vs., say, the Knicks at 8:00 and at 6:00 you'd see Philadelphia against Syracuse."

"Syracuse? When the fuck did they play in the NBA?" Joe Dunn asked.

"In those days the National Basketball Association never went west of the Mississippi. The East was the nation," Walt said. "Anyway, the point is the average guy like us could afford to go to the game without mortgaging his house."

"The fuckin' quality was probably better too," Joe Dunn said. "Now there's ninety-nine teams in the league with all those gunners tossing up three-point shots instead of passing the ball."

"Any guys that look like me playing in those days?" Cal asked.

"One or two on each team, Cal. They were just coming in, setting role models for your Blacks too," Walt said.

"Role models?" Joe Dunn snickered. "Today, if they go on strike for more dough, they can all use the occasion to visit their bastard kids all across America."

Staying within the prescribed limits set by the company, Dunn turned right on Massachusetts Avenue, heading east.

"Last stop of the day coming up," Cal said.

"T.G.I.F.," Walt responded.

"Let's hope these college broads are still wearing those short summer skirts," Joe Dunn said.

"Fuckin' pervert," Walt responded.

"We'll be there in five minutes," Dunn replied.

16

Upon checking in the previous evening, Tony Amonti had paid his bill in advance in cash. At 12:30 P.M. on Friday, he simply exited the Copley Hotel and drove down Huntington Avenue to the Midtown Hotel, parking in the garage area below ground. The '99 tan Explorer he had stolen over on Massachusetts Avenue in North Cambridge sat between two small cars, but there was an empty space diagonally opposite so he eased his Mustang into it. As he approached the van, he noted the New Hampshire plates, which he had stolen near Portsmouth, glistening in the semi-darkness.

He removed the "hotel guest" sign he had stolen from another car from the visor, and walked across to his Mustang, placing the sign on his dashboard. He then backed the van up and headed up the ramp to Huntington Avenue. No parking lot attendant, probably the only lot left in Boston of that type.

Heading west on Huntington Avenue, he turned right on Longwood and then right again onto Boylston. At the Jersey Street intersection, he slowed and parked across from the Red Sox ticket office. From around the corner, carrying a large gym bag, came the old timer. He slid open the door and sat in the rear. From directly in front of Tony, Johnny Casey crossed the street and came around to the passenger seat side, tossing his gym bag into the rear.

"Let's roll, Mr. Cheney," Fleming directed. "Normal speed. We don't need trouble before we even get there, but we want to be there fifteen minutes before the Brinks truck."

He pulled one of the large blue duffel bags toward him and unzipped it. "Here's the masks," he said, passing them around. "Mr. Lieberman, Mr. Cheney, this is a Glock 9mm semiautomatic. I prefer this mid-sized model because of its shorter barrel. It makes the weapon easier to conceal." He pulled the square, chunky slide and chambered the first round. He repeated the process with the second Glock. "Remember now," he said, handing the weapon in his gloved hand to Johnny. "They'll be three Brinks guys with the truck.

"If Mr. Bush is right, the driver and the guy in the passenger seat will get out of the truck once they drive down the ramp. At the end of the ramp they'll be automated glass sliding doors that lead into the student center. We must hit them before they enter the building. We don't want any action, any shooting going on where the students are milling. In fact, if we do this right, they'll be no fuckin' shooting at all."

"What about the third guy, the one in the rear of the truck?" Johnny asked.

"Mr. Lieberman, that's your job. When the two dipshits head to the back of the truck, they'll open it up and just for a minute, tops, the third guy will get out with the replenishment satchel for the ATM machines and then accompany the passenger side guy inside the center. Normally, the driver will get back behind the wheel and stare at the young broads until the other two get back.

"I'll take the driver and the passenger side guard as soon as they open the back door and Dick Tracy #3 steps out. Your job is to rivet on that third guy, and help me get all three disarmed and on the ground.

"Mr. Cheney, here's your Glock-9, just in case. When they're down, you'll have ninety seconds tops to fill these two duffel bags. And then we're off on the road to Morocco, as Hope and Crosby used to say. Simple. In and out in two minutes. And then two minutes more for the drops." Vic felt confident, in control once again, ready to experience the action. "Questions?"

"The money's loose inside there?" Tony asked.

"It's secured in short tan mail bags. Throw them in the gym bags, or if you have to, toss them in my direction if the duffel bags can't hold it all," Fleming replied.

Johnny Casey felt the beads of perspiration running from his temple, down his face.

"Questions, Mr. Lieberman?" Fleming asked.

"I'm fine, Mr. Gore," Johnny responded.

"You sure, son?" Fleming asked, his voice a mix of concern and empathy.

"I can handle my part," Johnny retorted, straining to gain control of himself, to think and act logically and to demonstrate to Brian, to Gore, especially to himself, that this could be his first real success since 1984.

17

"Look at the ass on that chickadee," Joe Dunn said, as the truck moved slowly into the turn from St. Botolph Street across the Robinson Quadrangle toward the student center. Just another forty yards now.

"Chickadee?" Walt Cochran repeated derisively. "I haven't heard that term since the 1930's."

"Yeah, well, everything old is new again," Dunn laughed.

To his right, five or six smiling students, still dressed in summer finery, walked briskly in two's and three's toward the least used entrance to the hub of the campus. To his left, three or four vehicles, some marked with the identifiable university logo, and some vendors making deliveries, were parked just off the ramp. He drove directly toward the down ramp and stopped ten yards in front of the automatic doors.

As he parked the vehicle, Dunn spoke through the window to Morgan. "You ready with the bags, Cal?"

"All set, Joe. Just the two today, right?"

Dunn looked at the manifest on the dashboard. "Right. $300,000. $150,000 in each. You guys go look at the latest in fashions and fill me in when you get back along with some coffee from McDonald's in there. Okay?"

Without waiting for an answer, he opened his door, and at the same time, Walt followed suit. From inside, Cal moved to the back door to await them.

Twenty yards to their left, Tony Amonti observed the situation. "Here they come!" he bellowed.

"On with the masks," Fleming ordered.

"Now when the driver opens the rear door, and all three are out of the truck, we go. Understood? Keep down low," he ordered Johnny.

Glancing through the front window, his hand covering the mask, Tony Amonti first noticed the dark guy—one of them

Indians from India he would learn later—and the pert white girl giggling and laughing as they approached the truck maybe thirty yards on its right side.

"Two kids on the right," he warned Fleming. "It's a go—all three are out of the truck."

Moving rapidly, Fleming and Casey exited on the right and left side of the van on a dead run for the short approach to the truck. With their focus on removing the bags from the rear, neither Cochran nor Morgan saw them coming. But Joe Dunn spotted them almost immediately and went for his holster.

"Touch that fuckin' gun and I'll blow your head off, asshole," yelled Vic pointing the machine pistol at Dunn.

"Hey, what the fuck..." Cal Morgan began as he wheeled to face them.

"Get those hands up," Johnny ordered. As all three compiled, the Indian and the girl walked right into their path. "Hey, is this a joke?" the Indian asked, his face breaking into a smile. "You men are American presidential candidates? This is a joke, right?"

"All of you down on the ground," Fleming yelled as Tony joined them.

"We're cool, sport," Tony spoke to Fleming as he climbed into the truck.

The Indian boy still stood, smiling. "Vice President Gore, is it? The joke is over. Unmask yourself," he said, taking two steps toward Fleming.

In a flash, Fleming lifted the butt end of his weapon and smashed it against the side of the student's face. He crumbled to the asphalt, blood gushing from his ear.

"Oh, my God, Raymond!" the girl screamed from the ground.

"Shut the fuck up, and just lie there," Fleming instructed.

Inside the van, Tony filtered quickly through the shelves on both side of the truck. Disregarding any paper, bearer bonds or the like, he placed the bags of cash into the two gym bags.

"Thirty more seconds, Mr. Cheney," Vic yelled.

Johnny focused on the three guards who lay on their stomachs as Vic leaned over them, lifting their weapons from their holsters one by one. He glanced around every few seconds, assuring himself that no one else was on a path to either enter or exit the building.

"Done!" Tony yelled, as he placed the two bags at the rear of the vehicle and then leaped out.

Fleming threw the guards' weapons up on to the overhang above the ramp and yelled "Mr. Cheney, Mr. Lieberman, both of you go!"

Waiting until Tony had the van in motion, Fleming eyed all five of his captives. "Now just lie there until we're gone. Don't force me to shoot one of you. It's not your money, so don't try to be a fuckin' hero." He noticed the Indian student did not stir much at all.

Backing up, he scanned the area from his left to his right, retreating quickly now as Tony pointed the van toward their route out.

Fleming moved into the van. "Let's go!" he ordered.

As Tony exited the parking lot, he could see five or six newcomers racing toward the Brinks guards, now on the rise, looking about, orienting themselves to the scene around them.

"We have maybe two minutes, Mr. Cheney," Vic said, discarding his mask as the others followed suit. "Give me your weapons," he said, as he unzipped the third gym bag.

―――――

At that very moment, Brian Hughes grinned at Perry Johnson across their table near the main entrance of the cafeteria.

"Well, I kind of thought you would have news today. That's really why I asked you to join me, other than for the pleasure of your company of course," Brian beamed.

"Why I must say, you're taking it better than I had anticipated, Brian." Johnson nervously ran his index finger along the rim of the paper cup. "Remember now," he said, looking up, "the college tenure decision is not necessarily my decision or that of the provost. We'll recommend separately to the president and the trustees."

"Perry, let's not bullshit a bullshitter. If the tenure committee voted against me 6-3, I'm on life support. I know it, and I think you know it."

"I'll review the dossier fairly, Brian." Johnson stated it firmly, as if all the gods on Olympus would bear witness to his integrity and independence.

He had no balls at all, the original Mr. Go-Along to get along, Brian thought, eyeing the main entrance to his left, where a stream of humanity came from out of the sunlight. To his right, the east end of the building, there was much less traffic—normal, he thought, but he anticipated that at any moment that would change.

It was time to eat some crow.

"Well I thank you for that, Perry. And whatever the outcome, I hope you know I appreciate your willingness to help with the recommendations if things don't turn out so well."

Dean Johnson smiled for the first time. "That's the spirit, Brian. Don't lose heart. Let's just see what happens next."

Yeah, like you won't go immediately back to your isolated office and begin writing a letter supporting the committee's decision, Brian mused.

"Hey, what's happening back there?" a blond male with four eye piercings yelled out to no one in particular.

"What? Where?" A couple of other males yelled above the normal din.

"Jesus Christ! Something's wrong!" yelled a pretty young girl dressed in shorts.

Like the roar of the crowd at a football game, the vocal alarm rose in its intensity as groups of students began moving rapidly toward the east end.

"What's that all about?" the dean asked.

"Some problem, from the reaction," Brian answered.

"Let's go see."

18

Exiting the parking lot, Tony turned right onto St. Botolph Street, followed almost immediately by a sharp, quick left onto Gainsboro Street and a right onto Huntington Avenue. Driving within the rules, he reached the Midtown within two minutes of their departure and eased down the ramp to the underground parking lot.

In the rear, Johnny Casey threw the rubber masks into one of the gym bags as Tony braked the vehicle in exactly the same spot from where he had started a little more than an hour and a half before.

"Don't take those gloves off—any of you—until we're out of here," Fleming ordered.

Johnny Casey felt exhilarated, the adrenaline pumping, their achievement now coming home to him.

"We did it! We did it!" he yelled excitedly.

"Let's go," Tony said calmly.

Stepping slowly from the van, Tony pointed toward his Mustang, parked diagonally across from the van. "Mr. Lieberman, you grab one bag and I'll get the other. Don't hurry, man. We're just two businessmen looking to have a workout."

At the Mustang, Fleming entered on the passenger side as Johnny sat in the rear. Once they were settled, Tony moved carefully up the ramp, back onto Huntington Avenue. From the distance, less than a mile up the road, they heard the incessant screaming of sirens and then saw, across the divided highway, two, then three Boston police cars racing toward the scene.

At Copley Square, Tony slowed the Mustang at Fleming's request. "I'll take the T home, Mr. Lieberman. Mr. Cheney, leave my vice president across the river with the other bag. Best we split now. See you both at the rendezvous—unless you want to be impeached," he laughed as he stepped out.

19

"They were the fuckin' candidates that's who they were!" Brian Hughes heard the excitable blond yelling at the rotund Boston policeman. She stood near the east entrance as a paramedic team administered first aid to a dark-skinned student.

"No need to swear, young lady," the cop scowled at the small, pretty, pert woman.

To his right, a tall, slightly heavy, plainclothes detective spoke with blue-suited officers as he pointed to various parts of the compass. Abruptly, in small squads of two and threes, they moved in harmonious response, some toward the parking lot exit, others toward the surrounding buildings. To Brian's left, four or five Boston regulars were questioning a small band of witnesses, or at least some people claiming to have been at the scene.

"What do you mean candidates?" the red-faced patrolman continued.

"Just what I said," responded Miss Pert and Nasty. "The three of them wore those fuckin' rubber masks—Gore, Lieberman, Cheney. The one with the Gore mask smashed my boy friend across the face. He..."

"Hold on," the cop interrupted. "Captain!" he signaled to the detective giving the marching orders.

Brian and Perry Johnson stood in the second row, right in the path of the now non-functioning automatic doors. They were separated from the inquisition only by the two policemen who held back the crowd.

"Yeah, Bunky?" the detective asked as he approached.

"Frank, this young lady says they wore rubber masks—Gore, Lieberman, Cheney masks. It's her boy friend who got whacked. The paramedics just whisked him away. We got the all points out. The wits say they were driving a '98 or '99 Ford Explorer."

"Let's get out of here, Brian," Dean Johnson whispered into his right ear. "Nothing we can do."

Brian touched his arm. "Just a minute or two more, Perry. This is interesting."

Behind the detective a police line separated the gathering crowd of students and employees from the investigators. The line parted for two middle-aged men, both dressed in charcoal gray suits.

"Oh, fuck," the Boston detective said to no one in particular. "The Feebs have arrived."

The better looking of the two special agents grinned as he approached, extending his hand.

"How you doing, Frank?"

"Mikey Fallon. Now we're all saved," the detective responded sarcastically.

Fallon laughed and turned toward his companion. "Paul Harper, meet Frank Sheridan, head of Boston's armed robbery unit. The scanner says they're out and loose, Frank. Is that right?"

"Gone with the wind, Mikey. We going to work this together?" Sheridan asked.

"Absolutely. Let's you and I continue to destroy the impression that law enforcement agencies can't cooperate. We're all such selfish bastards, right?"

Not waiting for a response, Mike surveyed the area, looking back to the police line and then around the perimeters at the small groups interviewing, and to his front where a group of about fifty people inside the student center strained necks to observe events.

Brian watched intently as Fallon ran his eyes over the group. He locked on Fallon, who, in turn, froze on him for just a moment. The excitement built in Brian, its effect dizzying. As Fallon turned back toward the Boston cops, Brian felt the dryness mounting in his throat. "We should go now, Perry," he said, trying hard to contain his exhilaration.

20

As its name implies, the Hilltop Steak House sits on the crest of a hill on Route 1 in Saugus, ten miles north of Boston. Home to America's largest volume restaurant, its front exterior consists of a long lawn punctuated with rows of plastic cows with an array of similarly plastic cactus plants tossed in every few yards. Its extensive parking lot, containing space for at least a thousand cars, runs alongside the restaurant and deep beyond its rear, for a distance of at least a quarter mile. A perfect place for the division of their booty, Brian had decided.

A half-hour early, he drove slowly into the lot, past the huge corps of Friday night humanity streaming toward the enclosed porch and the long lines waiting to enter. Most of them, based on the overhangs in their midsections, about as much in need of a large steak as a dose of arsenic.

He drove toward the rear of the lot. At the very end, he executed a U-turn so that the front of his vehicle faced Route 1 and the entrance. While waiting for the others, he scanned the radio dial, listening to the various news reports of the robbery. Slick and quick, most commentators agreed. Had to be professionals for sure, related the commentator on WBZ. They all seemingly relished their use of the appellation "The Candidates," some of the conservative talk show hosts delighting in drawing a comparison between the bandits and the real life politicians. All crooks, they bellowed, appealing to the baser feelings of their audiences.

Brian drank from his Dunkin' Donuts coffee cup, smirking at the conversations as he flicked through the frequencies. Nitwit radio, he almost said aloud. The fraternity of the miserable. Dumb bastards with no brains calling in to even dumber hosts with even less.

From the entrance, motorists sought an open spot, but few meandered toward the back of the lot. He watched carefully for the three drivers who would. Within five minutes they appeared, each facing front and parking a short distance away from him. He waited until the others had entered Fleming's SUV and then glanced about for a minute before he left his own vehicle and approached them.

"Greetings, Mr. Bush. We hope you didn't have too hard a day today," Fleming joked as Brian sat next to Tony Amonti.

"Well, it's this vision thing, the thinking for you guys that takes most of my energy," Brian replied. "You people hear the new reports?"

"Away clean, and the jokers don't have a clue," Tony said.

"Only for the moment," Fleming replied. "Don't get cocky. You never know what they know. They're not going to release it to those media assholes anyway."

Brian glanced at Johnny Casey. "Everything okay, Mr. Lieberman?" Although Johnny nodded, he seemed too quiet, too contemplative.

"Let's do the division and get the hell out of here," Tony said.

"I'm for that," Fleming said. "Guess how much is in this bag, Mr. Bush?" he asked.

"Close to a half million. Maybe three quarters of a million?"

Vic pointed to the seat beside him. "In this one bag is $1.3 million."

Brian turned toward Johnny. "And how about the other?" he asked.

Johnny drummed his fingers on the bag. "Would you believe $1.5 million?"

"You're shitting me!" Brian yelled. "Almost 3 million!"

"The early radio broadcasts said $2 million," Johnny said.

"You know, I hate to spoil this love-in, but what guarantee do I fuckin' have that there wasn't $5 million in the two bags?" Tony asked Brian.

Brian gathered himself before answering. "You don't, Cheney. But I trust these two, as you should. In a day or two, you'll hear media reports of the real number, and then you'll know for sure. If I wanted to rob you, Mr. Cheney, you wouldn't be here now. And I'd be taking more than a one quarter share."

"You okay with that, kid?" Fleming asked, turning in his seat.

"I'm cool," Tony replied. "I just want to feel comfortable about this, that's all."

"Good. Then let's take our $700,000 apiece and go away happy," Brian said. Both Vic and Johnny handed set packages to the others and to each other.

"One more thing," Brian said. "No spending of this dough yet. Understood? Any large spending will only call attention to us. Agreed?"

"Fine," Tony said.

"All set," Johnny agreed.

"He's right. Don't change any habits. The Feebs will be networking for anybody who's spending large stuff and so won't the locals," Vic said.

"In about a week, I'll call us all together to talk over that second hit," Brian continued, "For that one I think we can count on another $2-3 million. So in a week and a half, we'll have $1.5 million apiece and then, we're done. We go our separate ways."

"Sounds great, sport. I'm all for that," Tony said.

"Then we'll see you all soon," Brian said, as he placed his package under his arm and opened the door.

21

The approach always fascinated him. About a mile from the Sagamore Rotary, the bridge loomed like a giant hovering over the flatlands of Route 3, its lights at dusk illuminating the blackened sky. The Sagamore Bridge, gateway to Cape Cod and the resultant break from stressful Boston to peace and tranquillity. Tony Amonti aimed the Mustang toward the apex of the bridge, enjoying the long ride up and the feeling of relief and accomplishment now that the job was done.

He stayed within the speed limit, conscious of Bush's warnings about their behavior over the next week. He looked back to be sure the trunk was secure. He was both nervous and full of himself. $700,000! The most he had ever made in a single year was the $50,000 in '97, the year he won a few small prizes back in Iowa. Right from the farm to the Des Moines Fair Grounds. But like a successful rookie in baseball, the sophomore jinx had set him back. And for the last three years he had struggled. Maybe it was the cars he drove, or maybe he just didn't have it. But now he had $700,000, with another $700,000 or so to follow.

When he entered Dennisport, he headed for the ocean, turning down Old Wharf Road to the trailer park, looking forward to seeing his boy and in some way conveying the good news, at least the good news about life changing for them in the very near future. It was only when he was nearly alongside the trailer that he realized that it lay in pitch darkness. Where the hell was the harlot now? And what had she done with Doug?

Unlocking the door, he snapped on the kitchen light. Dirty dishes were strewn about the small countertop, Burger King wrappings tossed on the floor. Across the small aisle, breakfast dishes lay unattended on the small, chipped round table. "Sandy? Doug?" he yelled. No response.

Where could she be at 7:30 P.M. and with no car? If she had taken Doug into some bar—.

He slouched onto one of the wooden kitchen chairs, running his hands through his hair, trying to think clearly. A little boy, a little confused boy, slow to understand, his boy, out there somewhere, probably frightened by whatever environment that slut had introduced him to.

Suddenly he heard the slight tap on the door. "Yes, come in. It's open," he said.

"Mr. Amonti?" An old woman with receding, thinning hair, stepped into the kitchen, tugging Doug behind her.

"Daddy, you're here!" Doug blurted it out, practically tripping over the woman as he skittered around her.

As Tony rose, the boy leaped into his arms. "Hey, sport, where you been?"

"With the nice lady, Daddy. She gave me some ice cream."

"I'm Margie Adams," she announced, casting a disapproving glance at him.

"Please, Mrs. Adams, sit down here," Tony offered, brushing bread crumbs off the kitchen chair onto the floor.

"Someone left this poor child all alone all day," she replied rigidly, holding to her position near the trailer door.

"I don't understand, Mrs. Adams. My companion was with him..."

"Your companion? I don't know where she might be, Mr. Amonti, but I do know this boy needs a mother, a guardian. Your companion,—she emphasized the word, clearly connoting her disdain—left this boy all alone. I heard him sobbing this morning—wailing is probably the better word for it—right through the door. All alone, and the poor boy not being fed, not in school, where he should be."

"Sandy went away, Daddy. She said she won't be back. And I was scared," Doug said, still at his father's side, the blue eyes dull with that deer-caught-in-the-headlights look he so often displayed.

"Mrs. Adams, I don't know how to thank you. It was so kind of you to..."

"And I want to be kind, Mr. Amonti," she interrupted gruffly. "You ever need any help with that precious child, you call me. I'm only over there you know," she said, pointing toward the door.

"What do you say to Mrs. Adams, Doug?" Tony asked, bending to kiss him on the cheek.

"Thank you, Mrs..." he stuttered.

She smiled broadly. "Adams. But you keep calling me the nice lady, Doug. I like that better. That boy may be a bit slow, Mr. Amonti, but he loves his daddy, I'll tell you that. That's all he talks about is his daddy."

"Can I offer you a drink or something, Mrs. Adams?"

She shook her head vigorously. "I really have to get back and watch my programs. 'Who Wants To Be A Millionaire' is on tonight. And the answer to that is I do," she beamed.

"Well then, thanks again," Tony said, moving to open the door for her.

"I meant what I said, young man. If you ever need me, I'm in number six just over there," she reiterated.

"You're so very kind, Mrs. Adams," Tony said.

Closing the door behind her, he turned and gestured to Doug, beckoning him to fly into his arms once again. "Hey, we missed school today, sport. You need to get to sleep."

Doug rested his face on his father's shoulder. "Do I have to, Dad? Can't I stay up with you?"

Grimacing, Tony sat down on a kitchen chair, balancing Doug on his knee. "How's school going, anyway, sport?"

Doug lowered his head and looked off into space. "All the kids make fun of me. They call me "retard" and stuff like that. When can we go away like you said to that place?"

"California?"

He gestured wildly with his hands. "Yes! Tell me about it again!"

Two and Out

"Well, like I said, San Diego, California, has beautiful, sunshiny weather, beaches with golden sand, and..."

Standing up, Doug bounced on his toes. "Daddy, when? When? Let's go now."

Tony smiled at him, laugh lines breaking on his face. "In two or three weeks, Doug. Daddy has some business here for a couple of weeks. Then you and I can go to Disneyland on our way to San Diego. What do you think of that, sport?"

But suddenly Doug stopped his bouncing. "Do I have to go to school there?"

"Of course you do, Doug. But we'll find a special school, one much better than here that you'll like. And we'll be together every day. You and me always."

Doug charged into his lap once again. "Daddy, I love you."

22

"So let's add up where we are," Mike Fallon said, standing aside of the flip chart in the conference room at FBI headquarters.

A sheet of light was spreading in the east at 5:30 A.M. Outside, as the sheet spread, the late summer wind rose gently. An hour earlier he had arisen on this Saturday morning, assured himself that Rita was sleeping comfortably and then slipped into Jessica's room, stirring her carefully, whispering into her ear that he needed her to organize morning activities. On his way downtown, he reflected on the burden he was placing on a young teen, a beautiful girl who at this time of life should only be worrying about her studies and her appeal to young men. Somehow, in the future, he vowed he would make it up to her.

"Where we are is fuckin' nowhere, that's where we are," Paul Harper said, pushing back from the coffee-stained portable conference table.

Disregarding him, Fallon turned to the flip chart and the notations he had made earlier. He tried to concentrate, to show some leadership to a team that he knew wondered about where he was at. He pointed to the face page.

"At two o'clock, the Brinks guards show on the east side of the student center. Right on time, and they all exit the truck against company policy, open the rear door, and three masked guys are on them like fleas on a dog. According to the guards, they came out of a Ford Explorer parked just twenty yards away.

"The Candidates—for now that's what we'll call them—are there two minutes tops with minimal conversation. No names used. No excessive violence except for the student, who according to his girlfriend, advanced on them.

"He's fuckin' lucky to be alive," Harper interjected.

"The Boston cops find the stolen Explorer four hours later at the Midtown, and our perps are long gone. What's the status there, Dave?"

A young, thin, bald man, dressed in shades of brown and tan, responded. "The van was stolen from an insurance salesman over in Cambridge. The mobile techs dusted it and we're awaiting results. Our guys lifted a lot of prints, but all the witnesses at the school report they wore latex gloves.".

"How about fibers?" Fallon asked.

"We should know something in a day or so," Dave Cameron responded.

"My guess is we won't find much. According to the Brinks guys, they wore sweatsuits, standard stuff that's probably been burned already. But they'll be fibers, maybe something else," Mike said.

"The Boston cops fed us the transcripts from witness testimony," Marilyn Nelson offered from her position across the table from Harper.

"And?" Fallon asked.

"The three guards thought they were real pros. Fast moving, and as you said, hardly any conversation took place at all. The blond girl with the Indian student was too pissed off to notice much. She and the guards gave us some descriptions, but not much that's helpful." Marilyn Nelson sipped from her coffee cup. She had a small head, with a tidy nose, thin lips and was very blond. She was a Swede, one of the small-boned Swedes with small breasts and narrow hips. And sharp.

"All three of the perps were of average height, one a bit blocky—one of the guys who was holding weapons on them," she continued. "Not much at all to go on. The rubberized masks covered their hairlines."

"Next point," Fallon continued, "the firepower. The Brinks guys say that all three of them carried weapons in their right hands. The lead guy carried a machine pistol and the other two what looked like Glocks, probably nines or forties.

"Out in the open like that, that makes sense—nines. But with no shots, we have no chance to match up," Harper said.

"We're damn lucky there were no shots," Fallon said, staring him down.

"So like you said, Mikey, let's add it up," Nelson proffered. "Definitely pros, all the way."

Fallon flipped the chart and walked toward the small table on the edge of the room and poured himself some black coffee. "We know eight out of ten times there's some inside connection with these crews. Somebody inside knows enough to help plan it out." He pointed to Nelson. "Marilyn, take two or three of our guys and link up with that guy Stanton, the head of the University's security police. He looks like he knows what he's doing. Find out who's working over there with any kind of police record, and look into who's left there lately, who's disgruntled with them, or holding a grudge against them—that kind of stuff. Also check on the Brinks employees, all of them, but especially the three guards."

"Jesus, there's thousands employed at the school alone, and probably hundreds that left there within the last year," she replied.

"Then link up with the Boston cops too. If it's a manpower problem, use Stanton's people as well. Really bleed this one, Marilyn. Chances are there's an insider involved."

Moving back to the chart, he turned to Cameron. "Dave, you keep on the forensic stuff and while you're waiting, get the three Brinks guys back in and see if they remember anything else a day later. And go back to the Indian kid and his girl. Jog their memories. Try to sift something out here. Something that just hasn't hit the surface yet.

"Paul, you get on the networks. Coordinate with Boston and go over the usual suspects around town. And get into our database. See who's missing in action nationally, who's been active with armored car robbery in the last five years, at least. And talk to Boston about the weapons. Who's selling? Who's buying?"

Two and Out

"I'll need some agents—a dozen or so," Paul said.

"We're talking top priority here. I'll clear it with Morris. You know, and I know, that time's critical here. What we find out in the first couple of days makes it or breaks it. So let's get moving, and I'll see you all back here at 8:00 A.M. Sunday for a rundown."

"Another short day at the ranch. Right, Mikey?" Harper rejoined as they all stood.

23

As Johnny Casey walked by, Sonny Rossetti, Paulie Ayala's dumb gunnie, stuck out his forefinger and simultaneously effected a noise like a gunshot.

"Practicing your craft, Sonny?" Johnny asked, not waiting for an answer.

"Fuck you, Alky," Sonny replied.

Johnny continued toward the rear door and knocked.

"Come in."

Paulie Ayala sat behind the ornate oak desk, resplendent in his Armani suit, the early morning sun surrounding him as it reflected through the huge plate glass window. Behind him, Lake Suntaug wound its way toward Lynnfield.

Ayala looked up from his papers. "Well, well, priest. Come to pay your sinner's debt, huh?"

Johnny approached the desk and tossed a manila envelope onto the blotter. "$15,000, Paulie. Debt and vig paid in full."

Paulie opened the envelope and began counting. "You know, priest, I'm impressed. I really am. But then, I knew you'd be good for it."

Johnny started to edge toward the door and then stopped. "Then why do you always have that goon outside harassing me?"

Shifting in his chair, Ayala continued counting the packets. "Sonny? He means no harm. He's just protecting my interests." Looking up, he winked at Johnny.

As Johnny opened the door, Ayala stood.

"Hey, Johnny. It's Saturday. How about your BC Eagles against Virginia Tech this afternoon? Want some of that?"

"I'm off it for now, Paulie," Johnny responded, remembering Brian's admonition about spending, regretting the fact that already he had to pay out $15,000 against instructions.

"Well, if you change your mind, kickoff's not till 4 P.M., and Tech's a twelve point favorite. Think Tech can cover? That fuckin' Michael Vick is something else."

"BC can handle twelve," Johnny replied.

"I say they can't. I'll even give you thirteen on a good-sized bet."

Johnny turned to face him. "You're on for $10,000."

"Great, priest." Ayala walked toward the door and as Johnny stepped through signaled to Sonny.

Lumbering forward, Sonny stood in front of his boss. "Your friend there, the alky priest, has come into some form of inheritance, I think. Ask around. See what you can learn."

Sonny looked dumbfounded. "Ask where?"

"Forget it, you fuckin' moron. I'll do it myself," Ayala said, shaking his head and slamming the door behind him.

John A. Curry

24

"Rose of Washington Square" was definitely one of the most musical of Faye's films, Vic Fleming thought, as he fixated on the 1939 movie on his VCR. It had been Darryl F. Zanuck, in charge of production at Fox, who admitted that no one could sell a song as well as Alice Faye.

Was it those expressive eyes or the slight mouth tremble that sometimes bothered critics that made it so? Or was it the body stance? She almost always stood with her weight supported on one leg with the right leg bent at the knee. She displayed this same position in film after film, witness now her rendition of "I'm Always Chasing Rainbows."

As the images rolled on, he glanced at his watch. Phil Hanrahan would be here almost anytime. He cut the power with the remote control and turned on the table light. It had gone well, he felt. Almost without a hitch, and they were each $700,000 richer. For the fourth or fifth time he reviewed events in his mind, running them through as he did the old films he loved, remembering the scenes, pausing to savor the scenes.

It had, indeed, gone well. Despite his arrogance, the professor had foreseen the details, as well as provided a gem of a mark. They had struck on a Friday afternoon, a day when the campus was less populated, with both faculty and students scheduling themselves an elongated weekend. Their timing, too, had been precise and on target, again thanks to Brian's careful plotting. The use of rubberized masks, the getaway details, and especially the utilization of personnel who held no criminal records was ingenious, and very probably foolproof, he felt.

The people they had recruited had performed above his expectations. Mr. Cheney, whoever he was, appeared a bit fiery and impatient, yet in excellent control of himself. And the one Brian called Mr. Lieberman had surprised him. Although obviously jittery and unsure of himself, he, too, had shown some

Two and Out

charlies at critical points, not panicking when that dumb fuck Indian had approached them, keeping quiet and keeping talk to a minimum. No harm in his being nervous, in fact being somewhat nervous kept a person focused.

As he and Brian had discussed, he would call his friends in armed robbery at the beginning of the week, the old thirty-year-vet just inquisitive about Friday's heist. What do you guys have, old friends? And how about the Febs—what if anything, were they onto, besides pushing you guys around?

He walked toward the front door, flipping on the switch to light the encompassing darkness. A quiet night in Revere. An oxymoron?

Crossing the living room, he walked behind the portable bar and prepared the whiskey sour for Phil and the Jack straight up for himself. When the bell rang, he called out, "It's open, Phil."

As Hanrahan closed the door, Vic gestured him toward the bar seat. "Make yourself comfortable friend," he said, passing the gray man the mixed drink.

"How went the battle, Captain?" Hanrahan asked.

"Just fine, Phil. That envelope on the chair, that's for you."

Hanrahan turned to look behind him. "Captain, that's not necessary."

"Phil, it's to show my appreciation." He had been sure not to use any of the robbery money to show his appreciation.

Vic downed the Jack in one motion. "I need you to make contact with the same guy one more time. Pass some instructions on to him again."

"No problem, Cap. Just tell me where and when."

"In about a week, Phil. Now please take the money."

"It went well according to the news reports," Phil said, as he picked up the envelope.

"Couldn't have gone any better," Vic replied.

"Well, I'm happy you're thinking of getting out of this fuckin' weather, not spending many more long winter's nights here, Captain. A man like you—a friend like you—shouldn't be alone like this. Maybe in California..."

John A. Curry

"I'm looking forward to it, too, Phil," Vic interjected. "This retirement shit is fuckin' boring and with Sally gone, there's nothing here for me anymore, y' know?"

"Well, I'll miss you Captain," Phil said, extending his whiskey sour toward Vic.

"I'll have another Jack on that, Phil. You come out and visit some time. See LA. I'll show you the sights."

25

Brian Hughes sat in the fading afternoon sun at the Red Rock Bistro in Swampscott, the restaurant perched at the top of the sea wall, his view unobstructed on a marvelous early fall Saturday. Below him yuppies strolled on the sand at low tide, holding hands, as dogs of all sizes, perpetually in motion, chased the sea gulls, never ever with success.

To the north, above the beach, he could see the outlines of the huge Boston buildings, the John Hancock and the Prudential Center, and the financial district itself. To his right, the long sea wall ran from Swampscott back toward Lynn. Amateur runners and disciplined walkers mingled together, squeezing in their exercise before their Saturday night fun.

"When I was a kid growing up in Lynn, this place was an ice cream stand—Doane's," Johnny Casey said, trying to sip his VO and ginger slowly in front of Brian.

They sat apart from the two noisy couples at the far end of the restaurant, just a few steps from the entrance. At the maitred's station, a haughty young woman was having great trouble understanding why she couldn't bring her poodle into the dining area. They were practically outdoors anyway, weren't they? What was the problem?

"Will you listen to that fuckin' idiot," Brian said. "First the goddamn beasts are pissing on the beach or having a dump where people walk and now they want to come in and have a steak, too. Did you read the other day about people now bringing their mutts onto planes and into first class? Next, they'll be sitting on the pilot's laps or having a shit in the aisles."

"I'll take it you're not a dog lover," Johnny laughed. "Laura has a dog."

"How's she doing? Laura, not the dog," Brian added.

Johnny set the VO down. "I called her again today. She won't talk to me."

Brian studied his friend carefully. In just seconds the manic had faded into the depressive. It had always amazed Brian, despite his readings on the subject of mental health problems, how quickly these changes occurred in those who suffered with the malady.

"She'll come around, Johnny. It's hard for her, too, you know," he said quietly, his empathy for his friend coming through.

Johnny displayed his hangdog look. "I've fucked up my whole life, Brian. You know to me she's sort of a redemption, a new chance for me to make things right. To do something right. To make another human being's life better because I'm there." Glancing up, Johnny signaled the effeminate waiter. "You want another?"

"I'm all set, John." He decided to change the subject to try and move to a happier topic. "We pulled it off, Johnny. We fuckin' pulled it off. A whole day gone by, and it looks like we caught them all with their pants down."

Johnny's mood did not change perceptively. "It's only been a day, Bri. I wouldn't celebrate too soon."

"Well, by Monday we'll know more. I've got a way to find out what they know, but my gut's telling me they don't know jackshit."

Johnny frowned, the lines above his eyes coalescing. "I don't feel as good about it as you do."

Brian sighed and then bit his tongue. "What's wrong, Johnny?"

"I'm confused. I felt good about it yesterday, y' know? But today..."

"Good about what? Your involvement, right? Johnny, you did things right. You came through like a pro. Be fuckin' happy!"

Johnny sat still while the waiter deposited his third VO and ginger. "Brian, I was trained at BC to live a clean life, not to sin and so weren't you, too. Then we go out and rob people. It's a moral crisis for me."

"The hottest places in hell are reserved for those who, in times of great moral crisis, maintain their neutrality," Brian quoted.

Johnny smiled. "Richard Pryor say that?"

"Dante."

"Bichette?"

Brian grinned at him. "No wise ass. Dante. Didn't you learn anything at BC? Move off the dime, Johnny. That's what he meant. You can't worry about decisions you've already made. We've got enough to concern us, going forward. You made the decision to get involved. Let's not track backwards."

Johnny diverted his gaze toward the elongated windows and the ocean itself. A hundred yards away, four or five young boys braced themselves for the dash from seashore to the undulating waves, undoubtedly aware that in all probability this was their last swim of the season.

"I won't stay in neutral, Brian," he finally said. "I just have my ins and outs, you know? I just don't feel 100% good about being a fuckin' robber. So shoot me."

"Now that's the best thing you've said all afternoon," Brian said, reaching across the table and pumping his hand.

"Fuck you," Johnny replied, the manic expression coming on, the eyes lighting up, the grin spreading as the old ghosts receded, assisted by both friendship and the VO.

26

"Why can't I get my tongue pierced?" Jessica asked, as the Sunday morning sun poured through the kitchen window, highlighting myriad specks of dust on the dining room table.

Mike Fallon cast a disapproving look at his two youngest daughters who giggled in anticipation of his answer from across the table.

"Because your mother and I don't want you walking around like some Zulu. Tongues weren't made to decorate," he answered calmly.

"Paula Stickney is having it done," Jessica replied, just as calmly.

"If Paula Stickney should jump off the Tobin Bridge, we all should follow? End of discussion, Jessica."

"Amen." Rita Fallon stood in the doorway dressed in a frilly orange nightgown covered by a long blue robe.

"Mom! You're up!" Jessica bellowed, running to embrace her, followed rapidly by Nicole and Melissa.

Mike marveled at the change of direction. With most teenagers the issue at hand needed to be addressed, triggered by a pervasive selfishness not allowing them to see beyond their personal issue, in this case, the desire to walk through life with metal attached to one's interior parts. But Jessica continued to show him some increased maturity and the ability to understand the relative importance of events about her.

"Feel like some coffee?" Mike asked.

"Without my Jo, it's no go," she smiled.

"I'll get it," said Jessica.

"Ma, Jessica wants to get her tongue pierced," Nicole related mischievously.

"I heard, dear, and as your dad said, the answer is no."

Placing the coffee in front of her mother, Jessica leaned to kiss her. "It doesn't matter," she said.

"Stephanie Marks has one on her tit," Nicole blurted out.

"Nicole! We don't talk like that in front of Melissa—or anyone else for that matter!" Rita scolded.

"I'm sorry, Ma," Nicole said.

"What's a tit anyway?" Melissa asked.

Rita looked across at Mike. How to handle? The child psychology books would urge direct, honest involvement, but her instincts told her otherwise. "Her chest, Melissa. Stephanie wants to put a design on her chest, near her stomach."

"Oh. On her boob!" Melissa offered.

"Right." Rita looked aghast at her husband. "You going in today?" she asked, deciding to change the subject.

"Just for a couple of hours, to see where we are with the Brinks robbery. But if you're not feeling..."

"I'm fine, Mike. You go ahead. Is it a particularly tough case?"

"Too early to tell, but these first few days are always critical," he replied, sipping his coffee.

"Well, come home soon, Mikey. There are people here who love you," she said.

He stroked her hair and leaned across her shoulders to kiss her. "And don't I know that," he said.

"Like we figured—no prints at all," Dave Cameron reported from his seat at the conference table.

"And the fibers?"

"Plenty picked up, but it's going to take another day. Could be somethin' helpful out of that."

"Push them, Dave. We need the analysis fast." Fallon frowned. "How about the three Brinks guys?"

Cameron leaned forward and spread his hands. "Their stories haven't changed. They're suspended by the company for violating policy. The leader, Dunn, still claims he figured it was an easy assignment, a chance to get out of the truck and look around at the babes. Still says the three bandits were on them quick and just directed them to lie down. The only names the perps used were the names of the politicians themselves. His story's confirmed by the other guards and the girl."

"How's the Indian student?"

"He's doing fine," Cameron replied. "Fuckin' lucky. He ought to pray to Allah or Gandhi, or whatever the fuck he prays to, that he's still on this side of the mountain."

"Anything else, Dave?"

"Nada."

"Marilyn? Your turn."

From the doorway, Sam Morris moved into the room and took a seat. "Mind if I sit in Mike?" he asked.

Fallon tried to hide his real feelings. The principal coming in to observe the teacher. The concerned boss keeping a tight rein on the problem employee. Whatever. He shrugged his shoulders finally. "Go ahead, Marilyn."

She sat more erect now, opened her notebook, and made reference to it as she reported. "I met with Stanton, the Northeastern head of security. We spent most of the last two days going over employee records. There's two that are well worth pursuing—and that's just what we're doing—assuming there aren't 5,000 others who lied on the original application. But we're running all employee names against our file anyway.

"Probable #1 is a guy named Justin Kines, a custodian, convicted of armed robbery of an armored vehicle over in Somerville in '68 after a long record of similar perps. Old now. He's been out of Walpole for five years after serving almost thirty. One of the soldiers of fortune from Charlestown who believe armored car robbery's a rite of passage for a Townie. He's looked clean since then."

"He sounds real interesting," Fallon said.

"Probable #2 is Melvin Taylor, a food services staffer. Out of Mission Main, down the street a mile. Black guy who cut his teeth on Annunciation Road running with a gang of armed robbers called the Pit Bulls. Boston says they're a nice group of gang bangers. Cut your balls off as soon as look at you. He served ten years for armed robbery. But Taylor's been employed for three years now with no record. I asked Boston to call in Kines. He'll be here sometime today."

"Anything from our data bases or Boston's?" Morris asked.

Harper nodded. "We've been on the networks. The hot dog locally is Billy Flanagan from over in Charlestown. He's had a history with any number of crews and the word on the street is he's formed his own now. Former paratrooper with a solid appetite for violence. He's on parole now."

"What about the national data bases?" Morris asked.

Harper held up the computer printout. "We've got agents checking into at least eight possibilities—crews with an MO similar to our darlings."

"You still convinced these guys are pros?" Morris directed his question at Fallon.

"There's no reason to think otherwise, Sam," Mike replied calmly. "They planned like pros and performed like pros. In and out in two minutes and off the streets in another two minutes. No prints, no early forensics, no early word on the street. It's all leaning in that direction."

"We're watching for a show of big dough spenders around town," Nelson added.

"With Flanagan, we're looking to see if there's heavy spending among those close to him," Harper added. "But it's only been a couple of days."

"Bring him in so we can roust him a bit," Fallon directed.

"How's Boston cooperating?" Morris asked.

"The head of their armed robbery unit is a guy named Frank Sheridan. Good guy I've known for years," Fallon replied. "I don't catch any resentment toward the Bureau."

"We've been in touch with their string of informers as well as our own. Maybe something will develop there," Harper said.

Morris pushed his chair back and stood. "Weapons checks going on?"

"We're on it, Sam," Mike replied. "Both Boston and our guys are checking with the sellers. We'll see who's been buying Glocks or machine pistols lately."

"Well, good." Morris said, moving to the door. "You've got plenty to do, and we're now almost forty-eight hours away from the event. Let's hope something breaks soon. Every hour works against us."

"Let's talk to Kines, Taylor, and Flanagan today," Mike directed as they all rose from their chairs." "Marilyn, you and Paul take Kines and Taylor. I'll get on Flanagan."

27

Johnny Casey awoke on Sunday morning, trying to remember what had happened. After he and Brian left the Red Rock, he had driven over to Eastern Avenue to Monte's and sat at the bar watching the BC game. Now, as he placed his bare feet in the slippers and stood, he remembered. Virginia Tech 48, Boston College 34. Plus 14 points. Fuckin' Michael Vick and the Hokies. Plus 14 meant his $10,000 was down the drainpipe by one point. One damn point!

He must have drowned his sorrows at the bar because he could not remember much else. How had he gotten home? He wasn't sure.

The sing-song of his slippers slapping against the linoleum kitchen floor was the only sound he heard as he headed in a slow, veering course toward his coffee maker. From Lewis Street below, he caught the sight of a young boy exiting a car, delivering the Sunday papers. Little lazy bastards, he thought. When I was a kid, we walked, and we walked with the heavy bag of papers draped from our shoulders. Now parents in Mercedes drive their little cherubs up and down the street as if they were delivering mink coats. Oh, well, he thought, it takes a family to build a village.

From the living room, the telephone rang, its volume level penetrating and overwhelming. He had deliberately set it high for fear that he might miss an important phone call while in one of his frequent fogs. He let it ring a second time, trying to determine who might be calling him at nine o'clock on a Sunday morning. Ayala looking for his $10,000? He didn't need that call right now. Maybe it was Brian, but he very seldom called, and for the last three months not at all.

On the third ring, he quickened his pace toward the bedroom and picked the phone up. "Hello," he muttered.

"Johnny, this is Donna. How are you?"

Surprised, he almost dropped the phone, but then composed himself. "Hey, Donna."

"You all right, Johnny?" she asked, a trace of annoyance in her voice.

"Donna, I'm fine. Really. You just surprised me, y' know? It being Sunday morning."

"Well, the reason I'm calling is I wondered what you had planned for today."

"Planned?" he repeated, wondering where this was leading. "Not much, probably watch the Pats on TV."

"You sure you're okay? Not drinking or anything?"

"Donna, for Christ's sake. What do I have to do? Pass a physical?"

Donna paused for a moment. "Laura wants to see you, Johnny. For the last day or two she's asked me if you could take her to the movies over in Danvers at Liberty Tree Mall."

What had it been? At least a year since he had last seen his daughter? He didn't know how to react, and so he reacted poorly. "I don't know, Donna," he hesitated. "She wants to see me?" he asked, the surprise now creeping into his voice.

"Yes, Johnny. Isn't that a good sign?"

"Do you have any idea why she changed her mind?"

Donna skipped another beat before answering him. "She's almost thirteen years old, Johnny, and confused. She's hurt and hateful one minute, and happy and loving the next. She's a kid."

"Well, I thank you, Donna. I'm sure you..."

"It's her choice, Johnny. You treat her right, and make sure she has a good time."

Why was it that she appeared to be lecturing him one minute and then could be understanding and sympathetic the next?

"What time does she want to go?"

"The movie starts at 3:20 P.M."

"I'll be there at quarter of."

"Have her back here by 6:30, okay?"

"Fine, Donna, and thanks."

"So what are we going to see, princess?" he asked as they drove along Route 128 into Danvers, the honky tonk of the Liberty Tree Mall appearing out of the flatlands to their left.

"I'm not your princess," Laura replied coldly, her eyes riveted on the curving ribbon of highway, her concentration intact.

"Your being a princess is in the eye of the beholder. To me, you're a princess," he answered, almost defiantly, emphasizing each word.

"Well I'm not," she countered angrily.

"Okay," he sighed. "So let's get back to square one. What do you want to see, Laura? Is that better?"

Apparently not. She did not respond.

Johnny Casey tried to remember his child development lessons while pushing into the background the child psychology his father and the nuns had practiced on him. Talk sassy to an adult and a backhander would straighten out your recalcitrant ways, as defined by them, not by the child.

"I want to see The Perfect Storm," she announced out of the blue, as if any other option were not to be considered.

He decided to demonstrate his intellectual side. "I read Junger's book," he said.

"Who?"

"Junger."

"Who's he?"

"The author Sebastian Junger. The movie is based on his book."

"I think the movie came first, and he copied it," she declared firmly.

"Whatever, princess. I could be mistaken."

"Don't call me that name," she said, wrapping herself into herself, squishing almost into a fetal position.

He decided to retreat and play catcher to her pitcher.

John A. Curry

They walked through the entrance to the movie complex after he paid enough money for a luncheon at Pier 4 for tickets to the movie. "Want some popcorn?" he asked.

"No."

"Your tickets are to theater #2," a pock-faced young adolescent who just barely qualified as an usher-customer services representative indicated. "It'll be available in a few minutes."

Johnny Casey scanned the indoor marquee, noting that at least twenty different movies were playing, some on three different screens.

"I think we're straight ahead on the left," he said.

They entered a graham-cracker box of a theater with maybe ninety seats, eighty of them within five rows of the screen. Instantly, he recalled the movie theaters of his youth, massive cinema palaces with thousands of seats, with the option of near screen, mid, or rear orchestra, and balcony seating. To enjoy this movie, he would have to visit the Pearle Vision Center over in Saugus first. Stop bitching, he urged himself.

In the second row, he tried to concentrate on the plight of the six swordfishermen caught in the storm of the century. Thank God he had not had any VO, or else the endless streams of water crisscrossing the screen would have capsized his stomach as well as the boat. He glanced at Laura, who seemed lost with the crew at sea, her admiring gaze concentrated on George Clooney and Mark Wahlberg.

When it ended, and lights flooded the near empty theater, he decided to initiate conversation once again.

"You like that, Laura?"

"It was okay," she said, her glance diverted here and there, everywhere, but never on him.

"Well, they were heroic men, weren't they?"

"They were dummies, Dad. Real dopes. Going out to the Flemish Cap when a major storm was coming down. They weren't heroic at all; they were just six dummies."

Two and Out

Talking to pre-teens was such fun, he thought, as they headed back to Lynn. She sat silently, adrift somewhere in space, for the balance of the ride. When they arrived home, she virtually jumped out of the car without a word. He watched her bound up to the front door, seemingly oblivious to his feelings, to his desire to connect. What was that old GE slogan? Progress is our most important product? You couldn't prove it by him.

28

"So what can you tell me about last Friday's Brinks job?" Mike Fallon asked, pacing back and forth across the small interrogation room in the huge Boston Police Headquarters building on Ruggles Street.

"Fuck you, cop," Billy Flanagan responded. He was almost as tall as Mike. He was slightly heavier, which could have been due to the new muscle he had developed over the last year through weight training, or to the huge appetite with which he had struggled most of his life. His black hair, a bit prematurely gray, was swept back from his forehead and held in place by spray. According to his record, he was thirty-three years old, but he looked like fifty-three. He was dressed in a plaid shirt, chinos, and Nike sneakers.

"Mind your manners, Billy, and answer the man's question," Sheridan replied softly, before Mike could. If any sixty-year-old man could be said to have an innocent face that would be the head of Boston's armed robbery unit. His soft voice, sweet smile, and sympathetic manner had fooled many a thief into a confession he seemed to think he was entrusting to a priest. Flanagan eyed Sheridan disdainfully and then directed his attention to Mike. "I don't know nothin' about it."

Mike pulled up the seat and sat directly across from Flanagan and Sheridan. "Is that right, Billy? Our sources tell us you've formed a new crew over on Monument Avenue, a few gang bangers for the big jobs like last week's."

Flanagan pointed to the Newports on the table. "Can I have one?"

"Be my guest," Mike replied.

He lit the cigarette slowly and then inhaled deeply. "Your sources are full of shit, cop. No way am I involved in that takedown."

"Where were you last Friday afternoon, Billy?"

"Like I told the detective here, I was havin' a late lunch around 1:30-1:45 at the 99 over on Rutherford Avenue. You checked it out, right?" he asked Sheridan.

"We did, Billy," Sheridan said. "There's three or four witnesses say you were there. All Townies."

"What's there now, laws about where a person's witnesses come from? Besides which, if I'm in Charlestown at 1:45 P.M., there's no fuckin' way I'm over on Huntington Avenue a few minutes before two o'clock. So like I said, cop, go fuck yourself. You ain't pinning this one on Billy Flanagan."

Mike steepled his fingers beneath his chin and leaned forward across the table. "You know, Billy, I've been investigating armored car robberies for maybe fifteen years now. So we're not turnips off the truck. You could be sitting at the 99 enjoying your diet of fuckin' fried clams and chasing them down with a couple of boilermakers, while some fellow assholes are heisting the truck over at Northeastern. The record here says you're a planner known to participate, but not always. So what's it prove whether you were on site or not?"

Billy Flanagan placed his thumb and forefinger over the lit end of the cigarette and put it out. "You're barking up the wrong tree, copper. I don't have any crew, and I was nowhere near Huntington Avenue on Friday, and I didn't plan shit."

"So let's assume for the moment you weren't involved, Billy," Mike shifted gears. "What do you hear about the heist on the streets?"

Flanagan smirked as he dropped the crushed cigarette into the paper ash tray. "What do I look like—the fuckin' information bureau?"

Mike tapped the file in front of him. "You're due in court on a charge of domestic violence in a month. Your lady over in Charlestown got the shit beat out of her and says you helped separate a couple of her teeth. Pretty fuckin' brave ex-paratrooper, hitting a woman. This one has some balls though, Billy. She's in protective custody and is going to nail your ass."

Flanagan averted his stare. "Maybe," he responded.

Mike looked at Sheridan. "What about it, Frank?"

Sheridan reached for the cigarettes. "Violation of parole if it sticks, and there's also two friends of the victim willing to testify they saw Mr. Macho here clock her with a closed fist. Not too sharp, whacking her in the fuckin' McDonald's across the street from the Fleet Center."

"They was mistaken," Flanagan replied evenly. "She slipped on some fuckin' grease on the floor."

"I don't think so, Billy. I think you're going down what with a restraining order out on you and all. She's scared shit, Billy, and wants you in Walpole for a while."

"She slipped," Billy repeated calmly.

"No, you slipped," Fallon replied, elevating his voice. "And maybe you slipped last Friday, too, Flanagan. We're going to be all over you and your boyos for the next few weeks. You won't be able to take a piss without company. If you were in it, we're going to find out."

He stood and picked up the personnel file. "As for the girl, between Frank here and me, we'll see you go away, Billy. No fuckin' way you're not going back in the slammer." He paused for effect. "Unless you suddenly come up with some information that's helpful to us. Something that points us in a direction."

Flanagan glared at him. "I told you I ain't no fuckin' songbird."

Suddenly, Fallon's beeper went off. "We're done here, Captain. If Joy Boy here doesn't have a change of attitude, I'll manufacture two more witnesses on the D.V. charge. I'll speak to the judge as well. We'll have his ass in Walpole within a month."

"You prick!" Billy screamed, losing control for the first time.

"You're going to love Walpole," Fallon said, heading for the door.

In the corridor, he called Nelson's cell phone number. "Yeah, Marilyn?"

"How did it go with Flanagan?"

"He's a hard case. We need to pressure him all around. We'll see."

"I called you about Kines, the custodian with the long record."

"Yeah?"

"I don't think there's anything there. He's a burnout. He acts like a guy just wants to be left alone. Livin' out his life, y' know? Everyone around him—his parole officer, neighborhood minister, new girlfriend—claim he's completely reformed. He even reported to the University that he had the long record. I think he's a clear example that some of them change."

"Where was he last Friday?"

"Working as always. Never misses a day. He's also assigned to the building over on the Fenway—Kerr Hall. During the course of the day, he never even comes near the student center. I don't see him for this."

"Okay. Let's forget him for now. What about the other active employee? What was his name? The Pit Bulls guy."

"Taylor. Melvin Taylor. Harper's seeing him as we speak."

"Okay. I'll catch you later. I'm going to check in on Rita. See you on Monday at 9:00 A.M. at the office. Can you reach the others and let them know?"

Nelson thought hard for a moment before she asked. "She doing any better, Mikey?"

He seldom wanted to talk to anyone about his feelings, but suddenly he realized if he could speak to anyone it would be Nelson. Yet he decided to give his standard reply. "Thank you for asking."

"Sure," Nelson replied slowly, and then gathered her courage. "You know Mikey, if ever you need a shoulder to lean on—and I don't mean literally—I'm here for you. Y' know, a cup of coffee or something?"

"I know," he said, before pushing the "end" button. Too many well-intentioned people, too many people focusing on him when he had trouble focusing period.

29

On Monday morning, three days after the robbery, Tony Amonti playfully hoisted his son onto his shoulders and raced along Glendon Beach, his start and stop tactics sending Doug into fits of ecstasy.

"Go, horsey!" he yelled.

And as Tony accelerated for ten yards or so, he would exhort "Stop, horsey!"

"Horsey is getting tired, Doug. How about a little rest for Daddy?"

"No! Up horsey and run faster!"

From the east the sun resembled the emblem on the Japanese flag, with spidery beams emanating from the red core ball. From the shore, the sea ran flat to the horizon. At seven o'clock, the wind was surprisingly light, a precursor of a marvelous late September day.

"You have to get to school, sport. Or have you forgotten?" Tony asked lifting Doug high onto his shoulders and sprinting once again.

"Do I have to, Daddy? Let's just stay here."

As Tony stopped running, he sat Doug on his shoulders and then grabbing him by the waist, deposited him on the sand.

"Look, Daddy. There's the lady!" Doug announced, pointing south toward the jetty separating the public from the private beaches.

"Hello, Mrs. Adams," Tony yelled, as he simultaneously waved. Accompanied by a young thin woman, she walked briskly toward them, her pants pulled up above her knees, her feet slapping the shallow water.

"Hello, Tony. And Doug! How are you and why aren't you getting ready for school?"

Doug shyly slid behind his father. "Daddy, I know that other lady," he whispered.

Two and Out

Tony hoped he was not staring at the dark-haired woman dressed in tan slacks and a short-sleeved white blouse. She held her sandals in her hands and walked on the sand, being particularly careful to avoid the on-rushing tide.

"Meet our neighbor, Grace Fletcher, Tony. Grace, this is Tony Amonti and his son and my good friend Doug."

"You live in the trailer park?" Tony asked.

"Actually on Glendon Road, right over there. First house behind the restaurant."

"Daddy! Daddy!" Doug beseeched him.

Tony bent to his son. "What is it, Doug?"

He pointed to the young woman. "She's my teacher!"

The young woman smiled broadly at Doug. "Good morning, Doug," she said.

"You really are his teacher?" Tony asked.

She brushed a long strand of hair from her eyes. "That's right. Not his regular teacher, but Doug comes to me from his regular second grade class for help with reading and language skills."

"Well, it's a small world!" Mrs. Adams exclaimed. "I've known Gracie here since she was the young boy's age, cavorting in these waters. I remember when your dad was hoisting you up on his shoulders, young lady."

"That was a long time ago, Maude," she replied smiling.

Tony noted the sun slanting directly into her eyes, accentuating their blueness, contrasting that blue with the raven-like black of her hair.

"Actually Mr. Amonti, I'm pleased we've met like this. I was going to call you regarding Doug."

At the mention of his name, Doug moved more directly behind his father, his body now almost perfectly still.

"About Doug?" Tony asked.

"He tells me you're going to California soon."

"That's right, within the month," Tony replied.

"Well I'd like to speak to you about his progress, about the things he'll need to work on whatever school he attends."

Tony gripped Doug's hand and gently moved him to his side. "I can stop by if you like."

"How about tomorrow at 2:30?"

"You're on. I'll be there."

"Well, fine. And I'll see you in school, Doug," she said warmly.

"You make sure you go today, young man," Mrs. Adams added, as Doug moved back behind his father.

"How goes the battle, Frank?"

"Now this couldn't be that late great crime fighter Vic Fleming, could it? How's retirement treating you, Cap?"

"It'll be treating me a lot better when I can get the fuck out of here and move to some place with sunshine, Frank."

"Well, I envy you Vic. A couple of years more of this bullshit and I'll be joining you. You been following the Pats?"

"Yeah, been watching them every Sunday. So far this guy Belichick doesn't impress me. He looks like a scared rabbit in the interrogation room when he faces the media."

Sheridan laughed loudly. "You ain't shittin! What the hell does Kraft see in him anyway? What did he do in Cleveland?"

"One good season out of five," Vic replied. "I think we really miss the Tuna."

"God dam Parcells is moving the Jets right past us."

"Got time for lunch today, Frank? It's on me."

"Jeez, Vic. I hate to say no, but we're in bed with the Feebs on the Brinks job. There's no time to take a whizz, never mind a lunch break."

"Yeah, I've been following it on the tube. Media doesn't have much to say. Anything happening?"

Sheridan didn't hesitate for a moment in discussing the case with his former boss and close friend. "You know a guy named Mike Fallon with the FBI?"

"I heard of him. Never met him," Vic replied.

"He's a good guy considering he's with that bunch of bureaucrats. It's his crew leading the investigation, working with us."

Vic paced his apartment, pulling the long telephone extension with him. He had long ago realized that with important phone calls, it is critical to be on the move, never relaxed. He needed to be mentally alert, to be cognizant of any nuances while appearing to be only mildly interested in the conversation.

"They got anything yet?" he inquired. "You and I both know the first few days on these armored car jobs are critical."

"Not much at all. We've checked out the inside possibilities, and so far come up with nothing. No leads from the witnesses, either. They were real pros, we think, so we've lugged in Billy Flanagan for one. Remember him from over in Charlestown?"

"Yeah, the former paratrooper, right?"

"Right. We're twisting his balls both to see if he was involved—which I doubt, by the way—and whether he can help us."

"So no word on the street?"

"Nada. Fuckin' morgue out there so far."

"You got your own theory on it, Frank, or does Fallon have one?"

Sheridan reflected back to his time working with Vic Fleming. A tough commander like Parcells, but one who always drew your best thinking, a leader respected for his ability to listen to others' viewpoints before coming to a conclusion of his own.

"Yeah, Vic, I do. Fallon thinks they're pros for sure, probably with an insider—either at Brinks or Northeastern—involved. Personally, I think it's an outside crew, some new outfit in from Detroit, Chicago, someplace. But I don't think they're local. Flanagan and the likes of him are too fuckin' dumb to have pulled this one off."

"Interesting. You're making my old juices flow," Vic laughed.

"Yeah? Well remember what that president of BU said about guys your age."

"Who? You mean John Silber?"

"Yeah. That's him. Silber. He said, 'When you're ripe, you're ripe.' You old guys shouldn't hang on too long after retirement, was what he was saying." Sheridan laughed.

"Screw him," Vic replied.

"Hey, I got to go, buddy. How about a rain check on that lunch at Ambrosia?"

Vic laughed. "I never mentioned Ambrosia. McDonald's was what I was thinking."

"Well think again before you call again, you cheap prick."

"You know what I just said about John Silber? The same applies to you, Frank."

"Yeah, what was it that guy Lenny Bruce used to say about people saying "Fuck you" to you? 'Why get angry?' he said. 'Fuck you is a nice experience."

"Get back to work and catch some thieves, Frank."

"Fuck you, Vic."

30

Brian crossed at the State House and walked down the steps toward the Park Street Station. Around him, briefcase clad young professionals, both men and women, marched with determination toward the downtown buildings. No one looked at anyone else, he noted. Probably in fear that they might have to become involved or smile a bit and destroy Monday's mood. Personally, he himself loved Mondays more than any other weekday because he had no class schedule other than a graduate seminar at eight o'clock. The first workday of the week was largely his, contractually, to do his research or to work on his much delayed book. But on this particularly warm September day, he intended to do research of another type.

Traversing Tremont Street, he moved into the downtown, heading toward South Station, and his second visit to the train terminal in the last two weeks—both on Mondays and both to meet the Acela coming in from New York.

On Summer Street he blended with the crowd which broke occasionally to allow individuals access to the variety of coffee shops along the way. He stopped to buy the Globe from a newshawk across the street from the terminal.

That was how he first conceived the idea for the second and final score. From the newspaper. He had read of two Wells, Maine, men involved in a shoot-out with police at Chicago's Union Station. They had been traveling armed, wearing body armor, and carrying huge amounts of cash.

That had got him thinking. Train travel had to be attractive to criminals because of its relative anonymity. Airports require that passengers show photo identification and pass through metal detectors while car rental agencies demand a credit card and a driver's license. But on a train, there was no ID or luggage check. A dealer or bookie or any other criminal could travel with or without luggage and never fear detection. In time, he sensed, the police, whether the Drug Enforcement Administration, Boston, or Amtrack Security would catch up, but for now they were woefully behind. Unless the assholes committing the crime were stupid enough to flash huge sums of money around the railroad personnel, which was exactly how the idiots from Maine had been caught.

He had run his idea by Fleming during the summer. They had met at the Winthrop Arms Hotel over near Revere Beach, about a mile into Winthrop. From the lobby they could enjoy their drinks and gaze out over the water at the vastness of the great Atlantic stretched out before them, the coastline winding in and out as it touched Lynn, Swampscott, and Marblehead in the distance.

"It's very workable, Brian," Fleming mused. "How the hell did you think of the fuckin' trains?"

Brian held up a hand. "Maybe we found the venue, Captain, but I don't have a who or any idea as to who's carrying what?"

"What are we—Abbott and Costello? I'll find the who and the what through my own research."

And he had. Salvatore "Sally" Ayala, also known as "The Prince of Darkness," head of operations and subordinate only to Joey Sansone in the Mafia corporate culture of Boston. It had taken some time, but through one of his street sources, two or three of them left over from his days in narcotics, Vic had learned of Sally's frequent trips between Boston and New York, transporting cash to be laundered in the Big Apple for clean green coming back to Boston. Rumor had it that over two million dollars was involved with each transaction.

His source revealed that virtually every Sunday Sally Ayala would take the train to New York City and then return the very next day on the Acela. Vic had then sent Phil Hanrahan, a person unknown to Brian, on reconnaissance visits, first establishing the consistency of the pattern, and then trailing Sally and his female companion to Penn Station on the third Sunday.

Hanrahan had followed them to the New Yorker Hotel, just across the street from the train terminal. They had registered and ensconced themselves in a fourth floor suite. After registering himself, Phil sat in the lobby from 7 P.M., past midnight, waiting for any sign of activity. Vic had figured correctly that, whatever they did, they would not be out late, not if they were to catch the 6:00 A.M. leaving New York the very next day.

At ten minutes past midnight, Sally Ayala strolled into the New Yorker lobby, the blond on one arm and a Hartman light tan briefcase on the other.

Back in his own room Hanrahan had shaved and then sat up nursing coffee until 5:00 A.M. Thinking logically, he had decided to board the train without waiting for Sally and his blond. Three and a half hours later, he had disembarked quickly, and then stood in the rotunda of South Station scanning his newspaper, watching the other passengers leave the train. And there they were. He then followed them to the street where they hailed a cab.

Fleming never told him Hanrahan's name, but they had agreed that Brain should also scout out the situation, observe the marks himself, and establish a plan for the entire crew. And so here he was, sitting at one of the round tables facing track #8, gazing occasionally at both his Rolex and at the Boston Globe. At exactly 9:15 A.M. passengers began streaming into the rotunda from the sliding doors, forming a long ribbon, their eyes everywhere, looking for friends or for the way to new transportation.

He spotted Ayala and the woman, halfway back in the conga line. Brian had concentrated last week on the blond. Was she just the accompanying whore, or was she armed and potentially dangerous? This week, like last week, she wore a long black fall coat with full pockets and for the second week her hands never came out of the garment. He had to conclude that she was carrying.

Three things impressed him concerning Ayala himself. For one, he was both tall and thin, the antithesis of the stereotype of a Mafia figure. Through the long leather coat he wore, Brian observed his underdeveloped frame. Secondly, he was extremely observant. On both occasions he strolled across the rotunda, toward the Dewey Square exit, neither talking with nor looking at his companion. His gaze was focused on events around him, particularly those on his periphery. He swiveled his head ever so slightly to catch the crowd and its movements, waiting for any sign that his sojourn across the floor was being interrupted by counter-movement. As they passed his table, Brian was close enough to notice the long scar that wound from Ayala's right eye to the side of his mouth. Thirdly, his right hand never left the loose, full pocket of the leather coat. His left hand held the Hartman briefcase close to his body.

When they had exited the terminal, Brian sat thinking for another half-hour. Last week he had noticed that Sally Ayala never once looked behind him. Why wouldn't he be as concerned about his rear as he was his front and sides? Was there something else here—someone covering him from behind?

For sure. This time Brian had carefully scanned the group following behind Ayala. And he had settled on the short, dumpy man in another long, leather coat, his hands thrust into both pockets. He tried to observe the man as much as he could, but would still want to return a third time next Monday to both concentrate on him and on his movements.

He began to form a plan. He smiled to himself. The Dean would never appreciate that his kind of research was far more difficult than writing a book. And the tenure committee would give far less credence to this type of hands-on research than to some philosophical, theoretical presentation.

31

"Hey, moron!" Paulie Ayala yelled out to his muscle. No answer.

"Sonny! Are you fuckin' out there with your head up your ass or what? Huh?" he bellowed.

At that very moment the front door on the first floor of the Ayala Business Enterprises office suite opened. "Sonny! Get in here will you!"

Johnny Casey looked around the anteroom and, finding no one available, crossed directly to the closed door and knocked.

"Now you have to fuckin' knock?"

Opening the door, Johnny Casey hand saluted Ayala a la Terrell Davis and the Denver Broncos. "No one's out there, Paulie."

"What the fuck you want, priest?" Ayala said, cradling the phone in his left ear. He addressed the other party. "I don't know where he is, probably out playing with his meat somewheres. I'll have him call you back. Okay?"

Hanging up, he signaled Johnny forward. Johnny reached into his sports coat, found the envelope, and laid it on Ayala's desk. "Seems like I'm doing this a lot lately," he said.

Ayala presented his best smile. "The money from the Virginia Tech bet, right? I didn't expect to be paid this quickly, Johnny. No time to run up the vig, you pay me this quickly." He began to count the bills.

"It's all there, Paulie."

Flicking his fingers through the envelope, Paulie nodded. "And so it is. What you do? Come in to a large inheritance or marry some rich old crow?"

Johnny avoided his stare. "Neither. Just some good luck elsewhere. Some ponies running true to form down at Gulfstream."

Ayala eyed him suspiciously. "Really?" he finally replied. "Well, I'm glad your luck's changing. How about a bet for Saturday? Notre Dame? BC?"

Johnny shook his head vigorously. "I'm going to try to lay off for a while now that I'm back even."

From the outer room they could hear the door slam. Momentarily Sonny appeared in the doorway. "I'm back," he announced.

Ayala stared him down while he lit a cigarette from the pack on his desk.

"What?" Sonny asked defensively.

"You're back?" Ayala exploded. "I never even knew you left! That was my fuckin' cousin Sally on the line, your godfather wantin' to speak directly to you just five minutes ago, you fuckin' dildo. Where were you?"

Sonny studied his feet and then shifted his position ever so slightly.

"I'll see you guys later," Johnny said, pointing his index finger at Sonny and winking as he went through the doorway.

"Well?" Paulie demanded.

"I went to look at the ladies at the mall," Sonny stammered.

"What fuckin' ladies?"

"You know. The ones in their shorts that walk around the inside of the mall."

"You mean those old crows from the senior center? They must be between sixty and death, you fuckin' pervert!"

Sonny lowered his head, awaiting further abuse.

Paulie signed deeply and reached into his desk drawer.

"Call Sally. He's got some sort of job that needs doing. That is if you can break away from your mall dolls."

Grace Fletcher had this habit of hooking her hair behind her ear frequently as she spoke. She sat with Tony Amonti on the lower level of Michael Patrick's restaurant on Route 28 in

Two and Out

Dennisport. How did we get here? He found himself wondering as she continued to speak of her background.

This afternoon he had visited the elementary school a mile or two back on this same road. While they discussed Doug, he found her attractive in a tomboyish way. She kept her hair at shoulder length. She wore little make-up, but she had sharp, knowing eyes and a somewhat sad smile, as if she saw the humor and tragedy in everything at once.

She was professional while also being pleasant and gregarious. For more than a half-hour she had both spoken about and demonstrated Doug's slowness with phonics. He could not remember certain letters of the alphabet at all and regularly confused "a" with "o" and "j" with "g". But curiously, he was performing up to grade level in math. What he needed most was constant repetition with his letters. She had provided Tony with copies of basic phonics stories like "Sam I Am," emphasizing the short "a" sounds and with similar stories with word after word involving the other short vowel sounds.

In particular, she had expressed concerns about the boy's basic shyness and lack of confidence in himself. Did he play much with other children? She had inquired because, despite her efforts, he remained aloof from peers. Again, she had suggested some ideas to alleviate his son's problem. In passing, she had referenced her knowledge that his wife had died in childbirth. Above all, she had expressed a joy and an enthusiasm about working with Doug and the desire to continue his integration into the mainstream second grade class.

Caught up in her fervor and becoming increasingly confident, he had just blurted it out. "I'd like to show my appreciation, Miss Fletcher, for your help here. Would you have time for dinner some night this week?"

And in the manner of the modern woman she had surprised him with her reply. "I'd be happy to have dinner with you, Mr. Amonti, but you really don't have—"

"But I would like to," he had interrupted.

"How about tonight then?" she had quickly replied.

John A. Curry

They took advantage of the long break that the jazz quartet allowed itself, and as she played with her hair, she told him she had grown up in Sagamore, a true blue Cape Codder, attended Bourne High, and then the University of Massachusetts at Boston. Her parents now lived in Wellfleet, but she had treasured her independence and had found both the special education teaching position in the Dennis—Yarmouth public schools and the cottage rental in Dennis. She simply glowed when describing her work.

"How long you been teaching?" he asked.

She kept fussing with her hair. "It's only my second year, but I hope I always feel about it like I do now. Those children are special. Kids like Doug, you know? I see potential in all of them. We just need—parents and teachers alike—to draw it out of them. We don't all develop at the same pace and as long as we keep that in mind—"

She suddenly caught herself, the crimson flowing to her cheeks, the new hesitancy in her speech matched by her pausing with her hand in mid-air. "I'm sorry, Mr. Amonti. I -"

"It's Tony," he replied. "Can I call you Grace?"

She didn't hesitate for a second. "Sure. Now how about something about you before I go on babbling all night."

He smiled across at her, the dimple on his chin parting as his face broadened. "There's not a lot to tell," he said. "I grew up in Ames, Iowa, on a farm. My dad ran an auto body shop right outside the city, and from age five all I could think about was cars, fixing them, driving them, polishing them. I wasn't much good at anything else, though I did manage to get through high school. Worked for my dad until I got enough together to head for Des Moines and con some race track guys into taking me on as an apprentice driver."

Grace templed her hands under her chin and leaned forward as Tony paused for a bite of his scrod.

He stole a quick glance across at her as if debating whether to go on. "I had some success at first, enough to ask Claire, my childhood sweetheart back in Ames, to join me. We got married about eight years ago now, and then..." He looked away.

"It must have been very hard on you," Grace offered.

He averted her eyes. "Well, you don't expect to take your wife to the hospital knowing in advance that a baby boy will be coming home with you and then find that the world just blew up in your face."

He stopped himself not wanting to dwell on tragedy, not with her in particular. "But it brought me Doug," he said enthusiastically.

She went back to hooking her hair. "He loves his daddy. That's all he talks about."

Tony smiled at her. "Something tells me he kind of likes his new teacher, too."

She smiled across at him, a bright alert smile which made him reflect for a moment on Sandy and on the poor judgement he had shown, maybe out of sheer loneliness, in becoming involved with her.

"Where in California will you be going?"

"Probably San Diego. I can get more regular work out there as a driver or mechanic at the racetrack. Maybe I'll quit the driving altogether. I worry about the boy, y' know? If something were to happen to me. There's not much work here for me anyway. Mainly I want to get him into a good school environment."

"I have a close friend out there in La Jolla. If you'd like, I'll ask about the school situation for you."

He studied her face carefully. "I'd like that very much," he replied softly.

To their right, the jazz quartet returned and took their positions. When they started up, he was reminded once again why he preferred pop music. If more than a handful of the customers could identify what they were playing as "It Had To Be You," it would be a miracle.

Above the din she pointed to her watch. "Have to get up early tomorrow," she almost shrieked.

He nodded and beckoned to the waitress.

32

Johnny Casey sat at a small square table at Rolly's just off Wyoma Square in Lynn. The most popular breakfast spot in the city was filled with a combination of harried executives downing their coffee and donuts before work and clusters of retirees who settled into their seats, oblivious of time.

He sat by himself enjoying his coffee, and studied the crowd, noting the very careful attention paid to each customer by Jane Teal, the owner. He decided that family-run restaurants had it all over the chains up and down Route One. He thought of the television advertisements for the major chains, ones such as McDonald's, where bright, beautiful, cheery women who looked like vice presidents of the company greeted you from behind the counters. Yea, right. The reality was some ugly dummy who could hardly make change for a quarter would look sullenly at you and more than likely fuck up your order.

Suddenly his cell phone chirped and he answered it quickly, averting the disdainful look from the senior citizen couple at the next table.

"Hello."

"Dad, it's Laura," she replied nervously.

He fought back his surprise and tried to sound as if their communication was normal.

"Hey, prin..." He stopped. "Hey, Laura. What's up?"

"Can you come to Sacred Heart and get me? I tried calling Mom, but no one's home there."

"What's the problem, Laura?"

"I'm sick," she said.

"What's the matter? Flu?"

"No," she replied hesitantly. "I can't talk about it now, Dad. Can you just come?"

Two and Out

"I'll be there in the ten minutes," he said, cutting the connection and chastising himself for not being more sensitive to the fact that she was probably having her monthly visitor.

He paid his check and cut across Broadway to Boston Street, passing Manning Bowl, the scene of his outstanding high school football exploits. Within five minutes he parked aside the church and walked behind it to the school itself.

On entering the front door, he walked straight ahead to the principal's office where Mrs. Eagan waved to him from behind the glass partition separating her office from the secretarial station. Laura sat erect in a wooden chair, dressed in a blue plaid skirt and blue vest, the obligatory uniform for those enrolled in the middle school.

"I'm John Casey, Laura's father," he informed the pretty secretary seated across from Laura.

"You may go, Laura," she instructed, after first being sure that Laura identified her father.

As they left the building, Laura walked ahead of him, barely acknowledging his existence, her head lowered, her pace accelerating as they moved toward the car. He decided his best course was to say nothing for a while.

He drove for a couple of miles and then turned up Pine Hill. From the corner of his eye, he noticed Laura's hand held tight against her stomach. He decided to venture into the tiger's cage.

"Anything I can do to help, Laura?" he asked.

"No." But a soft no. Progress.

"Well if there is, you just ask."

She remained silent until they stopped in front of the garrison on B Street, just a few yards above the Lynn Reservoir. Tall pines surrounded the house and meandered from the yard straight down to the water.

"Well, okay, here we are," he said.

She opened the door, stepped out, and started to walk away. Suddenly she turned and said "Thank you" before heading down the walk.

John A. Curry

Mike Fallon did not look forward to the new day. He sat alone in his kitchen sipping his coffee, trying to focus on where they were with the Brinks investigation, or rather where he was as the leader of the investigation. He glanced at the clock above the stove, its luminous hands casting the only light about the room.

The headache had come on just before Rita and he lay down at eleven o'clock. He had stayed awake, his eyes closed, seeking sleep. Despite the pain, he had hardly moved, for fear of disturbing her rest. By 3:30 A.M., he was sure that the magical drugs had worked their wonders, allowing her respite from the demons. He had moved ever so slowly from the bed and, on reaching the kitchen, had quietly brewed himself some coffee.

Five days had passed since the heist. Five days with relatively little progress. He stared ahead into the darkness. Were they stymied due to his ineptitude, his lack of focus, his continuous worry about Rita, or was it just simply a very difficult case? At this early hour it was probable that Sam Morris was asking himself the same questions.

Fallon concluded it was the case, not him. In fact, for the past few days Rita had been in some form of remission, her spirits elevated. Five days into the case, he could feel himself being drawn in. He was concentrating more on his work. He noticed that longer periods of time would go by without his thinking of Rita. No, that wasn't right. She was always there, not locked far away in the recesses of his mind, but right there, ever on the cusp. But he could and was focusing on the case. It actually fascinated him, grabbing him and exciting him much as the Photographer case had more than a year ago. This crew was good, no question about it. They were a challenge, and he was coming alive. He had convinced himself, but how did Morris see it? And how about Nelson, Harper, Cameron, the others? Had they seen any return to form? How could a boss even ask?

Yes, it was the case now causing his pain. Why wasn't there some kind of breakthrough? He drummed his fingers against the coffee cup and began mentally ticking off the issues under investigation.

First, the witnesses. Nothing really from any of them. Just generic descriptions of height and weight. Secondly, both they and the Boston Police were depending on their stoolie networks for leads concerning purchases of weapons. So far, nothing.

Then the information from the mobile techs, the forensic evidence, was discouraging. There were no usable fingerprints. Although a large number of fibers had been found in the Explorer, he still guessed the crew had destroyed their sweatsuits right after the robbery. Some DNA tracings of skin found might or might not be of help if they could identify a strong suspect.

And then the most puzzling piece of all. Harper's network of agents had meticulously investigated the eight crews across the country, and from that, again, nothing. In most cases the crews hadn't even ventured outside of their own geographical areas in years, and in others alibis held up well. He stopped himself for a moment. Crews that heisted armored cars generally weren't your summa cum laude groups. They were essentially neighborhood guys, like the Charlestown Irish. Gangbangers trying to navigate a rite of passage or saloon hangers-on with a record looking for a score.

Something was different here. He could feel it in his bones. There were pros like the gangbangers and the passage guys, but there were also pros who could think and plan, pros who made few mistakes. And he was increasingly convinced that was what he was dealing with here. Maybe they had panicked Flanagan into coming back with some key information for them, but that was a long shot at best.

He couldn't shake the thought that an insider could be involved. But who? Nelson was a thorough agent, and she had assured him that all personnel records at Brinks and at the university had been scrutinized.

John A. Curry

From the east, the sun began its slow ascent from the horizon. He needed to see if Rita was all right and begin to get the girls started on their preparation, including their half-hour showers, for school.

So where were they? He liked an insider still. He would personally visit each of the three Brinks guards—Dolan, Cochran, and Morgan. Give them one more polygraph. Maybe something had gotten by Nelson and Harper. And they would roust Billy Flanagan a second time.

And one other thing. He would take Frank Sheridan up on his suggestion. He had asked the Boston detective if there was anyone on staff who was a top flight Boston expert on armored car robberies.

"Yeah," Frank had replied. "But he's retired. Friend of mine named Vic Fleming is the best."

He would arrange to see Fleming.

33

Salvatore Ayala strolled into his cousin's place of business on Route One in Saugus as if he owned the building, which he did. His entourage moved both ahead and behind him operating less as a security force and more as a band of brothers, hangers-on, like the group that had surrounded Muhammad Ali in his prime or Ray Robinson when boxing's all-time best had strolled the streets of Harlem.

Sonny stood up woodenly, like a programmed robot. Henry Miceli poked his advance guard partner in the ribs. "Look at the dumb fucker, will you, Jerry?" he snickered.

From behind them Sally Ayala raised his voice above the din. "Shut the fuck up, Henry. The kid's all right."

"Hey, Sally!" Sonny greeted him.

Sally moved to embrace his godson. "Sonny! How's your mother, huh? You takin' good care of her now?"

Sonny backed away shyly. "Of course I am Sally. I'm still living with her."

"How's things in Marblehead anyway?" Sally inquired.

"Good, Sally. Real good. Remember that old movie house, the Warwick? It's closed now."

"No shit. Like everything else—anything small and good gets gobbled up, huh?"

For the first time Sally noticed his cousin standing in the doorway of his opulent office.

"Paulie, for Christ's sake, you look like a million bucks in that Armani suit," he yelled out by way of a greeting.

Paulie looked at him as if confused. "What brings you to Saugus, Sal?"

"You guys wait here, and read a fuckin' magazine or something. Sonny, they give you any shit you just knock on the door."

As his cousin walked toward him, Paulie noticed the contrast in their dress. Instead of the Armani suits, European collar shirts and Gucci loafers that he favored, Sally most often wore Sansabelt slacks, neatly pressed, with an open neck dress shirt and royal blue coat sweaters. Sally was tall and thin with more gray in his short hair than would be expected for a man in his mid-forties, Paulie noted. But it was his hawkish face that you really noticed, with that long scar and the eyes, eyes so dark there was almost no delineation between iris and pupil. Weary eyes, slightly hooded with wrinkles at the corners.

"Please, Sally, sit over here," Paulie said condescendingly, pointing to two soft leather chairs in the corner of the room. "How about some coffee?"

Sally shook his head and sat on the edge of the chair. Paulie remembered there had always been a spring-loaded feel to Sally. He felt that at any moment his cousin could lunge right at him.

"I've only got fifteen minutes or so, Paulie," he began, drumming his fingers on the arm of the chair. "But tell me, things okay?"

Paulie tried to relax. "Couldn't be better, Sal. The whole North Shore's humming with the gambling, the whores, drugs. Fine."

He wondered what Sally was coming to. Just a bit of opening chatter, or was something wrong with what he was paying forth to Boston?

Unfortunately his worry surfaced. "Why? Somethin' wrong with our payments or something?" he blurted out.

Sally sat back in the easy chair and eyed him menacingly. "Relax, Paulie. I'm just askin' you how things are is all. If there was a problem, you and I wouldn't be talkin' like this, friendly and all. You get my drift?"

He had never known Sally to sit still very long, and sure enough ten seconds after easing back in the chair he was on his feet. He walked to the window and stared out at the lake. In the distance a fire truck careened down Walnut Street, heading

Two and Out

toward North Saugus. Paulie decided to sit quietly and wait for Sally's lead.

"You know Richie Speranza over in Medford very well?" Sally suddenly asked.

Paulie thought for a second. "I've met him a few times in Boston at those parties you and Joe Sansone have on Hanover Street and another time at Pier 4 at some fund raiser. Never had much to do with him, though."

Sally returned to the easy chair. "Well, that's good, cousin. Because if you had had much to do with him, maybe you'd end up where he's about to end up—with your fuckin' face bones broken in with a baseball bat."

"There's a problem?"

Sally nodded slowly and then spoke just as slowly. "A big fuckin' problem."

Paulie noticed the change once again. One minute his cousin was coiled like a snake, agitated, ready to explode and, then, in the next second, calm, almost relaxed. Neither mood lasted very long, therefore, it was important that the listener read him correctly.

Sally leaned forward once again. "Richie's got Malden, Medford, Somerville. You know that, right?"

"Yeah, sure."

"We got some good evidence about his skimming, along with his expanding into parts of Charlestown where a couple of our loony Irish friends are claiming they're paying me through him when they aren't."

"Jesus! I always heard Richie was a loyal guy, y' know?"

Sally began bouncing on his toes while still remaining seated. "I trusted that son of a bitch like a brother. He was right in my fuckin' inner circle, a fuckin' leader. Did I ever tell you that him and I went to grade school together?"

"I didn't know that."

"Well, we did. Over on Mission Hill with the priests and nuns. Back around 1960 at the time of Sputnik when the USA stopped holding its pecker and fought back. Him and I did a science project together. Copied some fuckin' rocket out of the encyclopedia and presented it to the class. In those days the more shit you copied out of the encyclopedia the more credit you got, y' know? Nobody asked you to think in those days, and now the prick isn't thinking too clearly either."

He paused and leaned back into the chair. "I want his lights put out, Paulie, and I want you to take care of it for me."

Paulie nodded. "Sure, Sally."

"You're probably wondering why I don't have one of my guys do it," Sally said, pointing back toward the door. "This is a family matter, a matter of honor. I want you personally to take care of this for me, and I want him to suffer, Paulie.

"I cleared it with Joe Sansone. Me and Joe were Richie's original sponsors. Did you know that?" he asked, his agitation showing in his tone.

"Nobody steals from me, Paulie. Nobody. As soon as anyone does, and thinks they got away with it, then you've lost control of the whole operation, y' know?"

He stood and offered his hand to Paulie. "Use a baseball bat and make sure he knows why it's happening. And make sure it happens sometime in the next two weeks. I don't like these problems lingering."

Paulie released his cousin's hand. "Consider it done, my cousin and friend."

They embraced for a long moment.

"How's my godson doing?" Sally asked as he turned to the door.

"Good on the heavy stuff, and a little slow on the thinking stuff," Paulie replied.

"Then make sure you use him on Speranza. He's family too. Tell him to take a few heavy swings for me."

"Thanks for taking her home, Johnny."

He looked out onto Lewis Street at exactly the moment that the streetlights came on.

"She okay, Donna?" he asked.

"Just her monthly period. Cramps and a little fear of the whole thing. She's fine today."

"Well, good."

"Did she have much to say to you?" Donna asked.

"Not really, but she did say thank you."

"Are you up for another movie this weekend?" Donna asked.

"What do you mean?"

"Laura wanted me to ask you. 'Bring It On' is playing."

"That doesn't sound like a very nice movie for a twelve-year-old," he said.

"It's not as bad as it sounds," she laughed. "It's about cheerleading competition among girls."

"I think she thought I was kind of dumb about 'The Perfect Storm.' How am I ever going to pass muster on a teen picture?"

"Well, I think it's great she wants to see you again," Donna replied in a much more friendly tone than he had been accustomed to in recent months.

Suddenly he felt terribly depressed. It came on him like a huge wave, his happiness and exhilaration about Laura's interest quickly overwhelmed by his conscience. How could he continue seeing Laura, maybe even form a relationship with her, when in just a few weeks he would be leaving for Florida?

"Johnny, did you hear me?" Donna asked.

"Donna, there's something I need to tell you about," he said softly.

"I'm listening."

"I've been thinking about giving teaching another try."

"You feel you're ready for that?" She asked the question in a supportive way.

"I'm trying hard. I've been cutting back on the gambling and doing a little better with drinking."

"I have mixed feelings, Johnny. You ought to be in AA, you know. You need a support structure behind you."

He bit his lip, trying hard not to start an argument with her. They had long ago agreed to disagree and try to remain civil. Even though he recognized his behavior was the major factor in their divorce, he had always resented the heavy control she liked to exert over those around her.

He thought it best to plow ahead. "Donna, there's something else. If I start over, I'm thinking about a new place, maybe Sarasota. Someplace where I can start fresh."

There was nothing but silence on the line. "Donna?"

"Are you serious?" she finally said.

"Right now I'm confused, you know? What with Laura wanting to see me and..."

Donna interrupted him. "Well you better get unconfused and fast. I'm getting sick of your act, pal. And you're not going to get Laura's hopes up and then pull out of town..." She started to cry.

"Donna, I'm..."

She slammed the phone down.

34

They stopped talking as soon as he entered the room. Moving briskly, Brian stopped at the lectern and withdrew the examination booklets from his briefcase.

A subdued groan permeated the amphitheater as the class observed the blue books. From the third row, Jerome Glass raised his hand.

"Yes, Jerome?" Brian asked as he started to pass out the test materials.

"You haven't said anything about the Brinks robbery last Friday. What do you think happened?"

Brian pointed his index finger straight at young Glass. "Right on, my friend!" he exclaimed. "You've anticipated our next term paper assignment."

Another collective gasp crossed the hall.

"Now, now, dear hearts. Let's not despair. And let's give Jerome credit for thinking. I want all of you to think about what may have happened, based on our past discussions, on your review of the literature, on your reading of the local papers. And perhaps some of you, that is those of you who expect to lead this class this term, who expect an "A", will think to interview some of those involved, for example the Boston Police or the university police."

"But what do you theorize, Professor?" Jerome persisted.

Brian finished passing out the booklets before answering. "I'll let you know after I read all the erudite explanations and laudable theories I'm going to receive from all of you. Papers no more than 2500 words in length—will be due two weeks from today. Now, let's get at the exam."

As they began to attack the two essay questions he had provided, he walked to the window overlooking the landscaped Centennial Circle below him. Behind it, and far below him, Ruggles Station, connecting the university to its Roxbury neighbors, loomed in the sunlight. He stared at the arriving and departing trains and busses and thought of his new plan.

Brinks was one thing, but Salvatore Ayala was decidedly another. There would be no statute of limitations for the Prince of Darkness if he were robbed of even one dollar, and if Fleming's sources were correct, if more than $2,000,000 was involved in these New York-Boston weekend exchanges, then Ayala wouldn't rest until he caught them. If they went ahead, the FBI, the Boston Police, and the Mafia would all be in pursuit, not exactly what he had envisioned some months ago.

He leaned forward, bracing himself on the window sill, looking to the west in anticipation of the Acela's arrival. Then he saw it, its sleek, long lines reminding him of the European bullet trains. He studied his watch and grinned into its face. On time, roaring through Roxbury on its way to its terminal at South Station.

He followed its glide, turning occasionally to observe the class in its deliberations. What was there really to be concerned about? It had been a full week since the heist and from all reports, the feds and the locals were clueless. Early reports of 'considerable progress' and of 'leads being investigated' had diminished to recent requests for any information from any source.

Quickly reviewing the Brinks job, he couldn't think of any red flags. As for Sally Ayala, he would plan just as carefully. No mistakes. They would relieve the Prince of his goods right in the middle of South Station. One or two more Mondays, one more careful look at both the victims and the location and the plan should be solidified.

And then they would strike—Bush, Cheney, Gore, and Lieberman together in Boston, united and civil, raising their own 'campaign' money. He laughed at his little joke. And Ayala would never find them, because he—Brian Hughes—was too clever to be found. Ayala could try, but good luck to him and the Red Sox.

Two and Out

At that same time, close to noon and almost exactly a week after the Brinks heist, Vic Fleming sat on a long wooden bench under a green pavilion along Revere Beach Boulevard.

On a beautiful cloudless fall day, he took small bites from the elongated hot dog he had purchased just across the street at Kelly's Roast Beef. He cursed himself for having ordered it with so much mustard and relish. When he raised it to his mouth, he found it difficult to control the droppings.

"You want another napkin?" Mike Fallon asked him, chewing on Kelly's traditional roast beef sandwich.

"I should have bought an extra shirt it looks like," Fleming replied, reaching for the napkin.

"Well, you're a cheap date, Captain," laughed the handsome special agent.

"So Frank Sheridan suggested you contact me?"

"That's right," Mike nodded. "He says you're the best at armored car robbery he's ever seen. Says you have a lot of the city's history on it right up here," he said, tapping his forehead.

Vic smiled his thanks. "Well, maybe at one time. But you guys must know from your own list of has-beens, when you're gone, you're gone. I've been out to pasture for some time now."

"According to Sheridan, only a couple of years."

"Agent Fallon..."

"Call me Mike."

"Mike, what is it you think I can do for you?"

Fallon surveyed his guest and lifted his soft drink. He had ordered a small Pepsi, but had received a tankard that could satisfy him and three others. "To begin with, I'd like your take on this heist. Did Frank call you this morning and go over the background?"

Vic sipped his coffee and blew into it once again. Maybe it would grow cold by dinnertime, he thought. "He went over it for an hour or so. I asked him a few questions in turn."

Vic looked at his watch and immediately regretted having done so. He felt more up tight than he thought he would when he had agreed to the meet. Yesterday, Sheridan had prevailed on him to give the FBI agent some time, and the prospect of gaining even more knowledge than he had garnered from his previous telephone call to Frank had infatuated him. Yet lurking in the background was this feeling that he couldn't shake. Warning bells were going off in his head. You're getting too close to them, they chimed. You could make a serious mistake. Was it even possible that he was being set up? That both Fallon and Sheridan suspected him? Impossible, he thought. What possible connection back to him could they have?

He had agreed to meet Fallon without even talking to Brian about it. In fact, for the last week, he had had absolutely no contact with Brian or with Lieberman and Cheney. Just as they had planned. No contact, no heavy spending and therefore no chance for error. And so far it had all worked.

"You in a hurry?" Fallon asked, acknowledging he had observed Vic looking at his watch.

"I've got a couple of hours, Mike," Vic responded calmly. "We retirees have plenty of time."

"You like it, retirement I mean?"

Vic looked across to Kelly's. At this hour, businessmen, housewives, retirees, school skippers—half of Revere—queued up in a long line extending around the corner, waiting their turn at the covered refreshment stand.

"It would be a whole lot better if the wife was still with me," he responded.

"I'm sorry, Vic. Frank told me of her passing. That's rough, just before retirement."

"I hear you have your own problems," Vic said.

Mike surprised himself by answering forthrightly. "Pancreatic cancer. She has maybe a couple more months, three at best."

Two and Out

Fleming rolled up his wrappers and tossed them into the barrel to his right. "You work your whole fuckin' life waiting for retirement, and then you face it alone."

"Any kids?" Mike asked.

Vic shook his head. "No. There was just the two of us. How about you?"

Mike stared at the sea in the distance. "Three girls—ten to fifteen years old. Good girls. They kind of help me through all this. Y' know?"

Vic nodded. "I might cut out for California in a few weeks. Maybe a change will do me some good."

"You from Revere originally?"

"Born and raised over on Shirley Avenue. Went to Revere High. Had a great guidance counselor there named Sammy Samuels. He pointed me the right way. Got me interested in law enforcement, instead of law breaking, which was my path until he stepped in." He paused and caught himself. "But hey, you don't need the story of my life. Let's talk about the case."

"So any ideas?" Mike asked.

"Let's start with the crime scene itself." Vic said, sipping his coffee now that it no longer tasted like boiling lava. "What about the masks? Any trace on them?"

Mike shook his head vigorously. "Nothing. They're sold in all kinds of costume joints all over America, even on the street corners adjacent to the White House. We asked big dealers around here if anyone had bought all four masks. No takers. We figure they were bought one or two at a time where nobody would notice."

"How about the mobile tech stuff?" Vic asked.

"Frank didn't tell you? There's nothing with the prints. We picked up some fabric and tracings of skin with the vacuums. The Explorer they used was owned by a clean freak so there's not a lot. What we do have has to wait until we find a suspect or two. My guess is the perpetrators burned whatever clothing they wore."

Vic pulled a pack of Newports from his shirt pocket. He offered one to Fallon who shook his head dismissively.

"I gather you shook the witnesses," Vic said.

"Over and over. The stories jibe. Very little variance among the principals."

Vic exhaled the smoke and then watched the thin cloud for a beat. "There's an insider involved," he finally said emphatically.

"My thought too," Mike responded.

"You're missing something, assuming your people checked on the Brinks employees and the University people. There's something there someplace."

Fallon swallowed some more of his soft drink.

"You'll be peeing all night, you drink all that chrome cleaner."

Fallon laughed out loud. "I paid for a small one. All these fuckin' places think small begins at $5.00 with $.50 increases to the middle and large sizes.

"The Brinks guys who were at the University are clean as snow. Dumb but clean. And Brinks employees, on the trucks or at the firm's various locations, have been very carefully scrutinized. If there's a bad actor, we're not seeing it."

"And how about the University people?" Vic asked.

"We think there's less likelihood of a contact there, but we tossed the personnel records there as well. Haven't found anything."

Vic thought for a moment. What he was advising was what every cop worth his salt would suggest. If he tried to turn Fallon away from the idea, the agent would think less of him.

"You're missing it, Mike. I suggest you go back over it. Frank says they were at BU before Northeastern, on a regular Friday afternoon run. Someone knew the pattern, and a crew was waiting for them. The timing's too precise. And as for the crew, my guess is it's a new crew, not Billy Flanagan or any of our locals."

"What makes you think that?" Mike said.

"Frank says you and him braced Flanagan."

"That's right."

"It's not his MO, Mike. His crew's usually half buzzed, their wives' names are Budwiser. And besides, one or two days after the job, Billy or one of his gang would be dancing on the bars over on Monument Avenue, spending down a good piece of what they stole.

"The scene doesn't fit any of the local crews I dealt with," Vic continued. "Flanagan, Joey Galvin over in Somerville, Brendan O'Leary in Medford—they would hit an armored car up in New Hampshire or maybe in Post Office Square, but they would have trouble finding BU or Northeastern, never mind thinking up a major heist on a college campus. And they wouldn't bother with rubber masks either, especially with presidential candidates' faces. The only politician Flanagan knows is Dapper O'Neil, and last I heard, he finally retired."

Fallon stood and placed his trash, including about eight ounces of his Pepsi, in the barrel. "Want to walk for a bit?" he asked.

"Fine with me," Vic said.

They headed north toward Point of Pines, the sun pouring its warmth on them, Indian summer all around them. Lone strollers, some supported by canes, walked toward them, and occasionally high flying skateboarders would zig zag through the old timers using them as pylons on their journey south.

"Do your national data bases show anything?" Vic asked.

"Not a lot. We've been checking out known crews with similar MOs, but it's slow work with little to show. Any other thoughts?"

Vic stopped to light his Newport. "I'm sure you guys are onto anything I might think of, but one thought that might have already crossed your mind."

"What's that?"

"How did they know the Brinks guys would all get out of the truck? If the guards had done what they were supposed to do and followed company policy, the driver would have stayed within the vehicle. Right?"

Mike moved quickly to his right to avoid an onrushing runner, a young lady dressed in spandex, racing along with a German shepard on a leash, the two of them taking up three-fourths of the sidewalk as well as freezing in place half the senior population of Revere.

"They claim they all got out to look at the college broads," Mike responded.

"Whatever the reason, I'd play the law of averages," Vic replied. "Probably few, if anyone, back at Brinks knew they would get out of the vehicle. So I'd still concentrate on the three guards themselves, and any friends they communicate with regularly. Y' know, people who hear them talking about the college cuties. Course, it's also very probable that someone followed them for a couple of weeks or three and observed their pattern. Which points me back to what I said earlier. We probably have a new crew in play here."

Fallon walked along without saying anything for a few minutes, mulling over Fleming's points. An insider? For sure they agreed. A new crew in play? It jibed with his own thinking. The three guards? Maybe they had missed something, some telltale sign. He would brace them one more time.

"Anything else?"

"Nope," Vic replied. "I hope I earned my lunch."

Mike paused near his car. "I'm grateful for the help, Vic. Can I call you if something comes up?"

Vic offered his hand. "Anytime, Mike. Anytime."

35

It happened on their third date because, by then, they both wished it to happen. Tony had taken her to the Olive Garden over in Hyannis the night after their dinner at Michael Patrick's. And then on Friday night, she had asked him for dinner at her place.

They had sat outside drinking Bud Light from the bottle and then walked across to Glendon Beach, savoring the serenity of the early evening. With the warm southeasterly flow of hot air that had come up from Florida, the beach remained inviting well into September.

They sat on the blanket. He was sitting so close, he could almost rub thighs with her. He did. Then he took her hand and gently ran it into the line where their legs touched, so she could feel them both at the same time, up and down, while she remained riveted, unwilling to remove her hand.

Breaking a long silence Tony said, "You're so very lovely. I think you're beginning to matter a lot to me." He turned to face her and moved his fingers along the line of her backbone. In the growing darkness, Grace placed her arms around his neck, giving in to the stillness of the water and the muscular person next to her with magnets in his skin.

"Let's go back to my place," she murmured in his ear.

Once upstairs in the cottage, she stood at the window to look out at the dark, serrated outline of pine trees in her backyard. He put his arms around her from behind, kissing her neck, touching her butt with his hands while he pressed himself against her.

"Tony, I'm not sure..."

He turned her and put a finger against her lips. She stared at him in the soft light, and she let go of her doubts. She let her worries fade away. She simply wanted him. His kisses fell like a gentle waterfall all over her body as she moved with them, letting herself be urged into the fresh bed. She put her arms around his strong, firm body and held on for dear life.

Afterward, they lay in each other's arms, content, at peace, enjoying the discovery of new love, not talking much at all at first. From the night the sound of crickets chirping mingled with the scent of pine needles and the laughter of couples moving along the street toward the beach.

"What are you thinking about, sport?" he finally asked.

"I guess I'm thinking about what you must be thinking of me right now," she said, sort of half asking rather than stating, as she rose up on one elbow.

"What I'm thinking is that I'm one lucky guy, Grace." He said it lovingly because he felt loving. "I'm not a guy that meets women easily," he said, rising on his elbow to face her, their bodies in a fetal position. "You have many guys?"

She ignored the question and placed her index finger near his mouth, tracing a line between his jawline and that sensuous mouth. "I've been hurt once or twice so I'm slow to commit, but here I am, not knowing you a week and in bed."

He pulled her hair, the wispy part that she herself was always fixing and kissed her softly on her lips. "With the loss of Doug's mother, I've mostly backed off myself."

"How about your lady friend that ran off on you and Doug?" She caught herself as soon as she asked and quickly added, "I'm sorry. That's really none of my business."

Tony waved his hand dismissively. "Sex, pure sex. I thought maybe it might be more, but that's all that it was. I made a bad mistake with her."

"And what's this?" she asked indignantly.

"I'd like to think it's something more, Grace," he replied softly.

She sat up in bed and placed her feet on the floor. "We sound like a couple of teenagers. I have no right to be pressing you."

She stood and found her halter and shorts on the floor.

"Where you going?"

"Don't you want something to eat?"

He glanced at the round-faced clock on her bureau. "I better get back to Mrs. Adams. She's been doing double duty every night this week."

She looked away from him. "That's probably best."

"Want to come back with me?" he asked.

She shook her head vigorously. "I need to get a few things done."

Standing, he slipped on his shorts and his Polo shirt. "Can I see you over the weekend?"

She stayed on the other side of the room. He didn't like the quiet interlude nor the distance she was putting between them.

"Call me, anyway," she finally responded, walking toward the hallway.

"Grace, I don't consider this another roll in the hay," he said, following her downstairs.

Once in the below-grade kitchen, she kept on the move, opening the refrigerator door, lighting the stove.

"Grace?" he implored.

"I'm sure you don't, Tony. It's not you. I'm just not sure I want to get involved and suddenly you're off to California a few weeks from now. Maybe it's better if it is just a roll in the hay."

He crossed to her and embraced her. Don't say much more right now, he cautioned himself. "I'll call you around noon," he said before kissing her cheek and moving toward the back door.

Like clockwork, Richie Speranza left Medford Square as he did every Friday night to have his hair cut, whether he needed it or not, at the Square One Mall in Saugus, about a mile up Route One from Paulie Ayala's office.

He drove up the ramp and parked his BMW in the open area near the Sears entry and wandered into the mall complex, fighting his way through the smokers crammed in the entrance and a clutter of teenage mall rats with those jeans that looked like they were designed by Omar the Tentmaker.

Impeccably dressed himself in a Paul Frederick open neck shirt covered by a lamb's wool red sweater and tan slacks, he snickered as he paraded by them. He walked onto the second floor by the escalator, mixing in with the throng of shoppers. About forty yards up, among a cluster of small shops, he entered Dick's barbershop.

"There's the fucker now," Paulie Ayala said, lowering his newspaper. He sat with Sonny on the long, wooden bench outside the Walden's bookstore and Sam Goody's.

"Where?" Sonny asked.

"You payin' fuckin' attention or what Sonny?"

"I'm payin' attention," Sonny answered defensively.

"Over there. Walkin' into the barbershop."

"Oh, yeah. I got time to buy the new Britney Spears record?"

Ayala slapped him on the arm with the rolled-up newspaper. "Keep up the bullshit, you dumb fucker, and godson to Sally or not, you'll be flippin' burgers back in Chelsea."

Sonny frowned and looked down at his shoes. "What did I do?"

Ayala didn't bother to answer but instead turned his attention to the passers-by. "Look at that fuckin' geek." He pointed to a teen-aged girl with spiked red hair and pale white skin. "How would you like to wake up next to her in bed?"

Sonny looked her over. "I wouldn't mind," he said.

Paulie gave him his best dirty look. He decided to change the topic. "You know, I've been thinkin' of our approach to this dirt bag. When he comes out of the shop, I'll start walkin' across so I run right into him. Then you join us, and we walk out to the parking lot with him. Then we get his ass into the car like I told you earlier. Think you can handle it without fallin' into a pile of shit along the way?"

"I'm cool," Sonny replied.

Paulie Ayala sat quietly for a minute. "On second thought," he said, "go and buy that record you want—what was it?"

Sonny perked up. "Britney Spears."

"Who the fuck is he?"

"It's a she."

"Whatever. Probably one of those transvestites. Go buy the record so it looks like we've been shoppin'. And hurry the fuck up."

Dutifully, Sonny stood and walked across to Sam Goody's while Paulie sat looking over the crowd. He felt behind his leather jacket for the Glock nine, assuring himself of his readiness. Did that dumb ass Sonny remember to bring the Louisville Slugger? No matter, he always kept an extra baseball bat in his trunk anyway.

The empty faced girl with the spiked red hair and the pale features suddenly appeared from out of a shop on the other side of the mall. Bouncing a copy of a teen magazine off her hip, she was joined by a gangling boy—maybe fifteen—with bad acne. They headed right for his bench.

"What did the geek do then?" the boy was asking as they sat next to him.

Her hand went to the ring in her nose. "Well, it's not so much what he did. I asked him, 'Are you serious?' y' know? Well, he said, y' know, 'I'm cool.' So I said, 'y' know, I think I am, too.' Y' know what I mean?"

Paulie tried not to look at them. If that fuckin' broad said "y' know?" one more time he'd clip her with the Glock instead of Speranza. He almost said "No, I don't know," but decided to keep the peace.

Where was Sonny? He almost hoped Sonny didn't appear, his joining up with these two linguists would really make their day. Then, suddenly, from the barbershop, Richie Speranza appeared, looking casually to his left and his right.

Paulie stood and walked toward him, being sure to time his interception. Speranza's handsome face lit in recognition as he saw Paulie approaching.

"Hey, Paulie!" he greeted Ayala effusively. "What are you doin' here? I thought you favored Louis' and Brooks Brothers and them other high-class places."

Paulie laughed and offered his hand and shook Speranza's firmly. "Sonny's with me. We stopped in to buy a CD. Hey, here he comes now," he said, spotting Sonny eyeing the two linguists, probably ready to engage them in conversation.

"Sonny, over here!" Paulie signaled.

Sonny lumbered toward them. "Sonny, you know Richie Speranza, right?"

"Yo, Richie," Sonny offered by way of greeting.

"What did you buy, Sonny?" Richie asked.

"They didn't have Britney Spears, so I got the new 'N Sync."

Whoever the fuck they were, Paulie thought.

"So how's things in Medford, Richie?" Paulie asked.

Richie waved his hand in a "so-so" manner. "Slowin' down a bit, Paulie. These two dumb fuckers runnin' for President are causin' everything to slow down a bit, us and General Motors," he laughed.

"You headin' out?" Paulie asked, pointing toward the parking lot.

"Absolutely. Let's go," Speranza replied. "I'm due over in Somerville in an hour."

As they exited, he asked, "What's happening in the Lynn area, Paulie?"

"We're doin' all right. Fuckin' spics can't get enough coke. Can't pour it up their noses fast enough. And the books are hummin'. Yeah, we're doing okay."

"Where you parked?" Richie asked.

"The Lincoln over there," Paulie said. Sonny fell back slightly behind Richie as they walked single file between cars.

"No kidding. That's my BMW over to your left."

Sonny drew the Glock and pressed it against Speranza's back. "Get in the fuckin' Lincoln, Richie."

Speranza froze in place as Paulie turned to face him. "Do as he says, Richie. We need to talk with you."

"You need a fuckin' gun to talk with me?" Speranza said, bile rising in his throat.

Paulie reached behind his back and pulled out his own Glock. "Just get in the car carefully, Richie."

From behind, Sonny patted him down. Then he stayed in position as Speranza entered the passenger door of the Lincoln and Paulie sat behind the wheel. They both kept their weapons trained on Richie as Paulie set the car in motion and Sonny sat in the rear.

"There's got to be some mistake here, Paulie," Richie said, his voice trembling. "What have I ever done to you?"

"This is not about me, Richie."

"What, then, for Christ's sake? Whatever it is, we can straighten it out."

"I don't think so, Richie," Paulie replied. "What it's about is you. You skimmin' from Sally. Knockin' down the points you owe him, as well as stealin' from the dumb Irishers over in Charlestown."

Richie turned toward Paulie, probably to offer some manufactured explanation, at exactly the time Sonny conked him with the Glock. He slumped to the side, almost falling into Paulie's lap.

"Good. That will keep us from hearing from him until we get there," Paulie said, as he crossed over the Essex Street overpass and headed north toward Breakheart Reservation. At the Melrose Fells Parkway he cut into Forest Street, the road leading into the deepest part of the recreational park frequented by joggers and swimmers. At this late hour he knew no one would be around, but he took extra precautions in any event. About a mile in, he left the main road, dousing the lights, cutting through a huge spacing in the tree line. He drove for another hundred yards through the brush until he was sure they could not be observed from the road.

They sat in silence for a brief moment. "What's the matter?" Sonny asked.

"Just listenin' for a second," Paulie said. "Get the asshole out of the car," he finally ordered.

While Sonny pulled and hauled Speranza from the car, Paulie kept his eyes riveted on the limp body. "And wake him up."

With Speranza prone on his back, Sonny slapped him across the face with his bare hand. Paulie reached under the seat for the two pairs of gloves and then stepped out of the driver's door and popped the trunk. He put on the gloves before grabbing the baseball bat and then motioned to Sonny. "Here's some gloves."

From the ground, Speranza slowly regained his senses and sat up groaning, reaching for his head. He rocked for a minute before looking at Paulie, remembering now, the terror right there in his face. He pivoted his head, catching a glimpse of Sonny behind him.

Paulie stood there, not saying a word for a minute, the Glock in his right hand, the bat in his left. Suddenly, Richie began to whimper. "You guys—tell Sally he's—got this all wrong. I can explain everything if only..."

"Time for explanations is over, Richie. Bottom line is you don't ever steal from the family. You know the rules."

Richie tried to stand, placing his weight on the bottom of his heels and half rising from his sitting position. And that's when Paulie blew out his right knee with the Glock nine. Screaming in pain, Richie fell on his other knee and grabbed for the source of his agony. Paulie leaned down and picked up the bat. He laid the Glock on the ground and swung the bat, taking one or two practice swings like Nomar Garciaparra on deck at Fenway Park, before swinging full force across Richie's jawline. As Speranza collapsed onto his back, Paulie threw the bloodied bat to Sonny.

"Hit a few home runs off his head, and then let's get the hell out of here."

36

Early Saturday morning, Johnny Casey decided to leave his Lewis Street apartment and walk to the beach. With summer lingering, dark clouds scudded across small patches of blue sky as he crossed Lynn Shore Drive. Other loners walked along either dejectedly or briskly, their body language connoting their status and the way the world was treating them. He headed north toward Swampscott, Kings Beach on his right. Joggers, both over and underdressed, ran at varying paces toward him, moving a bit away from the sea wall where, at high tide, thunderous waves caromed and then receded to the sea.

Why hadn't he heard from Brian about the second job? he wondered. It had been exactly a week since they had met for dinner at the Red Rock Bistro. How did he feel a week later? Manic and on, or depressed and down? He felt the smile spreading over his face. At least he could laugh at his own condition. At least he understood he was a confused, fucked-up guy. Brian must feel like he's baby-sitting me, he mused. One minute I'm up, exhilarated by the action, glad to be part of the crew, anxious for the money, and the next, down, unhappy with my involvement, sad-faced, moralistic.

How many years had he been seeing the nut doctors? Maybe three, he calculated. But that had been an in and out proposition too. More than half them needed help themselves. You couldn't put much stock in those weirdos. One guy—what was he a psychiatrist or a psychologist?—had started crying when he had related his estrangement from Laura and had blurted out "Me, too. My daughter won't talk to me either!" And how about the one over in Marblehead, the gay guy who had propositioned him?

At the Lynn-Swampscott line, he turned around and walked back toward Red Rock Park, with its circular stretch of grass surrounded by benches looming above the sea in the distance.

John A. Curry

To his left, three sea gulls carped and, in squadron formation, swooped to the waves, hoping for breakfast.

Apprising himself, he felt he was making some progress, and mostly on his own. Not with his mental state, which, he realized, would probably continue up and down, in and out, manic and depressive. He had read enough to know his was a forever condition. But he hadn't gambled for days now, and he had cut back on the sauce. The experts said that a person could never conquer these addictions alone. Who needed to conquer? He just needed to slow down. He was beginning to feel better about himself. It was through the inner strength that God provided him that he could win those two battles. And with those wins, he could return to the classroom. Make something of himself. With the new money in his pocket, he could even concentrate on helping others. God and his own determination would see him through.

He suddenly stopped and thought about his God. He walked to the rail and looked down at the waves crashing against the wall, timing his movements so as to coincide with the ebbing of the water toward the sea. But how could God approve of his being a thief? Would God remain disappointed with his desertion of the priesthood? Suddenly, his thoughts, the rolling waves, the undulating sea, brought on the depression. He stood back from the rail and resumed his walk.

And that's when he saw her. Her blond hair flowing in the light wind, Laura walked alone directly toward him.

"Hi!" she greeted him shyly.

"What are you doing here on a Saturday morning?" he asked, not knowing exactly what to say.

"Mom told me you always walk down here on Saturday mornings so I asked her to leave me off. We spotted you from the road. She's up there, see?" She pointed to the long string of parked cars on Lynn Shore Drive above the embankment separating the road from the walkway.

Donna returned his wave without much enthusiasm. "Can you drive me home later?" Laura asked.

"Sure," he replied. With that, Laura signaled to her mother, who then drove off from the curb.

"You hungry?" he asked, wondering what she wanted. He caught himself. His daughter had to want something from him? He felt ashamed.

"Could we get some milk and a donut somewhere?" she asked.

"Let's get my car," he replied.

They ascended the embankment and walked west above the beach. The sky began to thicken into dense rain clouds and within minutes began to unburden itself into a very fine drizzle. They hurried up Cherry Street, without saying a word until he challenged her.

"You up for a little run, or do we walk and get soaked?"

They jogged the final hundred yards, she giggling at their plight, he urging her on. "Can't you stay up with the old man?"

He went around to the driver's side, and just as he reached for the door handle, the sky opened up. Sheets of fat raindrops plummeted down. He dove into the car and unlocked the passenger side door. He banged his door shut sprinkling water all over the front seats.

Settling in, he noticed that she had become now very quiet. He didn't make a move to start the engine. He was busy with the rain on his face, with his sleek wet hair. Torrents of rain streamed down the windshield, blocking the world outside.

He decided that was how he liked it, stuck with his daughter in a very tight space. He was tempted to ask her about her life and to tell her so much more about himself. To explain himself so she would like him, maybe even forgive him. But where to begin?

All the windows were fogged up. He glanced at her as he started the car. She was busy studying the rain pummeling the windshield and didn't say a thing.

He drove to Vinnin Square in Swampscott, to the bagel shop that he liked, the one where you could sit at round tables on tall stools.

When they had ordered and taken their purchases into the far corner, he began cautiously.

"It's really good to see you, Laura."

She took a small bite of her jelly donut. "I need to talk to you Dad, so that's why I asked Mom to drive me over."

"Go ahead, Prin..." He caught himself.

"It's all right for you to call me that if you want," she declared very seriously.

"Mom told me she was mad at you again," she then announced.

He raised a quizzical eyebrow. "She tell you why?"

Laura shot him a glance. "She said you might be going away to Florida."

He sipped his coffee trying to anticipate where this was heading.

Laura fidgeted with her milk. "Mom still thinks I'm a baby. You know—when I was young, you weren't around much. Coming and going all the time so we never got to know each other. I think she thinks you hurt me then and now you'll hurt me again. You know, if you go away again."

Johnny set his cup down. "I'm not sure what I'm going to do, Laura."

She nodded, acknowledging his words, but not really absorbing them.

"Steve's kind of like my father now anyway. That's how I feel," she said, her eyes ever so slightly misty, but the voice sure of the message.

She stormed ahead. "I told Mom I'm grown up now. I'm not a baby or a retard. I told her I know you're going to go away again, and if you do that's all right with me. You're not like my real dad anyway, if you know what I mean."

Johnny sat in silence, wanting to help her understand, yet realizing that maybe she understood all too well. He just sat there, stung.

'So I don't really care if you want to go see "Bring It On" tomorrow or not. Mom says to tell you she shouldn't have hung up on you. She wanted me to tell you that."

He looked across at his "almost thirteen" daughter, as she liked to refer to her age. Having delivered her message, she sat more erect, more confident than she appeared an hour ago.

"I really would like to see the movie with you, princess. I'll pick you up at one tomorrow," he replied.

With absolutely no expression, she nodded. "Okay. Can you take me home now?"

———

"You guys done a good job last night." So surmised Sally Ayala with the phone call to his cousin at the same time Laura and Johnny left the coffee shop.

"You check for bugs all the time?" he suddenly asked.

"We're clean, Sally. Twice a day we have Stan check," Paulie responded.

"The wife beater?"

"He don't do that stuff anymore," Paulie said.

"Fuck him, Paulie. Once a wife better, always a wife beater. Get someone else."

"I hear you."

"You let our friend know what for?"

Paulie reached for the Marlboros on his desk.

"Of course. He understood why the home runs were being hit."

Sally snickered loudly. "Fucker," he said. "How did my godson do?"

"He was my clean-up hitter."

"Did you read the papers this morning?" Sally asked.

"Yeah, and heard the radio reports, too. The cops got no clue."

"Paulie, one other thing."

"I'm listenin'."

"You know that launderin' expedition I've been taking each weekend?"

"To the Big Apple."

"I'm promoting Sonny, Paulie. Bringin' him on to my side of things for a time. Takin' him with me to New York a few times, for back-up. Okay with you?"

Paulie knew enough not to disagree. "No problem, Sal. When you want him?"

"Tell him to come over Hanover Street to the social club on Saturday night. Bring some clothes for the short trip. I'll just need him weekends to begin with."

"He'll be there Saturday night."

"Thanks again, Paulie."

When Sonny wandered in around two o'clock, after his beauty sleep, Paulie told him of the conversation.

"New York? He's takin' me to New York?"

"Sonny, you ain't goin' there to watch the Rockettes' boobs, if that's what you're thinkin'. You're goin' as back-up to the man himself when he's carryin' some heavy dough so you show him you're the muscle and do that for him."

Sonny smiled and nodded. New York, back up to Sally himself. Maybe he would even have time to visit one of those gentlemen's clubs with the nudies cavorting on bar tops.

37

Mike Fallon decided to treat Joe Dunn to lunch at an upscale place. He chose Ambrosia on Huntington Avenue, about a mile up from the university itself. And he decided against inviting Nelson and Harper. The guard had seen too much of each of them and needed a change, a "good guy" who just wanted to take him to lunch in appreciation of his cooperation.

"Can I get a beer here?" Dunn asked as they settled in a corner fronting Huntington Avenue itself, the huge plate glass window offering a spectacular view of this resurrected section of Boston.

"You can get anything you want, Joe." He signaled to the waiter while a young boy poured water into long-stemmed glasses.

Smiling warmly, the tall, stately young man took their drink order and guided them through a long list of specials.

"I'll be back for your lunch order in a few minutes," he announced with great confidence.

"You didn't have to take me to lunch, Mr. Fallon," Dunn began.

"Yes I did, Joe. And please call me Mike. You've been extremely cooperative with our agents, and we just appreciate it."

Joe Dunn had the look of an innocent man, one who had nothing to hide. In truth, he had conducted himself in exemplary fashion throughout the ordeal they had subjected him to. He, like the two others, had been scrutinized, questioned, doubted, cajoled through endless days. He, Cochran and Morgan had agreed to take the polygraph test—each three times in fact—and had aced it each time. They had to conclude that the guards had nothing to do with the heist.

"You hear anything more about the suspension?" Mike asked.

The waiter arrived with the Budweiser and Mike's club soda. "What would you like, Joe?"

"I'll have the Cornish hen special," Dunn responded.

"The breast of chicken with the caramelized onions," Mike said, pointing to the menu and then handing it across to their waiter.

"You were asking about the suspension," Dunn said, reaching for the Bud. "My guess is we're out for three months, that's what they said to me was probable."

Mike lifted the tray of rolls and offered one to Dunn. "We've told your people that you've been very helpful to us, Joe. Maybe that will help."

"We fucked up good, Mr. Fallon. We deserve whatever we get. Never should have left the truck."

Mike signaled the waiter for another round. He looked around at the other tables. If presentation was any indicator of quality, then they were not going to be disappointed.

"What did you do before Brinks, Joe?" he asked.

"Military. I served twenty years in the army. Saw the world, including a little time in Grenada."

"Really? Combat?"

"A few shots is all. It was over practically before it started."

"Your family coming through this okay?"

He shrugged, avoiding Fallon's eyes. "I embarrassed them as well as myself, but, yeah, we'll be all right. One of the agents told me your wife wasn't well?"

The comment surprised Mike, and what surprised him even more was the change in his own reaction lately whenever the subject surfaced.

"She's not doing well at all, Joe. Pancreatic cancer. There's not much hope."

Joe eyed him sympathetically. "Maybe God will see her through. I'll pray for her, Mr. Fallon."

Mike smiled at Dunn and waited while the extremely efficient waiter presented their lunch. He thought of Rita every free moment—while walking, while shaving, while there were pauses in conversations like right now. But he was caught up in this case. He could feel it in his throat, the bile rising whenever he felt particularly down, the adrenaline pumping whenever he thought of a new angle. Prior to this heist, he had paid as much attention to business as to week-old bread. Now he was charged up, as he had been with the Photographer case.

And then he felt guilty. Why wasn't he focused completely on Rita? He was, he answered to himself and his conscience. She was always in his mind, in the forward recesses, or just there in the background, lingering and smiling, always smiling at him.

He knew that in part he had grown more accepting of her situation in the past few weeks. As they planned for her death, at her urging, he had begun to face the reality. And he knew why. Because she—his beautiful Rita—was manipulating the scene, readying him and the girls for what was coming. And her inquiring, probing questions about the Brinks case were simply to keep his mind on things other than death, he knew.

He poked at his chicken breast and smiled to himself. They shared all things, he and Rita. And they would share every moment they could until there were no more.

"How's the chicken?" Dunn broke into his reverie.

"Good, Joe. Yours?"

"Well, I don't eat Cornish hen regularly. It's different, you know?"

"No agenda other than the meal, Mike?" Dunn asked as he motioned to the waiter that he was finished.

Mike flashed him a wry grin. "None whatsoever."

"Can I ask if there's any developments with the case?"

"Lately I've been asking myself why I'm feeling pretty good about the case," Mike responded, "because my boss obviously doesn't. We're still chasing down leads, Joe, and waiting for something to break."

"Those guys knew what they were doing. That's one thing for sure. I've been around pros all my life, and they were pros," Joe said.

John A. Curry

"See the gentleman with the big smile sitting over there, two tables down from you?" Mike asked.

Joe Dunn turned to his right. "Yeah?"

"That's Eddie Andelman, the sports talk show host. WEEI is right in this building."

Suddenly a huge bulk of a man, probably one of the World Wrestling Federation stable, breezed by their table and approached Andelman.

"Eddie, how long you been waiting, sport?" he inquired.

Joe Dunn stared at them, transfixed to the point where Mike felt he had to say something.

"Joe, something wrong?" he asked.

Joe faced him, staring white faced. "That's what the one who was driving called one of the others," he finally said.

"What are you talking about?"

"Sport! I should have remembered. Like I told you guys before, nobody ever called anyone by name. But now I remember. The one who jumped into the truck. He called the leader 'sport,' as if it were an everyday expression with him. You know what I mean?"

Mike sat perfectly still, but he could feel the adrenaline beginning to course through his veins once again.

———

The call came on Saturday afternoon just as Tony Amonti stepped out of the go-cart with a shrieking Doug. They had looped around and around the miniature raceway on Route 28 in Dennis, father and son in one car, passing the others regularly while Doug, sitting in Tony's lap, alternated between driving and screaming.

"Can we go again, Daddy?" he begged as they disembarked.

"Of course we can! But we need to get another ticket. Let me answer this call first. You go stand in line and I'll be right there."

Doug ambled toward the ticket booth where a long ribbon of people stretched nearly out into the parking lot.

"Hello," Tony spoke into the cell phone.

"How have you been?"

The voice of the gray man. No name given or spoken.

"Fine," he replied.

"You remember the city where we met before?"

"Of course."

"Tuesday, 9:00 A.M. at High Rock Tower."

"No problem."

And then he was gone.

Tony searched for Doug, still halfway back in the line, bouncing on his toes. When he joined his son, he hoisted him to his shoulders so that he could watch the motorized carts flying around the turns, their drivers waving to family members lining the fences.

Tony thought of the call and of decisions made. How had he come to this point anyway? Just weeks ago he had up at Loudon, going nowhere but at least making an honest living. But just barely, he reminded himself. Basically a taxi driver was what he was. And trailer trash.

He had always dreamed of the big money, of California, and of new life. If he had the money, he could place Doug in a really good public school for those with special needs or a top quality private school. He could spend more time with his son. Maybe drive once in a while just for the fun of it. But then if he had the money, why take the risk? He could repair cars instead. He would be set for life.

If the new mark led to a similar payout, he would have maybe $1.5 million. He would be a millionaire. No more racing. No more short paydays. A life with Doug. Would Grace go with them? He would ask her.

Their relationship was more than a sexual one to him, and he sensed to her as well. But still, crossing the country with a lover and his son. Was the commitment there? He caught himself. Did he have a right to expect a commitment?

John A. Curry

He thought back to the first approach from the gray man. A message over the telephone at the track in Loudon. Would he be interested in driving for a crew and for a heavy price? Two jobs, and that was it. Two and out. He could make $1.5 million. Think about it. Further communications would follow.

A joke? For some reason he didn't think so. Why him? He had wondered. He had no criminal record at all. And then he realized that might be a reason for the interest.

The second contact also came by phone. Had he thought about it? Was he interested? Did he need more time? And finally a request to be at Lynn Beach on a designated date and be ready with an answer.

He didn't think enough then or even now about what would happen to Doug if he were ever caught. Then and now, there were maybe a million and a half reasons why he didn't.

38

High Rock Tower. It stands at the highest point in Lynn, dominating the downtown. From the tower you can view the complete topography of the city—its circuitous sea coast to the east, winding its way from Nahant to Swampscott, the majesty of the Atlantic in the distance; its rejuvenated downtown just below the tower, coming alive once again with the birth of new high-tech firms; its hill-topped terraces of gorgeous homes to the west along Lynnfield Street; its spew of three-decker apartments and moderately sized family homes over in West Lynn.

Johnny Casey was the first to arrive. He parked along Essex Street and climbed the hundred plus steps to the rocky grounds just below the imposing tower itself. From there he looked around the city, recollecting his childhood. From his boyhood home on Chatham Street he and his friends would come here in the winter with their sleds. Taking turns, they would post one boy at the bottom of the snow-covered stairs to warn of oncoming traffic while the others careened down the stairway right onto Essex Street. And in the summer, they would climb the steps of the tower, laughing and pushing one another as they ran to the turret and pointed out locations to one another.

He could see Green Street and the red brick building where he had attended elementary school. Now no longer a school, it still looked like it had decades ago when he knew it as St. Joseph's Institute. He smiled, remembering the little ditty he and his friends would singsong to one another, but never in the presence of the nuns or priests. "Rooty Toot Toot, Rooty Toot Toot, we are the boys of the Institute. First in war, first in peace, first in the hands of the Lynn Police."

With the thoughts, suddenly the demons came to visit again. He grew sad, thinking of the promise of his youth—his academic and athletic success at St. Mary's and at Boston College—and his situation today.

"Hello," a voice from the present, pushing the past back where it belonged. The young man, the driver, approached him from the top of the stairs. Behind him, Johnny spotted the old man climbing more confidently and briskly than had either of the younger men.

"Hey, man, good to see you again," Johnny replied.

"Where's fearless leader?" Tony asked.

"Not here yet," Johnny said.

Vic Fleming half raced up the final steps. He didn't even pause for breath, as he advanced toward them, saluting his greeting.

"The tower open?" Tony inquired.

"I don't think so. Been closed for years," Johnny said.

Vic walked around the perimeter, circling the tower. Like the others, he was dressed in a sports jacket with shirt, tie and slacks.

Johnny moved to the top of the stairwell. "He's starting up," he yelled to them all.

They congregated near the top as Brian bounded up the last dozen steps. He carried a tan Hartman briefcase, the deep expensive one, the one with the combination locks and fancy buckles.

"Good morning, gentlemen," he said, pointing to a spot about thirty yards away. "Let's gather over here. If anyone comes upon us—best bet would be a Lynn cop—we're members of the Lynn Historical Society, evaluating the possibility of renovating the tower and the grounds. I'll do the talking if we have to, but we should be all right here. Hardly anyone comes up any more." He pulled some documents from his sports jacket. "Here's material on the tower to make us look very official." He opened the Hartman and laid it on the ground. "Next Monday you're all going to be looking for this, so study it carefully. Tan color, Hartman label, seventeen inches across, twelve in length, four inches deep. Top of the line for today's executive."

He bent and closed the Hartman and then spun its two combination locks. "Empty today, but next Monday, one exactly like this will contain between $2-3 million dollars, and we're going to relieve its owner of its contents."

Vic Fleming broke the circle and sauntered over to the stairwell. Far below, there was no sign of activity on the stairs.

"Whose money are we talking about?" Tony asked.

Brian straightened and ran his fingers through his hair. "Any of you guys ever hear of Salvatore Ayala?" he asked. Vic stayed mute as he approached the group, and Tony shook his head.

Alarm bells sounded in Johnny's head. "Sally Ayala? The Mafia boss? You're thinking of whacking a Mafia chief?"

"Mr. Lieberman," Brian replied evenly, "there aren't too many honest citizens wandering around with maybe $3 million on their person these days, you know?"

Johnny hadn't had a drink now for over a week, but he suddenly felt hammered as his head passed from the exhilarating high he had felt yesterday to a downward roller coaster ride into another depressed state. Just like that, up and then down, the demons inhabiting his brain, picking away at his happiness.

He regained some measure of composure, at least outwardly. "Salvatore Ayala, the Prince of Darkness? How are we going to hit him, and more importantly, get away with it?"

Brian smiled as comfortably as he could. His eyes seemed to peel Johnny away in layers, and he had that voice you could listen to all night, the charm and the confidence, so sure of himself.

"We're going to hit him just like we hit the Brinks guys. Quick and fast, in two minutes flat, and he'll never know what hit him or who hit him. If the FBI can't figure us out, how's Ayala going to?"

Fleming spoke for the first time. "The vice president there"—pointing to Johnny—"is smart to be worried. Guy like Ayala will have no scruples, no laws, no due process holding him back from running down those who stole from him. But it can be done, long as we all realize there's no fuckin' margin for error with this guy."

"So what's the plan?" Tony asked.

"You guys ever hear of the Acela Express?" Brian asked.

"The new high speed rail service for North America?" Johnny asked.

"That's right. Amtrak has the Acela bombing along between New York and Boston at 150 miles per hour. Puts them right up there as a first-rate competitor against the airlines," Brian said.

"So?" Johnny replied.

"Next Monday, our friend Ayala, accompanied by a lady friend and one other guy as back-up, rides the Acela in from New York to South Station. He arrives there just after 9:00 A.M. with the girl on one arm, and his briefcase on the other. We grab it, and we're on our way.

"Mr. Gore here is on target. It is more dangerous than dealing with those sleepy-eyed Brinks guys, every step of the way. Ayala is going to be armed and so won't the girl. And the back up behind him. And they're all observant," Brian added.

"Jesus! There's not another target somewheres?" Johnny asked. He needed to let Brian know he knew Ayala's cousin, but decided not to mention it in front of the group. Brian had insisted they not reveal any personal identifying information, anything that might expose an individual member of the crew or compromise any one of them and, therefore, the group as well.

Brian didn't bother answering the question.

"So how do we approach him?" Tony asked.

Brian reached into his jacket and pulled out copies of his diagram of the inside of South Station, as well as the area outside. He passed one to each of them as he continued holding court. "When the trains pull in here, the passengers disembark, whatever the track, and enter the rotunda through these sliding doors. There's sliding doors all the way from track 1 to track 12.

"So far—every Monday, including as recently as yesterday—Ayala and his girl friend walk straight into the rotunda. See the large number of round tables between the sliding doors and Barbara's Booksellers right in front of Track number 6? Crowds gather at the tables, drinking coffee they purchase from the Au Bon Pain to the left of Barbara's—that is to your left, if you are a passenger disembarking—or from Southworth's Market over here to the right.

"I've been sitting at the tables watching the Prince and the girl. They walk through the tables and head straight back to the rear, exiting the terminal right near where the Greyhound bus people have their booth. They walk out to the street, turn left and head to the taxicab area."

"Do we hit them inside the terminal?" Tony asked.

Brian shook his head. "Too dangerous. Loads of people both coming and going toward the tracks. In addition, there's two or three Amtrak Police inside, some private security guards around, other regulars, like the porters, and all kinds of restaurant workers. Look at all the refreshment stands ringing the rotunda."

He pointed to the Greyhound bus booth. "Mr. Gore and I will be positioned here, talking business, hopefully looking like a couple of well-to-do businessmen. The booth's maybe twenty yards from the exit to the street. When the marks go by us, we follow them out."

"Isn't hitting them on the street just as dangerous?" Johnny asked. "There must be crowds out there as well."

"Good point, Mr. Lieberman. But there's where we luck out. First of all, the fuckin' Big Dig project is all over the downtown. There's high construction fences all along the exit route from the terminal. Look at the diagram. When Ayala is on the street, he immediately turns left. He's at the corner of Atlantic Avenue and Essex Street. He has to go maybe a hundred yards to reach the taxi pick-up area along Atlantic. For the entire route he—and therefore we—can't be seen from the street due to the construction fences. We hit him right here in that tunnel walkway."

"But there's others in the walkway," Johnny persisted.

"That's right. From what I observed, maybe fifteen tops. Most of the arriving passengers don't pass through the rotunda on their way to the taxi stand, but pass behind the sliding doors, toward Track #1. It's a more direct route. And another piece of good luck for us. Boston's not a big taxi town. There's only 4-5 cars lined up for the passengers anyway."

"We're still going to have to neutralize any passengers in the walkway," Vic responded.

Brian nodded in agreement. "You and I put on the candidates' masks as soon as we exit the terminal and fall in a bit behind Ayala and the girl. While you get the briefcase, I'll hold off any heroes in the crowd."

"We've got to get Ayala and the girl down quickly," Vic said. "What's your play there?"

"You take Ayala, and I'll take the girl. We clock them with our weapons so they're down. You grab the briefcase, and I'll cover you and get any bystanders down as well," Brian said.

"Mr. Lieberman," Brian continued," you've got to make sure that the back up is not a factor. You've got to follow him out of the terminal. Normally, he's about fifteen yards behind them. In all cases, we've got to get them on the ground."

"I'll take care of it," Johnny responded.

"When you whack him, any crowd members in front of you and behind us are going to become confused what with action in both directions. And that's good for us," Vic said.

"Mr. Cheney, your part now," Brian said.

"Can I express a little concern already?" Tony said, a smile forming along the lines of his mouth.

"Be my guest," Brian replied.

"Escape routes around South Station, especially around nine o'clock on Monday morning. The city's normally paralyzed anyway, and like you said, with the Big Dig going down all around the area, we might as well be in downtown Bangkok trying to get out."

"See the area right in front of the taxicab stand on Atlantic Avenue?" Brian asked.

"I'm with you," Tony replied.

"We're going to need you there, Cheney. Very early Monday morning. Around eight o'clock. We'll need a van, out-of-state plates. Can you get a van, steal some plates?"

"No problem so far. Except I'm still stuck on the streets of Boston with no place to go."

"Oh, yee of little faith," Brian laughed. "When we enter the van, you drive off on Atlantic, which is one way. You pass East Street on your right, because it's one way coming into us. The next right is Beach Street. We take that right up to Surface Road, turn left and there's the Massachusetts Turnpike West, right in front of you. Then..."

"Great," interrupted Tony, "and at the next exit on the turnpike, every cop between Boston and Metro West will be waiting for us."

Brain loved to demonstrate his superior intellect to this class as well as to his university students. "Did I say we were going onto the Turnpike? Did I?" he repeated, wagging a finger at Tony.

"Every cop between Boston and Metro West will believe we are stupid, and that we would take the fastest exit out of town. That's why, at the turnpike entrance, you'll take a right onto Kneeland, right into fuckin' Chinatown where you'll have parked a second stolen vehicle for us to transfer into.

"Everyone's looking for the van. Probably they might even have the plates phoned in by some witness. In the meantime, we're heading toward various drop-off points around the city while the police are off on their mission. What do you think of that?"

"A second car on Kneeland," Tony said, absorbing the idea.

"From there, drop each of us off around Boylston, Arlington, Charles Streets. We'll get away, like last time, on the subway," Brian said.

"It can work," Tony conceded. "When we leave South Station, we're going against the grain. Most of the traffic's coming into the city."

"Exactly." Brian waved a hand in Tony's direction, in acknowledgment of the superior student.

"What about clothing?" Vic asked.

"Wear long trench coats to hide the weapons and the mask. Cheney, you need a hat. Wear one of those broad-brimmed ones to hide your face from the taxi guys behind you and any passers-by."

Brian looked around, sensing some edginess that was not there ten days ago. "Look, it's a good plan. It'll work just like the Brinks job. It should take less than two minutes to grab the briefcase and reach Cheney here. And we'll be in Chinatown two minutes later, safe in another vehicle. And we each have another $600,000 grand or so like I promised you. And that's it. Two and out. You're gone from this area whenever you want after the payoff."

Fleming moved closer into the circle. "Remember, there can be no mistakes with this one."

"There weren't with the first one," Brian replied too quickly.

"But Sally Ayala wasn't involved with the first one. The prick will be relentless."

Johnny decided to ask the question rolling around in his head. "Mr. Bush, you've considered hitting on Ayala somewhere else? Like when he's in the taxi, or in his neighborhood?"

"I have," Brian answered. "We're better off where there's a good crowd, people minding their own business, bustling off to work on a Monday morning. He's also got too many people around him normally, particularly over in the North End. No, the train station's our best bet."

Johnny nodded slowly. "Okay," he said.

"We need one more run through on Friday, same time," Brian said. "You all know where Christie's is on Lynn Beach? We'll meet there, sit in a car, have some coffee, go over it all once more, pass out the weapons, masks and gloves, and then we'll be ready. What was it that U Mass basketball coach said?

He was right, you know. Preparation is far more important than the game itself."

39

"So what you're saying is they have shit," Brian said.

Vic stared at the VCR as Alice Faye stood in a belaced, beplumed gown of the Gay Nineties, a picture of loveliness. There was something wistfully plaintive in Faye's voice that tugged away at the love strings of a body's heart. Her singing in "Hello, Frisco, Hello," after an absence of a year from film making, seemed more composed, quieter, yet very effective.

He hit the remote and lowered the sound. "You want me to freshen that?" he asked Brian.

"I'm set," Brian replied. "Don't shut that down on my account."

"No matter. I'll watch it later," Vic said, turning it off altogether.

"You like the old movies, huh?"

Vic got up and strolled to the bar. "It's my hobby, my love, whatever you want to call it," he replied, indicating the videos—maybe 200 of them—set into two of his library shelves. "She's a special favorite."

"Alice Faye, right?" Brian offered.

Vic looked at him with renewed interest. "How would you know that? I mean a young guy like you. What are you, maybe thirty-five, thirty-six?"

Brian lifted his glass in a mock toast. "Thirty-eight."

"So still too young to recognize Alice Faye."

"Not really, Captain. I've got a good-sized collection, too. Mostly from the 60's on up. But I like the old stuff better than the new crap—DVD, widescreen, box lettering. Christ, half the picture's missing and the sound tracks are so loud you can't hear half the dialogue. Not that much of its worth listening too anyway. And the acting's worse."

Vic drank right from the long neck, taking a huge gulp. "I'm with you, son. Ever see 'The Postman Always Rings Twice'?"

Two and Out

"The one with Jack Nicholson and Jessica Lange, or the old one with Lana Turner and John Garfield?"

"You do know your movies," Vic said. "That movie points out what you're talkin' about. In the newer one, Nicholson's flinging her onto a kitchen counter and banging away at her. In the old one, the black and white, the sex is intimated and Garfield makes you feel his lust. Remember Lana Turner in that white bathing suit? The old one's a much better picture."

"You still going out to L.A. right after we hit Ayala?" Brian asked.

As Vic nodded slowly, Brian caught the loneliness in the man. He seldom smiled, joylessness being a big part of both him and his surroundings. He had never been to Vic's place before, but was not surprised to find drab furniture, too many dark colors, the lack of a woman's touch. That was it. There were two pictures of Vic with his wife in happier times, one at a picnic table with ten or twelve other people, probably other cops and their wives, and another with the two of them embracing, their love for each other obvious.

Vic didn't refer to her much at all, but his loss was in his eyes, in his posture—a retired cop with no one to care about him, and no one to care for. A man who had seen much of life and who knew there wasn't much more he wanted to see. At least not alone. Maybe the fantasies that engrossed him on the VCR would come alive for him in Los Angeles. The Faye movies were essentially films of love lost and regained, and of new love discovered and cherished. Whatever, Brian hoped the captain found what he was looking for in the City of Angels.

"Yeah, when I have the dough, the ability to live the way I want, it's always been my dream, y' know? Go out there where there's some warmth, a chance to meet new people. Spend my golden years in the Golden State. How about your own plans?"

Brian crossed his legs and finished off his glass. "I'm going to bounce around the country, Vic. Maybe start off in Las Vegas. Find a nice rental not too expensive near the Strip if I can. Stay for a few months. Take a fraction of what I've got and see if I can put it to work at the tables."

Vic furrowed his brow. "Not a good move."

Brian laughed his holier-than-thou laugh, the one that irritated. "I said only a piece, friend. A hundred grand or so. Don't worry, I'll save plenty to invest and then move around South America. In the end, I'll settle in Florida somewhere. Maybe Naples or the other coast. Miami."

Vic asked the question that had always been on his mind, although like some of the best lawyers, he knew the answer before he asked.

"Anyone close to you, Brian?"

Brian flashed that disarming, playful grin, the one that showed that he didn't take too many things too seriously. "Three people," he replied. "Me, myself, and I. And that's the way he wanted it to be, the way it had always been."

"No family, no girl?" Vic asked.

"My mother and father passed away some time ago. And no girl. No steady girl, at least. No ties."

Vic set his bottle down and opened two more.

"And I'm not gay, if that's what you're thinking," Brian added, laughter in his voice.

Vic passed the bottle along the bar. "That never occurred to me," he grinned.

"There's no such thing allowed in America anymore," Brian said. "A confirmed bachelor, I mean. Take the movies you and I both love. As soon as one of the big stars back in the 40's-60's died, some asshole declared him a homosexual—Cary Grant, Randolph Scott, Tyronne Power, Errol Flynn. I could go on and on. None of them alive to defend themselves. Fuckin' media. People suck. Yeah, I like to mix in with people, have fun. Been doing that all my life, but I also want my privacy more than anything else.

"With the money, I'll be able to live the way I want for a long while. No one to give me orders, discuss my credentials in private like at the university. I'll teach a bit in a couple of years or so, but I'll do it for my love of it, not to impress some sanctimonious asses deciding on my tenure as if they're better teachers than I when they couldn't hold a candle..."

He stopped himself right there. "How the fuck did I get started down that track?" he asked himself as much as Vic.

Vic shrugged his shoulders. "I think you were answering my question," he said.

Brian tapped his bottle with his thumb and began drumming. "Sounds like it was just a coincidence that the FBI called on you."

"No question in my mind. There's no suspicion there, and at least we found out where they are," Vic said.

"Nowheresville," Brian responded.

"So far," Vic said.

"So far," Brian agreed.

———

"What are we, ten days in now, Mikey?" Sam Morris was asking, standing very erect near his office window looking out at a weeping sky. The rain poured down in sheets, running diagonally along the glass.

Mike Fallon fingered his cup of Dunkin' Donuts coffee and blew into it before responding. "Ten days is right, Chief."

"Well, at least the guard finally woke up," Sam said, moving along the glass wall as if he might get away from the rain if he did.

"I called Billy Flanagan back in yesterday. Asked for his cooperation once again, or he was going down on the parole violation. I think he's a dead end, but he got the ultimatum—find me a fuckin' thief or go down."

"It's a long shot at best," Sam said.

"Maybe; maybe not. We're on the street with the stoolies on the 'sport' thing, passing the word. Somebody's going to be owed a big favor if they can help us find this guy."

"Where else are you looking?"

"Dunn told us the guy was the wheel man. We're asking around in general as well—mechanics, car parts stores, car clubs like the Corvette whackos. We passed the word inside Walpole. Maybe one of the cons there knows a guy."

"But so far nothing."

Mike let out a big sigh. "Jesus, Sam, it's only been forty-eight hours. Give it time."

"You know, and I know, that's something we don't have much of. Ten days with very little to go on. One asshole who calls people 'sport.' I'm going to look good bringing whoever he is to a prosecutor because him and 10,000 others call people 'sport'.

Mike placed his hands behind his neck and stretched. "You know as well as I do, if we find this guy and crack him, we could break the whole deal open."

Morris put both hands in his pants pockets and looked across at Fallon. "You think I'm breaking your balls on this, Mikey?"

Fallon shrugged his shoulders.

Sam turned and stared at the rain. "Well, I'm not. You've come alive on this, Mikey. I've noticed. Where we are is not for lack of effort on your part. I'm seeing some fire returning."

"Is this a good time to ask for a raise?" Mike joked.

"Well, let's not go that far. We'll talk about it when you catch this crew."

"And we will," Mike replied.

40

Brian parked his car in the huge lot on Market Street in Lynn and walked toward City Hall Square. As he turned left at the Square, he spotted Johnny sitting alone on a park bench directly across the street from the Lynn Public Library.

Who would he be today? Brian wondered. The animated Johnny, or the comatose one? He didn't have to wait long to find out, as Johnny bolted from the bench as he approached.

"What's up, John?" he asked.

"I need to fill you in on something I couldn't say in front of the others yesterday," Johnny began.

"Let's walk a while," Brian said.

They headed west along the Common. To their right, traffic moved along North Common Street toward Boston. To the left, the majesty of St. George's Greek Orthodox Church towered before them. At the huge gazebo directly in front of them, young Hispanic men played soccer, an audience of pretty young women urging them on, some pushing baby carriages back and forth as they watched.

"What is it?" Brian asked. He couldn't really figure out Johnny's mood. He seemed to be focused and normal.

"Sally Ayala? My bookie is his cousin Paulie over in Saugus."

Brian weighed the statement for a beat. "So?"

"They know me," Johnny replied, more calmly than Brian expected.

"Sally knows you?"

"No, I never met him."

"So this Paulie knows you?"

"Yeah."

"There shouldn't be any problem, John. This Paulie won't be at South Station. And you'll be wearing a mask most of the time."

Johnny didn't seem anywhere near as nervous as he had appeared yesterday at High Rock. "I just want you to be aware," he said.

At the gazebo, they turned around and walked back toward City Hall. "I've been seeing Laura lately," Johnny confided.

"How are things?"

"Well, it's hard to explain. There's a strain there, for sure. And she's hurt, and doesn't want to be hurt more, but we're connecting."

"You tell her about your plans to move to Florida?" Brian asked.

"Yeah. She says it doesn't matter, but it does. When she's hurt, she strikes back. Like most of us."

Brian glanced at him and poked him on the arm. "You look a lot better the last week or so, Johnny."

"I'm off the sauce. I'm trying to be good for her, y' know? As long as I'm around, I'm trying to make her proud."

"Who says you have to go to Florida?" Brian asked.

"I know. Lately, I've been thinkin' I might stay around. Apply for a job over in Saugus or Peabody. Lord knows they need teachers today. Problem is, I never know how I'm goin' to feel tomorrow, y' know!"

Brian had always marveled at the ability of those afflicted with manic-depression to understand themselves. Almost always they couldn't stop the roller coaster ride, but invariably they knew they were riding.

They turned up Market Street. From the open door of a small appliance store, sound boomed from a huge projection screen. On screen, an overweight woman pumped away on an exercise bicycle while simultaneously sending her e-mail. The broadcaster interviewing her seemed impressed at her ability to do two things at once. Jesus, no wonder we're a stressed-out society, Brian thought.

"You cool with next Monday?" Brian asked.

Two and Out

"Brian, I'm feeling great! Just because I asked a lot of questions yesterday doesn't mean I won't be there for us next week."

Brian tapped him on the chin. "I know that, Johnny."

———

Doug howled in delight as Tony and Grace pedaled behind him along Sea Street. They were headed for the Sundae School ice cream stand at the corner of Lower County Road, about a half-mile ahead. Having given Doug a fifty-yard lead, they couldn't seem to close the gap. He looked back over his shoulder once or twice, his training wheels banging noisily over the cracks in the sidewalk.

Tony and Grace feigned pedaling, yelling that they were closing fast as he shrieked. "We're right behind you, pal!" Tony screamed. "Only a few yards to go!"

He searched ahead, thankful there were few side streets between them and the stand and that traffic was slow at this time of day.

Once at the pebbled driveway leading into the stand, Doug stepped off his bike and raised his hand in triumph. "You beat us!" Grace exclaimed, turning in from the street.

"I won! I won!"

Tony leaned his bicycle against a wooden picnic table and fished into his pants pocket. "Don't forget to get some napkins, Doug," he said, handing two dollars to his son.

Doug leaned his face forward so that Tony could kiss him. "Thank you, Dad," he said before running off toward the short line in front of the huge red converted barn.

Grace smiled at him from across the table.

"What?" Tony asked.

"You know how I can tell you're a good man?" she asked.

Tony showed his dimple and shrugged his shoulders as he sat. "I'm just happy you think so."

"He loves you, that's how," she replied. "He loves you because he knows you love him more than anything in the world."

Doug waved to them from the line. "I think I'm getting to love his daddy, too," Grace said, placing her hand in his.

He decided there would be no better time to ask. "Can I ask you a big question?"

"Shoot."

"Would you come with us to San Diego?"

She quickly shook her head. "No. I can't do that, Tony. You know how he loves you and you love him and nothing could ever get in the way of that? Well, that's how I feel about my work here and the Cape. I'm one of that army of contemporary thirty-something yuppies who give most of their time and energy to work. I could never leave my children who need me, in the middle of the year, and I don't think I can leave this lovely place. There's no place like the Cape. Sometimes I can be alone and lonely here, but the sea, and the regulars here pick me up. I'm a Cape Codder through and through."

He cupped her hand, squeezing, not knowing what to say.

"Besides," she continued in a light banter, "I've only known you for two weeks. How do I know what your intentions are?"

"Your body," he said, going along.

"Just what I thought. Another guy just out for sex."

"You weren't complaining last night," he teased.

She touched her hair and played with the fringes. "No-o-o," she replied, smiling.

Doug walked back slowly toward them, licking his two scoops while he delicately balanced the cone.

"Let's just enjoy one another until it's time for you to go," Grace said, releasing his hand, a small tear forming in the corner of her eye.

41

Sally Ayala never failed to be impressed by the Acela. Three and a half-hours or less between Boston and New York with a 97 % on-time record. By the time you fought that miserable Logan Airport traffic, parked your vehicle, checked in, waited invariably for some sort of delay in taking off or landing or both, you were lucky if it didn't take four hours to New York.

He looked around as he waited for them to depart Penn Station. The oversized windows flooded the train with natural light. In business class the seats were extra wide and comfortable with plenty of leg room. Right at the seat he had access to audio entertainment, adjustable reading lamps and electrical outlets if he knew a fuckin' think about computers, which he didn't.

Carol was asleep already, and they had been in their seats no more than ten minutes. She sat in a fetal position facing the windows, probably dreaming of his sexual prowess last night, he thought. She could go all night too, but he wished, come morning, she could stay awake and face the daylight. Fuckin' vampire.

Some businessmen had already occupied a conference table with seats for four, not wanting to miss a chance to work all the way to Boston. The one with the lantern jaw held his small Hartman case on his lap. Sally tapped his own, mentally calculating that his held three clean and green million dollars. Later on, he would visit the Cafe car, watch some television and the panoramic view of the Connecticut coastline rolling by. Even taking a whizz was a pleasure on this train. The bathrooms were clean and featured backlit mirrors.

Suddenly, they started forward and within minutes gathered speed. Instead of the clackety clack of the old trains, he could hear just a barely audible hum. Amtrak had installed continuous welded rail along the Northeast Corridor, replacing the old joint-connected tracks and had added advanced soundproofing features on the train itself.

The train tilted along the way, bending with the curves, the new technology allowing it to keep its speed as it hurled itself ever forward toward Boston.

All these advances, and no security checkpoints, departing, boarding, or on arrival. Amazing. And never a sign of trouble either on the train or in the stations. Every weekend his trip went like clockwork. Bring the whore money, the shylock dollars, the drug bucks, the stolen paper, to New York and, for a fee, let the guys there launder it, do whatever they did. Once in a while he even brought the drugs themselves right off the fuckin' boats from South America to be sold in New York.

He looked around, priding himself on paying attention to his surroundings. He liked to read, see what the fuckin' Red Sox were doing early in October, which wasn't much whenever Pedro Martinez wasn't pitching. But he never read on the train. He paid attention to business, which is what he hoped Sonny was doing behind him.

"You want some coffee, Sally?"

Sally squinted as he looked up at his godson. He said nothing. Then with his index finger, he signaled Sonny to bend toward his left ear.

"Yeah?" Sonny asked.

"What the fuck are you doing here holding on to two fuckin' cups of coffee?" he whispered.

Sonny straightened and looked out the window for the answer, the coastline of Long Island Sound gleaming in the distance.

"I got you and Carol some coffee is what I'm doing." He shrugged his shoulders, trying to figure out what was bothering his godfather.

Sally gripped his arm, almost causing him to spill the joe.

"Listen, you moron," he hissed through clenched teeth, "you're supposed to be watching my back. Not down here lettin' half the fuckin' train know we're together. Where did you get the coffee anyway?"

Sonny frowned. "In the club car back there."

"You left my ass unprotected?" Sally asked, startled.

"No big deal, Sally. Who's going to rob us on the train? What they gonna' do? Jump off this thing at 150 miles an hour?"

Sally stared him down. "Y' know, Sonny, this may be your first and last trip to New York. Now get the fuck back there and stick that coffee up your ass along the way."

Sonny shook his head at what he perceived as a very unfair world.

―――

Brian sat in the Wendy's on Summer Street, pleased for the partly cloudy cool morning. No one would then find it inappropriate that he wore the long trench coat.

He sipped his orange juice and studied the Globe. Everytime there was a new debate there was a new Gore. He wished the vice president would make up his mind as to who he was before the Democrats blew the election. With Clinton having brought peace and prosperity to the country, winning the election should be a slam-dunk. He felt in his pocket for the Bush mask and fingered it. Maybe it was an omen of changes to come this fall.

He glanced at his Rolex and felt for the Glock at the same time. 8:30 A.M.—time for the short walk to the station.

42

Tony eased the black Mercury Grand Marquis into the vacant space on Kneeland Street at exactly 6:05 A.M. He sat for a while, acquainting himself with his surroundings. Even at this early hour, young Chinese professionals dressed in business attire wandered into coffee shops, greeting grandfatherly types who sat at round tables babbling with other seniors.

Opening the door, he began feeding quarters into the meter, enough to protect the space until Vic arrived at seven o'clock to replenish it. He looked up Kneeland Street toward Stuart, thinking of the escape route he had tested last Wednesday and Friday.

He was now a half mile, maybe closer to three-fourths of a mile, from South Station. When they had the briefcase, he would drive the Dodge Caravan from the train terminal to this place. Just one light to cross at Surface Road. They should be here within two or three minutes. If there was a spot for the van—a 50-50 proposition—he would park it, and they would transfer to the Merc. If not, he would double-park it anyway, which practically every one of these crazy fuckin' Boston drivers did anyway all over the city.

From here, he should be at the different drop-off points on Charles, and then Beacon, and then be on to Storrow Drive heading east within five or seven additional minutes.

He pulled the collar of his bomber jacket up and walked toward the Red Line station over on Summer Street. He should be in Quincy by 7:00 A.M. He would pick up the van on Hancock Street and be back in front of South Station by 8:00-8:15 A.M.

Two and Out

Vic Fleming boarded the Blue Line train at Revere Beach at 6:15 A.M., angling for a seat before the crush of humanity overwhelmed him. On a fall Monday morning there were very few left. Two teens on their way to some school in the city practically bowled over an elderly couple to gain the last two available seats.

He stood beside the old couple, the lady, probably in her eighties, straining to hold on to the strap above her. She bumped into Vic repeatedly as the train careened toward Beachmont.

"Would you like to sit down, Ma'm?" Vic asked.

"Oh, yes, thank you. But there are no seats," she replied, her hand quivering.

"Excuse me," Vic said, addressing the two boys lost in their own world, oblivious to anyone else, poking each other and laughing loudly.

"Yeah?" the blond one asked.

"Would you be able to give up your seats for these people?"

Looking like he had asked for the family fortune, the boys shook their heads and kept on talking to one another.

Vic leaned forward, speaking quietly. "Get the fuck out of those seats, or I'll yank your asses out for you." He opened his trench coat and flashed his badge, which was hanging from his belt.

Scowling, the two hyenas stood, and Vic gestured to the old couple. "Please sit down," he said.

"Why, aren't they perfectly wonderful young men. Thank you so much," she said to the two boys who looked at her like she had the plague.

———

At 7:00 A.M., Johnny Casey stood in a practically deserted Central Square in Lynn, waiting for the MBTA bus to Haymarket Square. He wore the Glock in the small of his back, just as the older guy—Gore—had told him to. He felt for his rubber mask in the left-hand pocket of his trench coat.

John A. Curry

He ran his hand over his face, feeling the clamminess, the cold dampness, not unlike coming off a drunk. But he hadn't had a drink now for more than two weeks, and curiously, he didn't want one. Not even this morning.

He was just nervous, wishing time forward. If only it were ten o'clock now, and this whole thing were over, with another $700,000 plus in his pocket. There was more risk this time, for sure. When it was over, he could consider his future.

But not right now. He couldn't afford to think of the future or of Laura, or of Sarasota, or of Lynn. Focus, he told himself. Not too up, not too down. Focus on the task at hand. The bus rolled to a stop right at his feet. He glanced once again at his watch. Hurry up and get here, ten o'clock.

Tony Amonti cursed the Southeast Expressway traffic as he veered into a new lane whenever he could to gain time. Calm down, plenty of time, he said to himself. At this hour, Mr. Gore should be in Chinatown looking over the Merc, preserving their spot.

The "Welcome to Chinatown" sign loomed straight ahead as he exited and looped the Dodge Caravan toward Surface Road. At Dewey Square, he turned right onto Atlantic Avenue and passed the small covey of taxis lined up outside the train station. Christ, he thought, if this were New York, they'd be a hundred of them waiting for passengers.

As he passed them, he kept his hand up close to his head and the soft fedora, although from the corner of his eye, he could see the drivers did not pay any attention, concentrating instead on racing forms or the sports pages. He noted the tall construction fence to their left, shielding from their view any passengers coming down the walkway from the station to the cab stand.

Pulling into a spot about thirty yards ahead of the line of taxis, he cut the engine and stared at his watch. 7:45 A.M. Before he exited the vehicle, he placed the "Massport" sign he

Two and Out

had lifted at Logan Airport, onto the dashboard and adjusted his soft hat.

Being careful not to turn toward the cabs, he sauntered down Atlantic Avenue heading west toward Chinatown.

On Kneeland Street, Vic Fleming stood in a doorway about twenty yards up from the Grand Marquis. Above him, a domestic argument raged in Chinese, with no subtitles. In the mix, he thought he caught a few "fuck yous," the universal expression of the angry.

Even at this early hour there were few remaining parking spots in the area. With the meters, and with any luck, there might be an opening for the Dodge when they arrived here around 9:20 A.M. No one seemed to pay him any particular attention. When he had worked narcotics, he had covered Roxbury; nevertheless, the criminal element here, as everywhere, could smell cop, retired or otherwise, in a quick second. He wasn't really comfortable loitering too long.

He glanced to his right and saw Mr. Cheney heading his way from the Surface Road crossing. No question, the kid with the Kirk Douglas cleft chin had been a real find. He had asked Phil Hanrahan to recruit someone with balls, someone who was a skilled driver, someone in need of money, but with no record. It had taken Hanrahan a month before he identified this kid up at Loudon on the racing circuit.

He had told Hanrahan he didn't want to meet the kid or know his name. As Brian had directed, they would keep knowledge of crew members to a bare minimum.

And they had themselves a success story. He wished he felt as good about the other guy-Lieberman. He hadn't performed badly at all, but his up and down behavior was worrisome. He had to pull a heavy load today, neutralizing the muscle. I'll have to watch him, Vic thought.

"You didn't look so good in that debate the other night, Mr. Gore," Tony teased, as he joined him.

"And you looked better than all three of the rest of us, Mr. Cheney," Vic countered.

"Think I should run for president?"

Vic laughed. "Don't get too ambitious, Mr. Cheney. You ready for today?"

"Fine. What the hell's that ruckus?"

Vic pointed upstairs. "Been goin' on for fifteen minutes minimum. Somebody cooked the wrong dish, near as I can make out. Best people in the world—the Chinese. They understand the need to respect elders, to value family," he added.

"Yeah?" Tony said. "Well, someone's not getting the message."

"Put this duffel bag in the Merc, will you? I'm heading over to the terminal now."

"It's 8:15," Tony said, "I'll get some coffee and feed this beast some more quarters, and be back over there at 8:45."

"Good luck, Cheney," Vic said. "And let's not get any speeding tickets."

———

Brian Hughes stood at the crosswalk next to One Financial Center and surveyed the entire area. Across the street the exterior of South Station looked old and drab, in contrast to a modern edifice like the financial center itself. To both his left and right, the largest federal construction project in the history of the state and the nation—$11 billion in costs and rising—proceeded as scores of workers labored to dismantle and depress the long stretch of roadway known as the Central Artery that connected the area north of Boston with the south.

Huge construction sites abounded as far as the eye could see in both directions. There hadn't been a major robbery in this part of the downtown for ten years, mainly because every right-thinking crook would find it clearly impossible to get away from this mess in any kind of quick time.

That is until he came along, he thought. He waited for the red light and crossed. Instead of entering the station directly, he turned to his right, walking once again now behind heavy construction fences masking him and any other pedestrians in the walkway from the taxicabs alongside the giant terminal. Somewhere in this distance of fifty yards they would intercept Sally Ayala, relieve him of somewhere between two and three million dollars, and then leave the city by going against the grain of the incoming traffic, and in two getaway cars, not one, and in just minutes to boot. At this early hour there were only four or five others in the walkway. A half-hour from now, he figured maybe twenty, tops.

He turned around and sauntered back to the main entrance at the corner of Atlantic Avenue. As he walked, he raised his arm and extended it for a minute. His hand, palm down, was as solid as a rock, his fingers straight as an arrow. No shaking, no nerves.

He grinned as he entered the terminal. Why should there be nerves? His plan was perfect, and it would be perfectly executed.

Directly in front of Brian, maybe fifty yards away in the brightly lit, festive rotunda, Johnny Casey spooned his coffee and watched both the sliding doors and the electronic board above them indicating the arrival and departure schedules. At the automatic doors there were far more people coming into the terminal than were heading out to the trains. From both west and south of the Hub, nattily attired executives—the men in blue, black or gray suits or sport coats, the women dressed in business suits or slacks of varying colors—marched into and through the terminal, side by side, unsmiling, looking neither left or right.

Somehow, the power look didn't go with the Nikes on the feet of many of the women, Johnny felt.

He drummed his fingers on the table and took a small bite of his donut. As he lifted his coffee, he almost dropped it, some of the joe spilling on his hand. "Fuck!" he muttered to himself, his nerves jangling.

He had to think of something good in his life, like Laura, like football. Yeah, that was it. Think of football and the days with Flutie, and then fuckin' perform like he had in '84. Bicknell, the coach, had praised him in front of the whole team following their return from Miami when they all watched the film together.

"Y' know," he had said, "Doug and the offense deservedly get great credit for their work down there, but watch how Johnny Casey handled that All-American tackle from Miami. He drove him back into Kosar all day long at critical times. There's a real All-American right here in front of me—Johnny Casey from Lynn."

Physically, he could still handle that big tackle from Miami or the muscle who would be coming in behind Sally Ayala. You bet your ass he could. It was the mental stuff that bothered him most, the ups and downs, the high and lows. But for the next hour or so he would perform in the same fashion as he had in the Orange Bowl. He lifted the coffee cup once more, and this time not a drop spilled. Fuck Ayala. He was ready for the kickoff.

From his position to the left of Johnny Casey, Vic Fleming could observe the entire terminal. He stood in front of the ticket purchasing windows, near Track 12, his eyes sweeping the rotunda. 9:00 A.M. Almost playtime.

Passengers scurried around him, some standing in line for tickets, others hurrying toward the trains as announcements boomed over the loudspeakers. He sipped his coffee while watching Mr. Lieberman, who was positioned facing the doors right in front of the track where the Acela would arrive.

The rotunda was extremely busy, but on a Monday morning, that was to be expected. He had to agree with Brian that the busier it was, the better. With a number of people in the walkway outside, there would be mass confusion when they hit Ayala. Yet large numbers could also produce a hero or two, and that could cause a real problem.

He threw the cup into a receptacle and looked toward Brain. Standing near the Greyhound ticket booth, Brian read his <u>Boston Herald</u>. He kept his eyes focused on the newspaper, never once looking up for Vic or Johnny. Like his crew, Brian wore a business suit, shirt and tie, and a long trench coat. To Vic, he looked like any other businessman commuter waiting the interminable wait.

From somewhere in space, the announcer's voice cut through to them. "The Acela—arriving in five minutes from New York on Track #8." A few people meandered from their tables or standing positions toward the sliding doors.

Vic watched the hands on his watch move for two minutes and then started toward Brian. When he approached, Brian looked up from his paper, greeting him effusively. They stood to the side of the Greyhound booth, maybe twenty yards away.

"Are you ready, Hessie?" Vic asked.

"Never felt better," Brian replied. "Spike Jones, right?"

"You never cease to amaze me, Professor," Vic said.

Tony Amonti sat erect in the Dodge Caravan, pleased with developments around him. Behind him on Atlantic Avenue, only four taxicabs were in line awaiting passengers. Although the fencing blocked his view of the walkway, there was little activity coming toward the cabs.

Fifty yards in front of him, a Boston cop directed light traffic around another piece of the Big Dig construction, his view back to Tony's position blocked by a huge caterpillar. No one paid him any attention, but Tony kept his Massport sign right there on the dashboard in the event someone became nosy.

He glanced at his watch. 9:15 A.M. The crew should be on the street in five to ten minutes.

"You sleep enough, Carol?"

"Don't yank my chain, Sally. I was tired, y' know? Christ, we go out all night, screw till dawn, and then take the milk train back here before I can even brush my teeth."

They stepped down from the train and began the long walk toward the automatic doors leading into the terminal.

"Where's the geek?"

Sally gave her a long stare. "That's my godson, Carol. Be kind, huh?" he said. "He's where he should be—twenty, thirty yards behind us protecting our asses."

She bumped him with her hip.

"Hey!" he cried indignantly.

"You have fun in New York?" she whispered.

"Of course."

"Then when are you goin' to leave that fuckin' deadbeat wife of yours. Huh?"

"Look, Carol. We have a good time, right? Let's not get into that every damn time we meet lately. Let's pay attention to what's goin' on right here."

"You worry too much," she said.

"When I'm carryin' Joe Sansone's money, I know I better worry."

The sliding doors opened and they entered the brightly-lit station. His eyes swept the area, his antennae up, searching for any sign of trouble.

Two and Out

Johnny found himself almost staring at the thin man with the long scar. He caught himself and lifted the <u>Globe</u> in front of his face. Ayala walked determinedly, his eyes everywhere, the Hartman clasped tightly in his right hand. The blond kept pace with him, her hands in the pockets of her long coat.

As they passed, Johnny lowered the newspaper and began the search for the back up. And that's when he saw Sonny, dressed in a long black trench coat lumbering toward him, almost at the doors, his eyes fixated on Ayala and the girl. Sonny Rossetti!

He could feel his breakfast rising in his stomach, surfacing to the edges of his throat. He battled back, trying to calm himself, remembering to pull the newspaper up as Sonny entered the terminal. He thought of Miami and 1984, and he relaxed a bit. He willed himself to regain composure. After all, he had met challenges on other days, and he could do so again today. Play had started, and he could and would perform. Standing, he felt for the rubber mask and moved in behind Sonny, probably a distance of about twenty yards as they headed toward the Atlantic Avenue exit. With his other hand, he gripped the Glock and thought of what Bicknell had said about him long ago on that film day.

When they saw Ayala and the girl enter the terminal, Brian and Vic shook hands and parted company, Brian taking a place in the Greyhound line and Vic standing alone, his back now to the oncoming Ayala, his eyes on his newspaper.

Walking briskly, Ayala never once turned around but occasionally looked to his flanks. The blond whispered something to him but gained no reaction. They passed Brian and headed for the Atlantic Avenue exit.

As Vic approached him, Brian stepped away from the line and fell in beside him. They exited to the street and turned left onto the walkway. Ahead, four passengers moved along in front of Ayala and the girl and two others trailed them. When Brian tapped Vic's arm, they simultaneously pulled the rubber masks from the trench coats, put them on quickly, and closed the distance between themselves and the marks. From the right, Vic skirted one of the pedestrians and smashed the Glock against the back of Ayala's head. As the blond turned at the sign of the commotion, Brian hit her with his weapon directly on the top of her head.

Ayala pitched forward, his hands instinctively reaching to break his fall. He slumped face down, the briefcase clattering to the ground. Vic leaned down for it as the blond girl fell backward almost into two women passengers. They began shrieking as the violence erupted.

"Down! Get the fuck down!" Brian ordered, pointing the Glock at the two women and at the four passengers ahead of Ayala in the walkway.

"All of you get down!" Vic yelled, addressing the half-dozen people behind him.

Sonny wondered about the commotion some twenty yards ahead of him. Some woman was screaming, probably from getting goosed or from having her tit brushed. Then it hit him. Sally was on the ground and so was Carol.

And then more than a few people in front of him were dropping to the ground, slow to follow the instructions of the two gunmen shielded by the crowd. As he reached for his weapon, his legs suddenly went out from under him. He fell to the asphalt, his fingers splayed apart, his world spinning, his head feeling as if it had been hit by a two by four.

"Let's move it, Mr. Lieberman!" Vic shouted. "Stay down, you fuckin' heroes," he yelled over his shoulder as Brian and he moved briskly toward the end of the walkway.

Sonny could hear the drone of voices seemingly miles away, sounding as if they were reaching him from underwater. He placed his hands on the asphalt to brace himself. He spotted his weapon on the ground and reached for it. Off to his left a guy wearing one of those vice presidential candidates' masks—the guy from New York or was it Connecticut?—stood staring, frozen like.

"Lieberman!" Vic screamed, turning, as Johnny just stood transfixed, not knowing why he just didn't go back and hit Sonny one more time. He couldn't move, and he couldn't respond.

Vic had now turned completely back toward Johnny, yelling all the time. "Come on, Lieberman!"

As Sonny staggered to his feet, aiming his weapon at Johnny, Vic raised the Glock and started squeezing the trigger almost before the gun was all the way up. The force blew Sonny backwards onto one of the women down on the ground, blood from the gap in his stomach spurting onto her face and clothes.

Johnny suddenly came alive again, running now toward Brian as Vic retreated along with him.

"Stay the fuck down!" Vic screeched at the group on the ground.

———

Tony revved up the engine at exactly 9:17 P.M., and within two minutes he heard what seemed like a gunshot burst. Yet what with the noise from the construction sites and the cacophony of traffic sounds, he could have been mistaken. Looking in the rearview mirror, he saw that nothing had changed. Both in back and in front of him, the hard hats continued with their hydraulic drilling, the cab drivers remained in line waiting for new fares, and traffic on the street remained light.

From around the corner, he spotted Bush, Gore, and Lieberman walking at a quick pace, but not calling attention to themselves by appearing to be in too much of a hurry. As planned, they had removed the rubber masks just before reaching the end of the walkway and the corner.

Grimacing, Bush sat down next to him as Gore and Lieberman piled into the rear.

"Go!" Bush said.

Tony pulled away from the curb and drove past East Street, taking the next right onto Beach Street. As he made the turn, through the mirror he saw two agitated businessmen come out of the walkway, pointing and screaming in their direction.

"Fuck! What the hell happened?" Brian yelled.

"I thought I had him down and out," Johnny stammered. "I..."

"You're lucky to fuckin be here," Gore replied. "I had to shoot the back-up or he would have taken this guy out."

"Jesus!" Brian screamed. "Is he dead?"

"I didn't stay around to find out," Vic replied. "Let's concentrate on what we're doing here, huh? Give me the masks."

Tony beat the light at Surface Road and took the left turn heading toward the turnpike. Again, the light was in their favor. He swung onto Kneeland Street, entering Chinatown. On his left, fifty yards ahead, he spotted an empty parking space, thirty yards behind the Mercury.

He leapt from the van and fed two quarters into the meter while the others stepped out and walked casually toward the Mercury. A few neighborhood residents, all of them elderly, walked along, engrossed in their own conversations. Looking back to Surface Road, Tony saw no sign of trouble. No blaring of horns, no police cars. No one yet in pursuit.

Entering the Grand Marquis, he noticed that all three of his partners had shed their trench coats, piling them on the back seat. In the front, Bush sat in the passenger seat with the Hartman on his lap.

Pulling away from the curb, Tony proceeded cautiously, occasionally glancing in the rearview mirror. He relaxed almost right away, as no one would now be looking for a Mercury sedan.

"We're coming up to Tremont," Bush announced. "Leave me right at the corner," he directed. "I'll see you guys tonight."

Tony slowed the Mercury as Brian exited, carrying the Hartman, walking now in the direction of Boston Common. He looked like any other businessman on his way to work, Tony thought.

On the move again, Tony crossed Stuart Street and turned onto Charles. Halfway down Charles he pulled over, allowing Vic to disembark with the duffel bag right outside the Public Gardens.

Starting off again, Tony turned left at the light on Beacon Street and within a minute entered Storrow Drive East. After passing Massachusetts General Hospital, he let Lieberman out, not too far away from the busses at Haymarket Square.

He studied his watch. Bush had called it right. They had been going against the grain of the incoming traffic. Only ten minutes had elapsed since they had left South Station.

43

Frank Sheridan fumed about his run of bad luck as he yanked the wheel of his unmarked Taurus toward the open space just in front of the taxicab area. Twice in a two week period. First the Brinks job practically on the doorstep of the new Boston Police Headquarters building next to Northeastern University. And now a robbery/murder one mile from the old headquarters on Berkeley Street. Jesus! Two major crimes right in his backyard, his jurisdiction. If this kept up, he would soon be directing traffic in downtown Dorchester over in Adams Square with some female rookie and him receiving the finger from all the future gangbangers driving by in stolen cars.

He bounded out of the car and flashed his badge at the red-faced young Irisher protecting the cordoned—off area.. Yellow crime scene tape stretched across the walkway exit and, at the other end, a bevy of officers prevented anyone from entering the tunnel. Along its length, blue-coated officers and some of his plainclothes staff spoke in small groups to potential witnesses, most of them agitated and distraught, pointing fingers or waving arms in exclamation.

He wiggled a finger at Tom Laitinen, the tall Finish-American who was his best squad member. "What the fuck happened here?" he asked as the tall blond approached.

"The dead guy's over there," he said, pointing to the place where the medical examiner bent over the huge frame of a man flat on his back, his long coat open, his green sweater rising up above a white shirt soaked with blood.

Laitinen looked at his small notebook. "Victim is Antonio "Sonny" Rossetti, out of Marblehead. He's..."

"I know who he is," Sheridan snapped. "Where's Ayala?"

"On the way to the Boston Medical Center along with a couple of the best wits. Fat Boy there fell on top of one of the females. With all the blood, she panicked, pushed him off her with the help of another citizen. The guy over there in the blue suit."

"Ayala say anything?"

"Not a word, although you wouldn't either, you got conked like he did. Same with the ho with him, Carol Riccadelli, his longtime squeeze."

"Did you notify Fallon?"

"He's on the way to the Med Center as we speak."

"No question the Candidates were the perps?" Sheridan asked.

"None at all," Laitinen replied. "They scooped up a briefcase. All the wits identified Gore and Bush as the leaders with Lieberman on scene as well. Cheney probably was out in front of the taxi area, driving the van. One of the wits described it as a Dodge Caravan, gray in color, but it was too far away for a plate pick-up. Turned right onto Beach Street. Probably headed for the turnpike. Haven't found it yet."

Sheridan nodded and moved away toward the young man in the blue suit. "What's his name?" he asked Laitinen, as they approached him.

Laitinen flipped his notebook. "David Gardner, Framingham. Works across the street at the Financial Center. Lawyer."

"Mr. Gardner, you okay?" Frank asked, concern in his tone. "I'm Captain Sheridan, head of our armed robbery unit."

The handsome young man flashed swamp green eyes at him. "I'm fine."

"Could you answer a few questions for me?"

"I already spoke to the investigator over there, Captain," Gardner replied, agitated.

"I understand, but it would help if you could take a minute or two. We'll need you downtown for a detailed statement later today anyway, Mr. Gardner. You know, as a lawyer, the importance of these statements."

Gardner settled back, leaning against the fence. "Go ahead," he sighed.

"How much did you actually see?"

"I was walking along with my colleague. We're both lawyers over there, across the street," he said, indicating the huge white edifice. "Suddenly, we saw some commotion up ahead of us, maybe twenty yards. Two men pushed their way through the crowd ahead of us, and the next thing I knew, one of them—the one in the Gore mask—was picking up a briefcase. You know the Hartman type, the big one? Well, he grabbed it, turned toward us, and ordered us onto the ground."

"The two men—they call each other by name?" Sheridan asked.

"No. Wait a minute. The guy in the Gore mask called one of the others 'Lieberman'."

"That's it on the names?"

Gardner thought about the answer for a moment. "No other names. It happened so fast, but no."

"How did the victim get shot?"

"From behind us the dead guy there fell, practically onto my back. Face down. The one in the Lieberman mask must have hit him, although I didn't see it. He went down face first at about the same time as Gore and Bush were ordering all of us down. Like they asked, we dropped to the pavement. The big guy got up waving a gun and the one in the Gore mask shot him. He fell on my colleague. There was blood all over her, gushing onto her suit, and she was screaming, so I helped roll him off her. Then, next thing I knew, some officers were on the scene, from the train station, I guess." He paused for a beat. "I think the guy froze."

"Who?"

"The one with the Lieberman mask. I was lying there on my stomach. I took a peek, and he took a few steps, and then turned around toward the big guy when he got up. He didn't say anything. Just stood there."

"Thanks, Mr. Gardner," Sheridan said. "Tom here will set a time for you to give us a full statement downtown."

He turned away, heading toward the medical examiner. Son of a bitch, he thought. Hitting Sally Ayala and his godson. The Candidates had to be tightly connected to the Boston Mafia scene, or they were some group of cowboys with plenty of balls. And what the hell was in the briefcase? Either drugs or money, for sure.

Sally Ayala sat on the gurney in the emergency room at Boston Medical Center, the ice pack pressed to his head. Although a curtain had been drawn around his station, he could observe the comings and goings through an opening. A bare-torsoed skinhead sat on another gurney right in front of the curtain. Sitting forward, the young Nazi displayed lettering on both biceps. "Jesus loves you," read the left one. "It's the rest of us who know you're an asshole," the right bicep answered.

The Black doctor parted the curtain and advanced without saying a word. "When can I get the fuck out of here?" Ayala grumbled.

"Let me look at that again," the doctor directed.

He stood next to Ayala and flexed his fingers through his hair. "Our tests show you suffered a mild concussion like..."

"Like a fuckin boxer, right, Doc?" Sally interrupted.

"You got it."

"Can I go now?"

The doctor stepped back and nodded. "Far as I'm concerned you can, but there's two FBI agents outside who want to talk with you."

Ayala winced. "Christ, my headache was just goin' away."

"They said they had just a few questions," the doctor said.

"Yeah, and my ass shits ice cream," Ayala retorted. "How's my lady friend, Doc?"

"We're keeping her overnight. She has a concussion, but she's not responding as well as you. She's disoriented, still sees the world spinning."

Ayala's mouth opened slightly. "You can bring on those J. Edgar Hoover faggots."

The doctor laughed hoarsely. "I'll let them know you said so."

He disappeared through the opening in the curtain, but was back within ten seconds. "Just a few questions today, Agent Fallon. We're releasing him, but he's not 100 percent," he was saying, as Fallon and Harper entered behind him.

"Well, well, Mikey Fallon and Paul Harper, two of J. Edgar's band of fairies," Ayala snickered.

"Good to see you too, Prince," Fallon rejoined.

"I don't like that name, Fallon," Ayala muttered.

Fallon laughed softly and sat down on the lone four-legged stool next to the bed. "We all have our crosses to bear, Sal."

"How you feelin', Sally?" Harper asked.

"I've been better, you know, like on those days in court when your boss Morris had to eat crow tryin' to get me indicted on some fuckin' trumped up charge."

"Racketeering. Violation of the RICO laws, if I remember right," Harper volunteered.

"Whatever. Me and Joe was declared innocent is all I remember. I pay the lawyers to handle the details."

"How's Joe these days, Sal?" Fallon asked, flashing a nice smile.

Sally's eyes narrowed. "You really care, Feeb? I'll tell him you was askin'. Can we get to whatever the fuck you want so I can get outta here?"

"The wits are saying the crew stole a Hartman briefcase, Sally. What was in it?"

Sally appeared to think a minute. "My laundry," he finally replied.

"Perish the thought," Harper said.

"Maybe he's being honest," Mike said. "His laundered money, he means, Paul."

"You're a riot in cell block 11, Fallon," Ayala said.

"I'm being serious, Sal," Fallon said, spreading his fingers palms down. "Either laundered green or drugs is my guess."

"Guess again, Mikey. You just struck out."

"Maybe you'll be the one out at home plate when Joe Sansone starts asking the questions," Mike said.

Sally Ayala frowned, his forehead buckling into a long series of wrinkles. "Anything else, Fallon?"

"What do you know about the Candidates, the crew that hit you?" Mike asked.

"Not as much today as I'm goin' to know," he responded. "They popped Brinks a couple of weeks ago now, right? What do you guys know is the real question."

"Maybe we could pool information Sally," Fallon replied.

Ayala laughed. "The word on the street is you guys got zero. No arrests and no suspects in two weeks means we would be pooling your nothing with whatever I come up with. No thanks, Feeb."

"We'll get them," Fallon replied tersely.

Ayala's face reddened. "They murdered my godson, Fallon. Did you know Rossetti was my godson?"

"You all were carrying, Prince. I'm not sure I'd call that murder," Harper replied.

Ayala tossed the ice pack on the bed, stood, and reached for his coat on the tree next to the bed. "I've got a license. You have any more questions see my lawyer." He parted the curtain and walked through without another word.

44

His timing was perfect. Brian sauntered out of the Super Stop and Shop on Boston Street in Lynn with his two bags of groceries at exactly 7 P.M. The stars were just beginning to shine in the city sky, winking behind a heavy cover of darkness.

His good mood had almost been shattered by the shopping experience. The middle-aged woman in front of him and the cashier had been wrestling over three or four coupons, whether they were good this week or next. He felt like tossing a dollar on the counter to settle the argument, or leaving the line entirely, but he held his temper. Besides, he wanted the groceries and he wanted some extra bags. Then he would look like any other shopper as he pushed his cart deep into what had to be the largest parking lot in Lynn.

He moved the cart along the side of the huge lot, where there were a small number of cars parked, but not nearly as many as in the front. Coming upon his vehicle, he opened the truck and pulled out the Hartman. Then he took the two bags of groceries from the cart and walked toward Vic Fleming's SUV a few spaces away.

For weeks he had wondered if the briefcase was electronically protected. If so, anyone who tried to open it without a key could get knocked on his ass good. A device like a stun gun could deliver 80,000 volts. Enough to knock him or anyone else out for a few hours.

So he had bought some heavy-duty rubber gloves, like the ones guys who work on the power lines use. It had taken him almost an hour to work the picks with the gloves on, but he had gotten it open. And sure enough, there was a battery in there that he then disconnected.

As he reached the SUV, Vic rolled down the window. "Why the groceries, Mr. Bush?" he asked.

"Put them where they can be seen," Brian directed. "Makes us look official in case anybody gets nosy. How about some help?"

"It's the other groceries I want to see," Fleming said, pointing to the briefcase.

Tony stepped out of the passenger side and came around to take the bags from Brian. He slid open the rear door and passed them to Johnny. Then he took a place in the rear.

Brian walked in front of the vehicle with the Hartman in his hand. He sat in front beside Vic and placed the case on his lap.

"What do we have, sport?" Tony asked excitedly.

Brian unlatched the case and opened it. "This fucking thing tried to electrocute me," he said.

"Stun-gun device?" Vic asked.

"Exactly."

They all strained to look inside. It was lined side to side with stacks of one thousand-dollar bills bundled in cellophane. Brian laughed as Vic's mouth dropped open.

"I counted the bricks. There's fifty of them. You're looking at exactly two and a half million in cash," Brian said.

Johnny spoke for the first time. "Why is everything so carefully arranged?" he asked.

"That's not unexpected. Ayala gave them either drugs or dirty money, and they gave him a neat package in return," Vic replied.

"I'm passing you twelve of these each and keeping twelve for myself," Brian said. For the next few minutes he divided the cash. "There's paper bags in there with the groceries," he said. "Pass them around, will you, Mr. Lieberman?"

Brian split one of the two remaining bricks and passed half to Vic. He did the same with the other one, turned, and handed the money to Johnny and Tony.

Brian threw his left arm over his seat. "So we now each have over $1.5 million apiece. What do you dildos say to that?"

Tony slapped his arm. "I never thought I'd see that much green in my whole life."

Brian stared at Johnny. He could tell his friend was now in his depressed state. "What happened back there?" he asked.

Johnny sat quietly, his bearing too erect, like a statue. "I hit him and thought he was down and..."

"The back-up wouldn't stay down," Vic interjected. "The goon got up and was almost ready with his weapon. I had to shoot him, or Mr. Lieberman here might not be with us right now."

Brian weighed Vic's answer and decided to let it go. "You hear the radio reports?" Brian asked instead. "The back-up was Sonny Rossetti, Ayala's godson. You should all realize Ayala, Joe Sansone, the whole familia, will come after us harder than ever. Be smart, and don't spend any of these large ones for a while."

"We should not meet again," Vic said.

"Exactly right. This is our last contact with one another. You won't hear from me again, unless I hear one of us is in some kind of danger from Ayala or the FBI," Brian replied.

Vic looked out the window into the dark night. "It's best we leave the area and soon," he said.

"That's my plan," Tony responded.

Brian stared at Vic, trying to catch his eye. "The shooting is bad business. We now also have the FBI with no statute of limitations."

Vic glared at him. "They have shit."

"But they have all the time they want now to turn shit into gold dust," Brian said.

"We'll see," Vic replied.

"Can you get rid of the briefcase?" Brian asked him.

"Leave it."

Brian turned and extended his hand to Johnny and Tony. "I promised you two and out. Now go enjoy the rest of your lives."

Tony pumped his hand vigorously. "Thanks, Mr. Bush."

"Pass me my groceries, and one of those empty bags, will you, Lieberman?" Brian asked.

He placed his money in the empty bag and then offered his hand to Vic. "It's been great. See you, Gore."

"I hope not, Mr. Bush. For all our sakes, I hope not."

"You fucked up, Salvatore. You fucked this up real good."

Joe Sansone's brow furrowed as he pointed his index finger at Ayala. He was a broad-shouldered man in his late 50s with a swarthy complexion, a flat nose, and long black hair. These features gave him the look of a peasant who had worked long, hard hours tilling the soil. He wore a plaid sports shirt covered by an old gray coat sweater, blue slacks, and red and white Nike sneakers.

"We'll catch them, Joe," Sally replied.

Sansone stirred his black coffee as he sat in his favorite and reserved booth at the Prince Street Social Club in the North End. He snickered at Ayala's comment and looked about the club, trying to control his anger. Near the front door the young bartender swept the linoleum floor, never once looking up from his labor and never straying more than a few steps from the door. There was to be no interruption to these proceedings, and even though he had locked both the outer and inner doors, he didn't need some loud paisan to begin pounding and send Joe Sansone skyward. Nobody needed that.

Sansone exhaled a loud sigh. "You'll catch them? Is that what you just said, Sally? You and what other fuckin' dope?"

Sally grimaced and poured the remnants of his beer into the glass. Across from him, the number one figure in their Boston family lifted his coffee cup to his mouth. As he did so, a trickle or two sluiced down his chin. He wiped it away with the back of his hand.

Inadvertently, Sally pushed his hand out as if putting some foul-smelling thing at arm's length. Fuckin' slob, he thought.

"What's the matter?" Joe asked him, his belligerence coming through strongly.

"Nothing, Joe. Nothing at all."

Sansone's lips thinned. "I want that fuckin' money back, Salvatore. You lose the clean money and get your own fuckin' godson killed in the process. Why didn't you have a handcuff on the case?"

Sally ran a finger along the scar on the side of his face and sat back in the booth.

"I didn't think that it was necessary," he finally replied.

"You didn't think period, Sal!" Sansone fumed.

"Whoever stole it will get a surprise. It was wired with over 80,000 volts."

Sansone snorted. "So fuckin' what? One guy gets knocked on his geester for a few hours, but there were at least three of them. You should have cuffed the case, Sal, and you shouldn't have had that retard godson of yours as back-up. That was another brilliant idea."

Sally had long since planned to ride the storm out. He bit his lip and sipped some more beer.

"You fuckin' better find them, Salvatore. What have you done so far besides sit there drinking your beer?"

Sally pushed the bottle to the side. "We've got our people out there talkin' and askin'. It's early, Joe. It's only been six hours since we were hit. I'm goin' to need time," Sally replied.

"Time? You don't have much of that. This crew hit the Brinks truck and all around town nobody knows shit after two weeks," Sansone said.

"We weren't lookin' for them then, Joe. We are now."

Sansone slurped his coffee and then swirled the contents as he nodded. "You're a cocky bastard with the other guy's money, Sally," he finally said.

"Joe, its the family's money."

Sansone set the cup down. "Is that right, Sally? Well, fuckin' allow me to personalize this a little bit for you. You lost it. Now it's goin' to be your money at play here. I want $1,500,000 from you, Sal, and by Wednesday. Two days, Sal. Your personal money."

Two and Out

"Joe, for Christ's..."

Sansone raised his hand. "Listen to me, Sally, and listen good. $1,500,000 by Wednesday. You're fuckin' lucky I don't ask you for the whole nut. Your money, Sally. And clean money, which is what you lost on me. You fuckin' catch these guys and get my money back and you get your money back. You don't, you forfeit the dough. And you've got two weeks, Sally. That's all. You and I both know we don't catch them by then, we might never catch them. Clear?"

"Crystal," Sally replied.

Sansone picked up his coffee cup and threw it against the opposite paneled wall. "Now get the fuck out of my sight."

45

Nelson wiped her lips with the napkin while Fallon pondered her question. Across the street a delegation of fathers and young sons, probably from a suburban little league, closed together as they crossed Jersey Street. From their car parked in the McDonald's lot on the corner, both Fallon and Nelson could observe Fenway Park straight ahead. A string of vendors lining the route to the ticket booths hawked everything from sausages to Red Sox caps to programs as the crowd hurried toward a rare Tuesday afternoon game.

Fallon wrapped the remnants of his cheeseburger and tossed it into the paper bag. "Early thoughts? It's the same crew for sure, with one addition this time—the guy in the Bush mask. The Cheney guy wasn't at the scene, but he had to be the getaway driver."

He looked across the street where one of Boston's finest was directing traffic. "And another thought."

"What?"

"Maybe there's a cop involved in this."

"What takes you there?"

"We've been searching for crews—both known and new—for two weeks now with nothing coming back from the street. Think about it. Why?"

"They're pros," Nelson replied.

He turned his body toward her.

"Marilyn, maybe not. I'm beginning to think otherwise."

As she stirred, shifting her weight, she exposed some thigh. He tried not to look, and he felt guilty about even noticing.

"On what basis?" she asked.

"Did you ever think that this is an entirely new crew, new not necessarily to each other, but new to the armed robbery scene. And that's why we're not picking anything up?"

"Where's the cop idea come in?" she asked.

"For one thing, the planning's first class. Meticulous, coordinated. Secondly, someone knew enough to hit Ayala on a Monday morning at South Station. If there's no one on the street who knows anything, then maybe, just maybe, someone with access to insider information is involved. A cop."

"How about someone within Sansone's own family? I still don't see the connection back to a cop."

Fallon raised a hand and rubbed his chin. "It's just a hunch, Marilyn. And I don't see someone ripping off Brinks or the Mafia without the word spreading if it were a maverick operation. No, I'm thinking this is all new—a new crew, with maybe some cop involved."

"There's been zilch on any known asshole using the word 'sport'," Marilyn said. "The word's out there, but nothing's coming back. Either it's too commonly used, or we just haven't caught a break yet."

Fallon tapped his fingers on the wheel. "It's light. We need some other connecting point, something more to go on and then maybe it'll tie to someone."

He looked at a young father holding the hands of a little girl maybe five years old, and a boy probably a year older. They stood at the intersection, the father pointing ahead, and then over to the right in the direction of the Green Monster, the famous Fenway left field screen. The children bounced in place on their toes, their body language indicating their delight in what lay ahead.

He thought back to another day, another golden weekday afternoon when his patrolman father had held his hand at this very same intersection in 1975. A day earlier, Freddy Lynn had driven in eleven runs in one game in Detroit, and his father had surprised a seven-year-old with tickets for the first game on the Sox return from the road. They had arrived at the ball yard early, in time to watch batting practice. His hero, Lynn, had sprayed ball after ball off the Green Monster, demonstrating his prowess as a left-handed hitter. And then Jim Rice had entered the cage, a right-handed terror, hoisting bullets into the left field screen. From the first base grandstand he felt that he could watch them hit forever, maybe never go home again.

"You like baseball?" he suddenly asked Nelson.

She was surprised at the change of subject, but recovered quickly. "Sure. My dad used to take me to see Fisk and Luis Tiant. They were my favorites. And then my ex and I would go occasionally over the years, y' know."

"You mean after he was your ex?".

"No! I meant while we were married. I haven't seen the asshole since we were divorced and hope I never do."

Fallon thought for a moment before he continued. "Could I ask what went wrong?"

Nelson looked at him before answering. "The usual. The Job. It ruins a lot of relationships. I was ambitious, anxious to join Justice, and he started looking in other places for some attention, which I wasn't providing."

Fallon stared at the crowds continuing to cross the street. "That doesn't excuse infidelity."

She laughed out loud. "I love you, Mikey," she teased. "So help me God. The world needs more guys like you. Does Rita know what she's got?"

He didn't answer. He just kept looking toward the crowd.

"Would you ever get married again?" he finally asked.

"What are you taking a survey, Mikey? No. The answer is no. Marriage is a great institution for the criminally insane."

"Don't you want happiness?"

She placed her remnants in the paper bag before answering. "Happiness? That's what I love about your kind of guy, Mikey. You equate happiness with marriage. You're loaded up with middle class values and morals. What's happiness anyway? You don't think I'm happy right now, living alone, no children to fret about, just being responsible for me, myself, and I, not having to worry about keeping some philanderer's socks clean for him?"

"Jesus!" Mike said, almost too loudly. "That's a hell of a way to look at life."

Two and Out

"That's because there aren't many guys around today like you, Mikey," she replied softly.

In the silence, his cell phone burped.

"Yeah? Fallon here."

"Where are you?" Harper asked.

"Boylston and Jersey," Mike replied.

"Want some good news for a change?" Harper asked.

"For sure. Shoot."

"Our friend from Charlestown is ready to meet. He has something for us. Says he and his lawyer want to sit down, the sooner the better. I'll tell you more when I see you."

"Set it up for this afternoon at 4:00 P.M.," Mike directed. "I'm on the way back now."

46

Tuesday was another perfect day in the Boston area, which meant they had used up all three of them. The sun was high in a cloudless sky, and the air brisk and cool as Brian and Johnny circled Lake Quannapowitt in Wakefield. They strolled on the Main Street side, heading toward one of the prettiest downtown areas in the Commonwealth. To their right, the lake sprawled, quiet, murky green and imposing. On the walkway, young mothers pushed strollers, while good-looking middle-aged women power walked their way past members of the senior set just out for the air, all of them grateful to be alive on such a fine day.

"You sure you're okay?" Brian asked.

"I should have put him down and kept him down, but I was shocked, you know?"

"So you knew the guy and he knew you?"

"That's what I'm telling you, Brian. Yeah, he worked for the bookie I told you about, Ayala's cousin Paulie. Christ, when I saw him coming into the terminal from the train, that's when I really froze. I barely got the paper up in front of my face before he saw me.

"That shook me, y' know? I followed him out, put on my mask, and thought I hit him real good. Right on the noggin. Then when he got up and looked at me, started to point his weapon at me, I froze there. I thought he could see me, recognize me right through the mask."

"It's over. Forget it."

Johnny gave out a loud sigh. "Seems like I can't do anything right lately."

"Stop feeling sorry for yourself, John."

About twenty yards ahead of them, three senior males sat on a bench enjoying the sunshine, arguing loudly about the individual merits of their heroes.

Two and Out

"Ted Williams was the greatest hitter who ever lived," the white-haired gentleman dressed in grey slacks insisted.

"Musial was Stan the Man," came the vote from another precinct.

"I'm for the modern hitters, guys like Garciaparra and Helton. They got to fly, play games at night, face fresh pitchers all the time," said the third.

"Helton?" the white-haired guy exclaimed, incredulous. "Are you nuts? He couldn't hold Williams' jockstrap. Playing in that air out there in Denver where a pop fly's a home run?"

Johnny burst out laughing and jabbed a playful finger toward the bench as they passed. "You tell 'em, pal," he said to the first man. "I vote for Ted."

Far above them a helicopter swooped over the lake heading for Route 128 to report the obvious to all commuters who could follow the too-brief, rushed correspondence of the reporter—Route 128 was slow today. Duh. Tell us when it isn't.

Johnny pointed toward another park bench. "Let's sit for a few minutes. I want you to hear something." They stopped at a place where the pathway circled back toward North Avenue and the other side of the lake.

"When you leaving town?" Johnny asked.

Brian shrugged his shoulders. "First I have to see the dean at the University and let him know I'm resigning at the end of the quarter. It'll be around New Year's Day when the term ends. Just in time to go out to Vegas, and then on to Aruba for a while. But I'll be here through the holidays. How about you?"

"That's what I want to tell you. I decided not to go."

Brian raised a quizzical brow. "Not going?" he repeated. "You thought it out carefully?"

"Brian, I'm not feeling sorry for myself. For one thing, I don't feel like I screwed up at South Station the other day. I was surprised by Sonny, that's all. And I felt I did my part at Brinks and at the terminal as well. When I say I haven't done much right, I'm reflecting more on Laura and on our relationship. I'm turning corners, Brian. I'm not drinking or gambling, and I'm feeling much better."

Brian noted the determination in his voice, the confident body language. He acted neither manic nor depressive and seemed more in control of himself than he had for so long.

"So I'm staying here, Brian. I'm going to make this relationship work. I'm going to be a father to my daughter finally. And I'm not being stupid about it. I'll always have the ups and downs mentally, y' know? But at least I'll be around, not drinking, not gambling. Show some character. I want to be around when she needs me."

Brian placed his hand on his friend's knee. "You'll make it, Johnny," he said. "I wish I could be around to see it."

"I'm going to try," Johnny replied.

Three miles away Sally Ayala propped his feet onto his cousin's desk, waiting for the expected reaction.

"You're shittin' me," Paulie finally said.

Sally wagged a hand. "I'm tellin' you I want $750,000 by tomorrow. That's half of what Joe wants from me."

Paulie tried to calm himself. "Salvatore, with all due respect, what the fuck have I got to do with your business with Joe?"

Sally wrinkled his brow. "You want to know what you got to do with this? I got to tell you that? You're family, for Christ's sake!"

"Sally, of course. But $750,000? And by tomorrow. I don't know if..."

Sally stood and ranted at the same time. "Mortgage your fuckin' house if you have to Paulie! How the hell do you think you got it in the first place if not for me?"

Paulie placed his palms down on the desk. "Sally, please sit. You're surprisin' me, y' know? Give me a little time to digest all this, will ya?"

Sally patrolled the floor like the sentinels at Arlington National Cemetery, back and forth. "Well digest it fast, cousin. The dough's due to Joe tomorrow."

"Nothin' on the street about who took the briefcase?" Paulie asked.

"And that's somethin' else I need from you," Sally replied.

"What?"

"I'm puttin' out the word that we're offerin' a $1,000,000 reward for information on who stole that case."

Paulie couldn't contain himself. "You want more dough from me?"

Sally stopped pacing and laughed. "Hold your piss, Paulie. I need you to get the word out around here, and with any contacts you have in town. $1,000,000 for information about who hit us."

At the risk of facing another explosion, Paulie decided to ask his question. "We're gonna' pay out another one million?"

"Maybe," Sally replied. "Probably not. We'll see. It'll depend on how good the info is. And on who delivers it. And on whether we get our $2.5 million back before those assholes spend it. But I'll tell you one thing."

"What's that?"

"I'm gonna cut the balls off every one of that crew and anyone associated with them."

47

Grace lay naked on the bed, on her stomach. Tony straddled her, kneading her shoulder muscles, moving his fingers into the crevices in her neck and then scratching between her wings.

"Do that again."

"Which? The sex?"

"You know what I mean, Mr. Innocent."

"I'm really not sure," he replied, leaning down to kiss the side of her face.

"Scratch. Around the shoulder blades," she answered playfully.

He moved his hands down and gently slapped her ass.

"Ow! That's not my wings!"

"Could have fooled me, angel."

"You can let me up now," she said.

"Only if I have a promise to get my just desserts later."

"You've already had your just desserts."

"Killjoy," he muttered as he rolled over onto the pillow, placing his hands behind his head.

The sun streamed through the window, slanting diagonally across the room as an extreme shaft of light, capturing large elements of fiber and dust in its course. They lay silently for a time.

He leaned over and began stroking her cheek with the back of his hand. "I love you," he said.

"I know," she replied.

"We should be together then," he said, knowing he had just introduced the mood breaker.

She placed her hands above the headboard without saying anything. She breathed evenly and stared straight ahead.

"Oh, well. I'll ask Mrs. Adams then," Tony finally said.

Grace laughed quietly. "She's been so good to you and Doug."

Two and Out

"I'll make it right by her before I leave," Tony replied.

She turned to face him. "You're a good man, you know that, Tony Amonti?" She cupped his chin in her hand.

"You don't know that," he said.

"Yes, I do. I can read character. And besides, children like you and they—the young ones—can't be fooled. They can smell goodness."

Tony leaned on his elbow and looked directly into her eyes. "You're what goodness is about, Grace, not me."

She touched his lips with her fingers. "Can I try to explain something to you?"

"Shoot."

Grace sat up so that she was looking down at him. "You know Cole Porter at all?"

"Shortstop for Detroit?" he laughingly replied.

"No, silly. The Cole Porter, the songwriter."

"He was before my time."

She shook her head. "He was for all time."

"What's he got to do with us?"

She ran her palm across his face and rubbed softly. "He wrote a song called "At Long Last Love" among many other great ones. No one before or since has had the way with lyrics that he had. In that particular song, he's debating whether he's found love or not. He says, 'Is it for all time or simply a lark, is it Granada I see or only Asbury Park?' Well, it's Granada, Tony. Since I met you, it's definitely Granada. No question, no debate."

"I love you, Grace," he whispered.

"And I you, Tony."

"Then come with me," he pleaded.

"That's what I'm trying to explain. That feeling of Granada, it's for you, Tony, but it's also for my Cape and my children. I'm just not ready to leave them."

"They'll be so many children, including Doug, out there who need a teacher, a good teacher, and we could build a life together. I've saved some good money and I'll catch on quickly there. I don't have to drive, Grace. I can make good money as a mechanic. It will be Granada out there for us."

She shifted her position and sat up completely, searching for her halter and shorts. She stood when she located them at the side of the bed. Bending, she slipped on the pants and hooked the halter.

"Tony, I haven't really asked you this as aggressively as I'm going to now. I don't want to pressure you, but what's so important about going out to California? You say you love me?"

"You know I do."

"Then why move, Tony? Stay here with me on the Cape. Make a life here."

"There's no real work here, Grace. I'm like a transient here, me and Doug just passing through. He's not happy here, and I've been talkin' so long about a new life out there—about Disneyland, about the Golden State, y' know, about a dream coming true—I don't want to disappoint him."

Grace nodded in agreement. "You have to do what you think is best for you and Doug. I understand that. And I need you to understand my position." She sat down on the bed and reached for his hand. "That's how we should leave it, at least for now. When will you be leaving?"

"Today's Tuesday?" he asked. "Right now I'm thinking we'll go in about ten days."

She leaned down and kissed him on the lips. "Then go with my love, Tony."

He pulled her down on top of his chest and embraced her. "Can I have my just desserts every day until then?" he teased.

"Wise ass."

48

Billy Flanagan had dressed like the choirboy he decidedly was not. He wore a navy blue suit, a Kenneth Cole white shirt, and a red and blue striped tie. Little Boy Blue, Fallon thought. At 4 P.M. on Tuesday afternoon, they sat side by side at a round table in a room on the sixth floor of the Hilton Hotel at Logan Airport. Across from them, Frank Sheridan poured water into tumblers while Flanagan's lawyer unzipped his briefcase and placed a yellow legal pad on the table. Martin O'Shea represented a number of Boston's leading criminals, particularly those of Irish descent. More often than not, he represented them well. He reminded Fallon of the actor Gene Hackman with his receding hairline, rounded face and alert eyes.

"We ready then?" O'Shea asked.

"It's your meeting, Mr. O'Shea," Mike responded.

"So it is, Mr. Fallon. First of all, my thanks to you and to Detective Sheridan for agreeing to meet us here. It's important to my client that we talk away from any public places where we could be observed," O'Shea said.

"I'll bet it is," Fallon replied.

O'Shea gave him a nasty look. "For the information Mr. Flanagan will provide, we want these trumped-up allegations regarding his having assaulted Patricia McCarthy dropped," he said. Billy Flanagan sat impassively, looking out the huge window at the planes taking off and landing.

Fallon left the response for Sheridan in recognition of his jurisdiction. But the detective's answer didn't surprise him. "That all depends on what information we're talkin' about, Martin. And you know, the DA would have to agree."

O'Shea doodled on his pad. "Fair enough," he said.

"So what do you have for us, Billy?" Fallon asked.

Flanagan adjusted his tie, his discomfort with both the cravat and the situation evident. "There's word on the street that one of the crew on the Brinks job calls people 'sport'."

Fallon looked from Flanagan to O'Shea. "Is he serious?" he finally asked the lawyer.

"What do you mean?" O'Shea responded.

Fallon shrugged his shoulders. "Detective Sheridan here and I put that word out. My grandmother up on Mission Hill and one-half of Boston might know we're looking for that guy."

"I can tell you a lot more than that," Flanagan replied in a huff.

"Like what?" Fallon asked.

"Like about the South Station heist, once you get that cunt off my case."

O'Shea raised his hand. "Let's go a little slower here, Billy. Let me give a little overview to see if we have any common ground here."

"But I..." Flanagan began.

"Go ahead, counselor," Sheridan said.

O'Shea placed his hands against his protruding stomach. "My client can tell you exactly what was in the briefcase confiscated at South Station. He can tell you much of the story behind how whatever was in the briefcase got there, and he can tell you from whence it came. All for a price, of course."

"What about the crew that lifted it?" Fallon asked.

"I don't know nothin' about them, but I do know they're not from around here. Nobody knows nothin' about no one," Billy said.

Fallon grinned at him. He felt like making a comment about Billy's butchering of the English language but decided to be prudent and stay on course. Instead, he looked at Sheridan who nodded imperceptibly.

"For that, you've got a deal," Fallon replied. "If Billy cooperates, we forget the McCarthy charges on the condition the DA concurs."

"I need to know that now, Mr. Fallon, before we can proceed," O'Shea said.

"Give me a moment," Sheridan said, heading toward the bedroom.

While he made the call, Mike walked to the window and stared at the activities out on the runways. Behind him, Flanagan and O'Shea caucused in the corner, their conversation barely audible. Mike considered Flanagan's words regarding the crew. Like theirs, his best effort concerning identifying them had failed. Who are these guys?

Sheridan came out of the bedroom forming a circle with the thumb and index finger of his left hand. "We're on with the DA," he said.

Returning to the table, O'Shea pointed to Flanagan. "Tell them what you know, Billy."

Flanagan still needed to be convinced that he would walk for fracturing his girl friend's bones. "I'm off the hook then?"

"Unfortunately, yes," Sheridan replied.

"One other thing. I'm protected here? I mean if anybody ever found out I told youse guys..."

"We protect our sources, Billy," Fallon interrupted.

Flanagan leaned back in his chair and rubbed his nose. "There was $2.5 million in the briefcase. Joey Sansone's money. For months now Sally's been bringin' their dirty money down to Manhattan and exchanging it for clean stuff. They use the train 'cause none of you dimwits knows enough to check out the trains. You can bring a howitzer on with you 'cause there's no security. Sally meets with Vito Forcelli down on Staten Island. You know him?" he asked no one in particular.

"I've heard of him," Fallon said. "One of the higher-ups in the Staten Island arm of the family."

Flanagan pointed a finger at him and grinned. "Right. Vito Forcelli, the baker. He's bakin' more than cookies down there. He's launderin'."

"How do you know the number is $2.5 million?" Fallon asked.

Flanagan was noticeably more relaxed now, the monkey of a few years back in the slammer now off his back. "Believe me, I know. This time it was $2.5 million, sometimes it's $2.0, sometimes $3.5—but always in that range. Comes right from a Sansone family member."

"Anything else?" Sheridan asked.

Frustrated completely with the tie, Billy unloosened it and pushed it into the side pocket of his suit. "Oh, yeah. Let me throw you guys a bonus, like a down payment the next time somebody accuses Billy Flanagan of a -what do you call it?— "alleged" crime. Joey's pissed at Sally. Real pissed. Wants his money back and soon."

The telephone screamed from the bedroom. "I thought no one knew we were here?" O'Shea asked belligerently.

Fallon stood and walked to the bedroom. Only Nelson knew he would be here.

"Mikey, it's Marilyn," she began. "I don't know how to tell you this..."

"What's the matter?"

"Is your cell phone working? I couldn't get through. Your day nurse called ten minutes ago. They've taken Rita to Boston Medical Center. She went into a coma, Mikey."

The grey man scurried along Marlborough Street toward the corner of Massachusetts Avenue. Vic Fleming waved to him from that position as Hanrahan advanced toward him.

"How goes the battle, Captain?"

"I'm only a few days from LA, so it goes fine, Phil. And yourself?"

They crossed to the Massachusetts Avenue Bridge, walking toward Cambridge. On their right, the greenish waters of the Charles swelled against the bridge and technicolored sailboats ran with the breeze down toward the Hatch Shell. In the distance, crews from Harvard and Northeastern raced in perfect sync, led on by coaches with bullhorns in following launches.

On the bridge itself the light winds whipped at the few strollers, a harbinger of the fall to come. That was one New England season he would miss, Vic thought. Nothing could beat October in New England.

"Thanks for coming out," Vic said. "I have a little going away present for you."

Fleming touched his arm while at the same time looking around before removing an envelope from his pocket. "That's $75,000 for you and the wife, Phil."

"Captain, that's a lot..."

"Hush, my friend. Just take it."

Hanrahan placed the envelope inside his topcoat. "Until we meet again, Captain, may God hold you in the palm of his hand."

Fleming liked to conduct business in public places, but away from crowds, and only with those he trusted. Maybe that's why the affinity with Brian. They thought alike.

"Where will you be stayin' in LA?" Phil asked.

"I don't know for sure, but I'll call you when I'm settled in. You come out and see the sites."

Hanrahan smiled broadly. "I'd like that."

Halfway across, Fleming signaled a reversal of direction. He wheeled, pushed along by the wind. "What went wrong the other day?" Hanrahan asked.

Fleming turned his coat collar up. "Just like it was reported. The back-up didn't stay put, and when he got up I had to put him down or one of ours would have gone down."

Hanrahan didn't respond right away. He reached for a cigarette, pausing on the bridge and cupping his hand to ignite it. "It's a bad business, Vic," he finally said.

"You hearin' anything around the rialto?" Vic asked.

"Just that Sansone and Ayala are out lookin'. But you knew that would happen."

At the corner of Marlborough, Vic extended his hand and then pulled the grey man into an embrace. "Take care of yourself, Phil. And don't spend that dough for a while. The Italians will be lookin' for big spenders around town."

Hanrahan's voice clutched as he tried to say good-by. "Captain, how does a person thank a friend for a million favors? You take care of yourself in L.A., and watch out for the young starlets. They could cause the death of you."

Fleming poked him gently in the stomach and turned away. Walking toward the public gardens, he never once turned around. If he had, he would have seen Hanrahan still at the corner studying his retreating form, deep in thought.

Had he heard anything around town among the sources? Yes. Sally Ayala was willing to pay $1,000,000 for useful information regarding the Candidates crew. He would have to pay the Prince of Darkness a visit.

49

It took Mike Fallon only ten minutes to reach the Boston Medical Center. With siren screaming, he tore through the Ted Williams Tunnel and across the Southeast Expressway to Massachusetts Avenue. He screeched to a halt outside the emergency room entrance and then raced into the area through the automatic doors.

He stepped into the path of the first identifiable medical team member he saw, an Asian named "Sanusi" according to his badge. "Dr. Sanusi?"

"Yes?" the MD responded, irritated to have been stopped so abruptly.

Fallon flashed his wallet. "I'm Special Agent Fallon of the FBI. My wife was brought in here in a coma about a half-hour ago. Could you tell me where she might be right now?"

Sanusi signaled him to follow through the maze of patients to the emergency room desk itself. He spoke to a middle-aged woman. "Mrs. North, a Mrs. Fallon. Where might she be?"

Looking to his right, Mike spotted Dr. Hazlitt coming from a room halfway down the corridor. He walked purposefully toward them and then straightened even more so when he sighted Mike.

Mike half-walked and half-ran to meet him. "Doctor, how's Rita? I just got the call and..."

And then Mike stopped. It was there in the doctor's eyes. Death. He didn't say anything, or do anything. It was just the way he looked. Grim, disconnected, sorrowful. Mike would always remember that look. The look that spoke for itself, the look that tore apart his world.

"She's gone?" Mike finally said.

"Let's sit over here," Dr. Hazlitt replied, grabbing his arm and aiming him in the direction of a small, private conference room.

"What happened, Jim?" Mike asked as they sat, and when the answer came, it came from somewhere else, out of the fog, from another planet. The doctor's voice seemed locked in an echo chamber so that Mike caught only words or phrases, not whole sentences.

"Nausea...abdominal pain early. Not uncommon to have only a little pain in late stages...hemorrhages...tumor..." each comment made in a soothing, kind manner, but each just devastating.

"But today seemed no better or worse than any other day," Mike protested.

Dr. Hazlitt nodded in agreement. "Things escalate quickly with this form of cancer, Mike."

And then they sat in silence, Fallon absorbing the news, trying to sift things out to no avail, the doctor solemn, performing the most difficult task of all for those in his profession—trying to explain the inexplicable and the inevitable and comfort the devastated.

The girls. Mike thought of his three girls. In the morning, they had left for school with a mother at home for them. And at 5 P.M. that same day, she was gone. God give him the strength to explain why to them.

———

Hello, Brian," Dean Johnson greeted him nervously. "Have a seat."

When Brian had scheduled the appointment, he sensed the reluctance of his dean to meet with him. Maybe he thought that Brian's tenure case was contagious, but more likely he desired as little contact with his faculty member as possible for the balance of the year.

"If you're here regarding your tenure case, I really can't tell you much more at this point. You know..."

"Perry, please," Brian tried his most soothing tone. "I'm here to ask a big favor of you, one that can ease this tenure consideration for both of us."

Placate. Condescend. Make the pompous ass feel important. Why leave an enemy on his way out the door?

Johnson relaxed a shade as soon as he sensed their meeting was not to be confrontational.

"What's on your mind, Brian?"

Brian leaned forward in his seat, frowning a bit, acting a lot, giving the desired impression that a monumentous, difficult decision had been reached. "I'm going to resign, effective the end of the fall quarter."

Johnson reacted as if Brian planned to swallow his children. "Brian! Whatever for? You have a contract with us you know."

Brian shook his head in agreement. "Would you allow me to explain?" he asked.

Sensing the issue was one he controlled, Johnson became much more noticeably sedate. He sank into his leather chair and templed his fingers. "I will listen," he said.

"Thank you," Brian replied, admiration for this concession expressed in his smile. "Perry, if I resign, a good number of positive developments occur. First of all, and most important to me, I stop the tenure process. There is then no blemish on my record. The clock stops, and my record here—one I continue to be most proud of incidentally—remains solid. Secondly, I can start anew on another campus. I've been thinking of the West, Perry. Probably Nevada. I'm single, I have the resources to relocate, and in less than a year I'll have my book in print and a good chance at tenure wherever I am. And you avoid a drawn-out fight in the spring, if my students become upset with a negative decision on tenure."

Johnson scowled as part of the act. In reality, Brian knew he would be delighted to see him leave and the sooner the better. "But your contract?" he said.

"That's the favor I'm asking, Perry. Couldn't you fill in with part-timers or with one person for the two remaining quarters?"

Johhnson reacted as Brian knew he would. His eyes searched the ceiling, his templed fingers came apart and then back together. He considered his navel. "If it's what you want, I can accept your resignation, Brian," he replied in solemn tones, like Moses parting the waters of the Red Sea.

But at least they were parting, Brian thought.

50

He decided all the girls would attend the wake. Actually, it had been one of those decisions Rita had made with him when they would lie awake and plan the future, knowing there was to be no future. She tried to make him comfortable about impending death and helped him understand the importance of discussing key matters together.

"We're fortunate we can plan," Rita had ruminated while they drank tea from her fine Irish service one night about a month ago. "For some, the end comes too swiftly. They have no chance to anticipate meeting God and attending to things here before the journey."

She had relaxed him with her strength, her courage, her wit. Together they had chosen the pictures to be displayed at her wake, the dress in which she would be buried, her desire for a closed casket, and especially her wish to be mourned at the Sweeney Brothers Funeral Home in South Quincy, a half mile from her childhood home on North Payne Street.

And the girls were to be present. They were old enough to understand, she had said, and she had helped prepare them for what was to come.

He stood with his children in a huge room filled with folding chairs as a long line of mourners edged forward to their position. He could both see and hear the milling crowd arriving in the hall, some laughing too loudly, some quiet and reverently solemn. Their dress was a mixed bag, some men and women in business attire, with others in the new look for church, wakes, and funerals—jeans, boat shoes, sneakers.

He accepted the condolences of those who flowed directly to the casket, knelt in brief prayer, and then rose to offer him solace. When finished greeting each one, Mike introduced Jessica to those who did not know her, and, in turn, she introduced her sisters. Occasionally, she would squeeze his hand, and he, in turn, would squeeze back.

The air was thick with the scent of roses, freesia, and gladiola, and the snippets of conversation from those in the folding chairs directly in front of them. "Pitino stinks." "Did you hear Harry's on the shit list?" "Paul's seeing that whore Cathy?"

He felt like screaming out something about the need for solemnity on the occasion of a soul departing. But he caught himself, because he could hear her voice, urging him to be both kind and understanding.

From the front row of seats Paul Harper caught his eye. He stood and approached the line. "Time for a little break, Mikey?"

Mike shook his head. "I'm fine, Paul."

"Go ahead, Dad. Take a couple of minutes," Jessica urged.

Mike grinned at her. "My girl can handle this?"

Jessica half smiled, gazing into his eyes. "I think so."

"I'll be back in five minutes," he said.

A gray-jacketed man helped clear a path through the hallway for them. At the rear of the building, they found the lounge area, a large room ringed with folding chairs with both a men's and women's room running from it. Two young men, about Jessica's age, sat together in the corner wishing they were somewhere else. He didn't recognize them.

"Anything I can do?" Paul asked as they sat on the opposite side of the room.

Mike almost found a smile. "No thanks, Paul. We're doing okay."

"Sam Morris came by, I see by the register," Harper said.

"This afternoon. Everyone's been by. Nelson was here this afternoon and earlier tonight. Crime must have taken a holiday."

Harper laughed. "Not much chance of that."

"Anything new on the Candidates?" Mike asked.

"You really want to talk about it now?" Harper asked gently.

Mike nodded. "You know she helped prepare me too, Paul. I thank God she didn't suffer at the very end."

Harper paused for a long moment. "Those girls are a great credit to her," he said.

"For sure," Mike replied.

The two boys decided that they had endured enough adult conversation and filed from the room.

"So?" Mike asked.

"The case? Not much the last couple of days, Mikey. Boston ran ballistics tests on the bullets they took out of Sonny Rossetti. They're from a Glock nine millimeter like we suspected. He got hit with a burst of three. The autopsy showed two of them cut into his stomach and liver. He was dead before he hit the pavement."

"How about the vehicle they left on Kneeland Street?"

"Nothing new. We've gone over and over it. Boston got a good amount of fibers out of it—you knew that, and you know we've got nothing to match the stuff against. We're still checking on the second vehicle, walking all over Chinatown, but so far no one saw anything."

Mike ran his tongue over his lips, trying to cut the dryness down. "This crew is really good, Paul. They're good, they're new, and they're connected."

"You think Flanagan was honest with you and Sheridan?"

Mike nodded. "Yeah, I do. It confirms my suspicions. They're a new crew and they must have watched Ayala for a few weekends. They knew what was in the briefcase, or at least knew something of value was in it. I'm guessing the former. They knew, like they did with Brinks, that millions were involved."

"Nelson says you think a cop could be involved?" Harper asked.

"I do."

"She's cross checking against those who know or worked cases involving Ayala and Sansone," Harper said.

"Good."

"You know we've had Ayala's phone tapped in the past. We can't get anything now. Either he's using new lines or his techs are constantly sweeping."

"He and Sansone are too smart to talk business at home or the office."

"Maybe. But there's a new wrinkle that's developed," Harper replied.

"What?"

"Word on the street from the snitches—ours and Boston's—is that Ayala's offering $1,000,000 for info on the crew."

Mike gritted his teeth. "That's good news. It confirms what we've been thinking and what Flanagan said. They're an unknown crew. Maybe Sally can help point us in their direction."

"Yeah, right." Harper replied. "And I'm Lana Turner."

"More like her sister, Stomach Turner," Mike laughed.

Harper tapped his arm. "One other thing. Joe Dunn's comment that one of the Brinks bandits called the other 'sport'? I got a call from the Loudon racetrack up in New Hampshire based on our inquiries. Some driver up there uses the term frequently. I sent a couple of agents up there earlier today. It may be something; it may be nothing."

Mike Fallon hung his head and stared at his shoes. "You know, Paul, I can see the break coming. Someone's going to turn soon, either because of the money or because of the pressure. We're close. I can feel it."

Suddenly she appeared in the doorway. "Dad, there's some people who want to see you."

"Thanks, Jessica. I'll be right there."

Johnny Casey sipped his club soda just a few feet from the Kernwood bar while he looked across at his daughter finishing her ice cream.

"What?" she asked as he stared at her.

"Nothing," he said. "I was just admiring you is all. Anything wrong with a father admiring his daughter?"

She smiled at him as she brought her napkin to her lips. "Mom says you're a charmer and to be careful."

"It's a wise woman who listens to her mother," he replied.

They sat at a square table in his favorite room, enjoying the early supper menu. He had done justice to the New England boiled diner, and she had romped through the spaghetti with meat sauce. Above them, some of his old friends sat on the stools absorbed in their own conversation, occasionally glancing at them but in the main allowing a father time with his daughter. In fact, he hadn't been drinking for days now, and he didn't miss it at all. The men were arguing about music, and their conversation permeated the half-full room.

"Sinatra was the greatest, no question," Scotty, a union representative, was saying. His gravely voice delivered his opinion in a staccato tone, each word standing by itself for the sake of emphasis.

"No, Crosby invented modern pop singing. He was the icon," Freddy, the good-looking, white haired lawyer responded.

"No way! Judy Garland!" Ray, the bartender, said.

"We're not talkin' women here," Scotty said, a bit too loudly.

Laura shot him a feminist look that would kill, but with his back turned, he wasn't aware.

Without warning, Scotty burst out in a passionate tribute to his candidate, with a rendition of "The Second Time Around," hoping to overwhelm the other voters. Laura shrugged her shoulders and giggled at the performance.

"Should I nominate Ricky Martin?" she asked.

Johnny swirled his ice cubes and laughed out loud. "No. They'll think you mean Dean Martin, princess. They won't know any modern guys. Having a good time?"

She nodded her approval and then cast him her most serious look. "Mom says you're not going away."

"That's right. I'm going to be teaching as a sub at the high school in Saugus. I found a job."

"So you'll be around." She stated it as if she were mulling it over, not wanting to show her feelings, for fear of experiencing disappointment tomorrow, next week, or next month.

"I'll be around," he replied softly.

"I have a project to do for English. You think you could help me?" she asked, taking a safe route away from the situation.

"Sure. What's it involve?"

"I have to write an original poem in iambic pentameter by next week."

Leaning across the table, he reached for her hand. "We'll work on it together. How's that?"

She kept her hand in his. "I would like that."

"Now, what's the name of this movie you want to see tonight?"

"Almost Famous," she replied. "It's about a rock and roll star."

"Don't say that too loudly in front of our friends," he laughed, pointing to the bar.

51

"Who wants to know?" the raspy voice replied.

"Just tell him someone wants to talk with him about the South Station hit," Phil Hanrahan said.

"I need a name, pal."

"No, you don't."

"And I need a phone number so he can call you back if he wants."

Hanrahan let loose a loud sigh into the pay phone. "Look. Let me try this one more time, and then I'm going to hang up if I don't get the right answer. Tell him he lost $2.5 million the other day. Does he want it back, or doesn't he?"

"Hold on."

Hanrahan watched the traffic flow along Route One in Saugus. The light rain whistled against the pane as he cupped his hand over the phone inside the CVS store. Gazing at his watch, he decided to give it sixty more seconds. If there was no response, he'd call again later on. Let the asshole answering the phone take heat for not connecting him. And whet Sally's appetite a bit, as well. And then his thoughts were interrupted.

"This is Salvatore Ayala. Who's this?"

Hanrahan hesitated a moment. "You don't need to know who I am, Mr. Ayala, but how would you like to know the name of the leader of the crew who robbed you of your $2.5 million?"

"How do you know it was $2.5 million? Who told you that?" Ayala replied querulously.

"The man who robbed you. The one who shot your associate, your godson."

Another pause as Ayala considered the source.

"I hear you're offering $1.0 million for information," Hanrahan continued. "I can give you the identity for that, and I'm sure you can take it from there, perhaps recoup all or most of your laundered money."

"How do I know you're legitimate?" Ayala asked.

Hanrahan replied quickly. "A fair enough question. You and the blond girl checked into the New Yorker last Sunday. You've been going down on the Acela on Sunday and coming back on Monday mornings for weeks now. When you leave South Station, you always walk directly through the terminal."

"How about you and I get together. I'll give you an address where we can meet. Say in an hour."

Hanrahan laughed into the phone. "My name's Tucker, not sucker," he replied. "Let me suggest something different. You take a day to gather the $1 million, and I'll tell you where to drop it. Within an hour after I get delivery, I'll give you the name, on the phone."

Now it was Ayala's turn to laugh. "I'm not partin' with a million big ones without meetin' with you face to face."

"No way," Hanrahan replied.

"You pick the place, my friend," Ayala countered. "Public or private, I don't care. I'll come alone, as you will. I'll bring half the money, but I need to know who you are, know something about you, what you say, validate your information before I hand across the balance."

Hanrahan pondered the comments. "I'll get back to you," he said and abruptly hung up.

"Hey!" Ayala bellowed into the dead line.

Hanrahan walked away from the CVS right into a driving rainstorm. Entering his Toyota, he sat for a minute watching the rain pelt against the windows. He needed to think, to handle this correctly. By reputation, Ayala was both smart and vicious. There was no margin for error.

Easing the car forward, he turned toward Boston and the Tobin Bridge. The ride would provide him with time to put the pieces together. Did he have to meet with Ayala? All along he knew that no one would just hand him $1,000,000. But he had tried anyway, ready to go to his back-up plan.

He certainly was expert in falsifying credentials so that Ayala would never know he was meeting with Phil Hanrahan. He would meet the crime lord in a public setting with plenty of people around, and he was sharp enough to reconnoiter the area ahead of time, as he had done at the New Yorker and at South Station, to ensure his safety.

Through the now misty rain, he could see the flats and the highs of Charlestown on his right. As a young boy, he has boosted cars from Monument Avenue and pilfered the pockets of tourists climbing around Bunker Hill. No way was he a novice in dealing with the likes of Ayala. But a person had to know his limitations, and he saw himself as a fringe player, not as an everyday regular.

Except for the counterfeiting charge from which Fleming had rescued him, he had never had a major encounter with the law. He suddenly felt a bit nauseous as he thought of Fleming. He swallowed hard and rationalized easily.

Why would he turn on his friend? For $1 million, of course. For a while he had thought of giving Salvatore Ayala the wheelman—that kid Amonti. And maybe he still would, but for some extra cash. The Mafia must be swimming in loose cash, so another $250,000 or so should be no problem.

First, he would see how his meeting with Ayala went down. At any rate, Captain Fleming had to be the ringleader. Hadn't he asked him to recruit the driver? Hadn't he asked him to follow Ayala? It was Fleming, the leader and the admitted shooter of the godson, who would bring the big money. Later he would worry about Amonti, after he had the $1 million.

He drove along the Central Artery and took that convoluted turn onto Atlantic Avenue and headed down Northern Avenue to Anthony's Pier 4 Restaurant. Once there, he sat at the bar, had Luca make him the first of three whiskey sours, and considered his options once again.

John A. Curry

He would never agree to meet in a private place. Never and ever. Such a setting was too much to Ayala's advantage. He might grab him and keep the money. No. It had to be a very public place for sure. If Ayala wouldn't agree to that, he would forget the deal. But how do you forget $1,000,000? With that, he could afford to live high—he and Dotty. They could visit California, like Fleming intended. Take that trip to Normandy. See Paris. Live the good life.

He used the swizzle stick to stir the whiskey sour. Through the large plate glass windows the sun peeked through the slight parting in the clouds, the first sign all day of a change in the weather. Tourist boats glided down Boston Harbor, their raincoated passengers waving toward the restaurant, like monkeys in the zoo, he thought. Look at me; I'm Sandra Dee.

He pulled the tickets from his sports jacket. Two tickets to the Red Sox game right in the first base grandstand for tomorrow night. What could be better? Although they were playing those banjo hitters from Tampa Bay—what did they call them, the Devil Rays? More like the Jelly Fishes, he thought—there would still be a good September gathering. They could sit for as long as they wanted, they would be surrounded by thousands, and when the business was done, he could get lost in the crowd, even if Ayala had someone watching them. But he had a strategy to ensure no one would be observing him. Would he be better off at the New England Aquarium? he wondered. Probably not. Good numbers of people, but it would be more likely someone could follow him after they conducted business.

He hated the idea of receiving only half of the money at the meeting, but Ayala's response was the expected one. He thought of Ayala's chasing down Fleming to get the names of the others. The gray man grimaced at the thought of Fleming suffering. But only for a few seconds.

Deciding, he went to the pay phone in the lobby and dialed.

"I'm looking for Salvatore Ayala, and this time I don't need any shit."

"Hold on a minute."

Two and Out

"Ayala here."

"Mr. Ayala, you like baseball?" he asked.

"Sure. Who doesn't?"

"I'll leave you a ticket for the ball game tomorrow night at the pick-up window on Jersey Street. It'll be there at 6:30. You be there with the money at 7:00."

"You're on, pal. $500,000 now and the rest later."

"Oh, and Mr. Ayala, I'll be watching you every step of the way. If I see you talking to anybody, or if you're with anybody, then I'm walking away and you'll never hear from me again. No one's to know where we're sitting. Understand?"

"Just be there with the information. I'll be happy to pay if it's good."

"Until then, Mr. Ayala."

Hanrahan hurried from the restaurant, noting the sun was spreading now, the clouds diminishing—a good omen of things to come.

"How are you, Mikey?" Sam Morris greeted Fallon.

It was now a week since the South Station heist, a Monday morning with a cool breeze wafting through the air tunnels between Boston's largest structures.

"I'm fine, Sam," he kept the response brief on purpose.

"Good. Good."

"We've had a possible break with the Candidates," Mike announced, standing in the doorway. "I thought you should know right away."

"Sit down," Morris directed.

Mike sat on the couch along the edge of the room. "It's from up at the New Hampshire race track. A guy named Tony Amonti has this big habit of calling everybody 'sport'."

"And?" Morris asked.

"That's it for now," Mike responded. "Nelson and I are going down to the Cape this afternoon. Look him up. He lives in a trailer park—Grinnell's—right off Lower County Road in Dennisport."

"Not much to go on, Mike. So a guy calls people 'sport'. That's it?"

Fallon looked at his boss sipping his coffee behind his desk. "He's a driver up there, Sam. He's from Des Moines originally. Been bouncing around the country."

"Any record?"

Mike shook his head. "None."

"Seems thin," Morris replied.

"Maybe it is. We've been watching him for three days now. He's had no contact with anybody except a woman who teaches school. He has custody of a young boy who's retarded, seven years old. He spends all of his time when he's not driving taxi with the two of them."

"How about phone records?"

"We checked. No calls to anyone interesting. In fact, he gets few calls and makes few."

"Bank accounts? Credit cards?"

"He's got a bank account with Fleet, $6,500. He owes a similar amount. No big transactions over the last few months."

Morris set his jaw. "Did I say it seems thin? It is thin, Mikey."

Mike tried not to sound defensive. "Sam, this may end up being an extended case. It took years with the Brinks job back in 1950, right? But I don't think so here. Ayala's got big dough out there. We're looking. In my gut, I think something's going to break. There's too much pressure being applied."

Morris decided to change the subject. "How are the girls, Mike?"

Recognizing the business part of their meeting had just ended, Mike stood. "I have the housekeeper there at 7:00 A.M. now, and she stays with them until 5:00 P.M. They're not happy about that part. Feel they can handle themselves after school."

"I'll bet," Morris laughed for the first time.

"I'll let you know about this Amonti thing," Mike said, turning to the door.

"We deserve a break, Mikey, but I don't think this is it."

"We'll see," Fallon replied from the doorway.

52

Standing in front of the souvenir shop across Jersey Street from the pick-up booth, Phil Hanrahan had a clear view of the entire scene. Having arrived at six o'clock, he had handed the jowly ticket agent ten bucks along with the envelope marked "For Salvatore Ayala." Then he had waited the half hour, observing the short line for any sign of the Prince of Darkness.

Across from him, entrepreneurs of all ages peddled peanuts, scorecards, and a variety of cholesterol inducing meats. In late September, the crowds had thinned from the early days of summer when the dream of the pennant or a wild card possibility was still intact. He munched on a hot dog and drank his Coke, having overcome his desire for a beer. He knew he would need a clear head tonight.

While he waited and watched, he thought about the wild card fraud being perpetrated on fans in many sports, including baseball, to keep the revenue coming. The more teams that could make the playoffs, the more money for the teams. In reality, losers were being rewarded. In this morning's <u>Globe</u> there had appeared an article about the Celtics' chances to win maybe 35 of 82 games and qualify, as an eighth place team, for the playoffs. Ridiculous.

At exactly 6:30, Sally Ayala turned the corner from Brookline Avenue to Jersey Street, carrying a tiestring accordian business folder. Striding confidently toward the window, he neither looked left or right. The mark of a pro, Hanrahan thought. He probably knew Phil was there somewhere, but he also knew that he would not be able to identify an observer in the vast crowd congregating on the street and on both sides of the road.

It took Ayala ten minutes to reach the window itself. He then walked toward the turnstiles with the grandstand ticket for Section 12, Row 11, Seat 23 in his hand.

Two and Out

Hanrahan crossed the street and presented his ticket for Seat 24 to an usher three turnstiles down from Ayala. They stood almost parallel to one another, waiting their turn to pass through. He was close enough to observe that Ayala spoke to no one. The Prince continued to look straight ahead, his hands thrust into the pockets of his leather jacket.

Phil kept about twenty yards behind Ayala as they ascended the ramp to the grandstand itself. When they reached the circumferential walkway, which led them from third base toward first base, Phil dropped further behind, lost in a maze of revelers either watching infield practice from the walkway or standing in long lines for refreshments.

When he arrived at Section 12, Ayala studied his ticket and then proceeded to the seat in Row 11. As soon as he reached it, he yelled to a vendor hawking peanuts about six rows below him. Without hesitation, the young man hurled a bag like one of Pedro Martinez's fast balls across the distance. Then Ayala sat, shelling the peanuts and motioning to the beer vendor as soon as he spotted him.

Slowly, Phil wandered along the walkway until he was above Section 13. From there, standing next to an uniformed Boston patrolman, he could look diagonally down at Ayala. He stood there as the coaches exchanged line-ups at home plate and while the National Anthem was being played. No one approached Ayala, and no one spoke to him. The Boston patrolman moved away from Phil, probably for a better view behind Section 12.

As Pedro Martinez strolled toward the mound at 7:05 P.M., Phil took a last look around the walkway. Along with him, only a woman in a wheelchair, a young boy holding his father's hand, and the Boston patrolman were standing in the area. This was working, Phil thought. He felt safe. He stepped toward the aisle to Section 12, descended, excused himself to the three or four fans in the seats between him and Ayala, and then sat down next to the man who could make him a rich man within the hour.

Ayala fidgeted in his seat and eyed the newcomer, but he didn't say a word, waiting for Hanrahan to take the lead.

"Salvatore Ayala?" Phil asked, extending his hand.

Ayala left it hanging in space. "That's right. Who am I talkin' to?" he asked as two young males dressed in Polo shirts and shorts asked to be excused. From the looks of them, they had paid five or seven visits to the beer line already, and the first pitch hadn't even been thrown.

The Prince of Darkness glared at them before standing and allowing them to pass, his body language connoting that he didn't intend to go through this exercise often. "Half these guys are fuckin' polluted before they arrive here. They had a sobriety test at the gates, the attendance would be cut in half," he said scornfully.

Below them the crowd stood and applauded as Pedro Martinez continued his warm-ups. The Dominican displayed his complete arsenal as the fans roared approval—a high, hard riser, a cut fastball, the best change-up in baseball, and a sharp curve.

"So what's your name?"

"Benson. Larry Benson," Hanrahan said.

"Yeah, and I'm Warren Beatty," Ayala replied sarcastically.

Hanrahan stood and pulled the small leather wallet from his rear pants pocket. He opened it and held the driver's license so that Ayala could read it.

"Lawrence Benson, 11 Granite Street, Peabody, Massachusetts, and a matching picture to boot," Ayala snickered. "That don't mean shit to me."

Hanrahan turned in his seat and spoke confidently, close to Ayala's ear. "I don't give a rat's ass what you believe. You want to do some business here or not?"

Ayala touched the scar on his face and traced it with his index finger as he spoke. "I've got a folder here with ten $50,000 bricks in there if your information's any good."

Hanrahan pivoted in his seat and looked around, particularly to his rear. Three or four fans were being moved along by both the Boston patrolman and Fenway security. No one would be allowed to stand in the walkway now that the game had begun.

"What are you worried about, Benson? If I wanted you dead, you'd already be dead," Ayala said.

"Who decides if my information's any good?"

Ayala squirmed in his seat and beckoned to the hot dog vendor. "One here with mustard!" he yelled. "Want one?"

Hanrahan waved him off. "No. Let's just get this business done."

Ayala bit into his hot dog. "I decide if your information's any good. What I want is a name, Benson. A real name, the organizer, and some more proof that what you say is legit."

"When do I receive the other $500,000?" Hanrahan asked.

Ayala straightened in his seat as if someone had slapped him. "In my business my word counts for something. You tell me how I can contact you, and as soon as I locate the name you provide, I'll be back at you. Worse thing a guy like me can do is renege. Have the word out on the street that I welshed. It ain't gonna happen. You'll get your money."

Hanrahan looked at the field just as Nomar Garciaparra laced a double off the center field wall sending two teammates across home plate. "I'll call you, Mr. Ayala. We'll arrange another public meeting like this."

Ayala laughed out loud. "You're a suspicious fuck, Benson."

Hanrahan set his jaw. "That's the way it has to be."

Off to their right, and down three rows, a big guy with an overlapping stomach and a ponytail down to his geester was arguing with his neighbors—a young suburban family—about his right to stand up and curse anytime he wanted to. Fenway security rushed to the area from both above and below them.

"So what have you got for me today?" Ayala asked.

Hanrahan reached into his sport jacket and pulled out a photo.

"Who's this?" asked Ayala.

John A. Curry

"Captain Victor P. Fleming, age 67, retired narcotics/robbery—homicide detective, Boston Police Department. He's the guy you want."

Ayala studied the photo intensely. "Yeah, I know of him. Never met him. Wasn't he a big guy on armored car robberies?"

Hanrahan nodded. "You're on target. Like I said, he's retired now. Lives over in Revere on Sargent Street."

"A fuckin' cop. Go on, I'm listenin'," Ayala said.

"He's someone I know. A while back he asked me to scout out your trips to New York. He and some others—I don't know them—took down the Brinks truck at Northeastern, and then hit you at South Station."

"You don't know any of the others?"

Hanrahan had anticipated the question. First, he would receive this $500,000. Then, when they found Fleming, the other $500,000. Fleming didn't even know Amonti's name. For his own reasons, Vic hadn't wanted to know. He would contact Ayala later—their relationship now cemented—and present him with Tony Amonti's name then, for another good piece of change.

"Like I said, I know Fleming."

"How do you know him?" Ayala asked.

"He did me a favor a long time ago."

Ayala laughed, that hyena laugh that made him sound like Richard Widmark in 'Kiss of Death'. "So now you're showing your gratitude, huh?"

Hanrahan didn't respond and watched the game instead. On the field, Martinez was mowing down the hopeless Tampa Bay batters—Castilla, Canseco, McGriff—all big swing, low contact hitters. No wonder the fans in Tampa Bay were staying away in droves.

"How about my dough?" he finally said.

Ayala handed the folder across to him. "So you followed me to New York, huh?"

"That's right."

Two and Out

"How did the cop know what was in the briefcase? How'd you know?"

"I didn't know, but somehow Fleming found out. Probably through his contacts."

Hanrahan untied the string and opened the accordion file. Pulling it close in to his body, he lifted one brick toward him and flipped through the packet quickly. Obviously he couldn't count in public, but he knew that it was all there.

"Satisfied?" Ayala asked.

"I will be when I have the rest of it," Hanrahan replied.

Ayala laughed the creepy laugh once again. "If you gave me the right info, you'll get your money. If you didn't, you'll be seeing me sooner than you think, Benson."

"We done here?"

"One more question," Ayala replied. "Do you know who killed my godson?"

Hanrahan nodded. "It was Fleming."

Ayala simply repeated the answer. "Fleming."

"You better move fast," Hanrahan said. "He's moving to L.A. Maybe he's already left."

"L.A.? Retiring on my dough," Ayala replied.

"I'm out of here in a minute, Mr. Ayala. You have any problem with that?"

"You go. I'll sit here for a while and watch Martinez some more. See how many strikeouts he racks up against this triple-A crew."

As he spoke, a Martinez fireball caught good-looking rookie Aubrey Huff standing still. As the first half of the fifth inning ended, a good portion of the audience deserted their seats for either the beer line or the lavatories. One inning a beer, the next a whiz. When their two friends from down aisle rose, heading their way, Phil Hanrahan also stood, grasping the folder.

"I'll be in touch," he said to Ayala.

"Benson."

"Yeah?"

Ayala waited while the two preppies passed by. "You guys should never have killed my godson."

Hanrahan looked at him as if he were crazy. "I wasn't there!" he said loudly.

"Have a nice night, Mr. Benson."

As he exited, Phil headed for the rear of the grandstand, mixing in with as many fans as he could. At the top he stood for a long moment observing the scene around him. No one appeared to be focused on him. After a minute, the Boston patrolman approached him, indicating he could not loiter.

Retracing his steps toward the exit, he walked briskly around the circumference of the walkway, pausing every now and then, ostensibly to look toward the action on the field. He could detect no sign of surveillance so he descended the ramp, still in the company of tens of fans.

Once on Jersey Street, he turned right, crossed Brookline Avenue, and walked directly into the cavernous parking lot. He edged along in the darkness, joined by a few families who had called it an early night what with the Red Sox winning 9-2 and with Pedro pitching. He passed between cars, turning occasionally to reconnoiter. Along with the fans, he noted a few security guards back at the entrance on Brookline Avenue and in front of him on Beacon Street. He spotted a Boston policeman behind him and to the right.

On reaching his Honda Accord, he inserted the key, opened the door and threw the file onto the back seat. And then he felt the searing pain in his back. He hadn't heard anything, or seen anything. As he turned, he felt his stomach explode and he slid between the parked cars. The last sensation he felt was some cold object being placed against his temple.

53

After five o'clock the cold air hit them straight on. Not cold cold, but fall cold. That time of year when the temperature drops drastically and surprises you once the sun goes down.

Nelson had asked him to put on the heater to take the edge off. For the last hour they had sat outside the Town Taxi office on Route 28 near the Dennis—Harwich line.

"Where the hell is he? He's supposed to be off duty at five o'clock," Mike said, frustrated.

Nelson sipped her coffee, trying to put some warmth back into her body. "Here comes a cab now," she said.

From behind them a gray Crown Victoria moved into the parking lot between the cab office and a boutique. A few seconds later a good-looking young man with dark hair and olive skin stepped out of the vehicle with his outer coat slung over his shoulder. He walked directly to the office.

"That's him," Mike said.

They got out of their car, crossed the street right in front of the boutique, and feigned window-shopping. Two minutes later Tony Amonti appeared on the sidewalk.

"Mr. Amonti?" Mike asked.

Tony turned toward them. "Yeah? Who wants to know?"

As they approached him, Nelson opened her pocketbook to show him her I.D. Tony tensed when he saw the movement toward the pocketbook. "Hey!" he yelled.

"Relax, Mr. Amonti. I'm Special Agent Marilyn Nelson of the Boston office of the Federal Bureau of Investigation." She flashed him her I.D.

Fallon reached into his back pocket and produced his wallet. Flipping it open, he displayed the badge. "Agent Michael Fallon, Tony. Agent Nelson and I would like a few words with you. Got a minute?"

John A. Curry

Tony knew he looked flustered and even astonished. But then again, who wouldn't? he thought. Nothing wrong with that. But now was the time for composure and perception, two traits that any driver careening around an oval at 180 miles an hour had to possess.

He stepped away from them a bit, registering continual surprise. "Sure, but what can I do for you?"

Fallon pointed to the street. "Any place around here where we could get a cup of coffee?"

"There's a Friendly's restaurant just past the lights. We can walk it in two minutes," Tony replied.

"Let's do that," Mike responded.

They paraded silently toward the small restaurant, a strategy on their part to sweat him, Tony felt. On the contrary, it gave him time to think, to overcome the initial surprise. What tie could they possibly have to him? Maybe they were here for something other than the robberies? Likely not. He'd soon find out. Stay composed, he told himself.

Fallon selected a booth in the rear and signaled the waitress. "Three coffees," he said.

While they waited, Fallon began. "Mr. Amonti, you been following the presidential election?"

Tony nodded and spoke slowly. "As much as most other citizens."

"Who do you like between the vice presidential candidates—Cheney or Lieberman?"

He had to be kidding, Tony thought.

"Cheney," he replied, without skipping a beat.

"Cheney. Really? Why him?" Mike asked.

Tony locked eyes with Fallon. "Because he's smart."

The waitress deposited their coffee and asked if they wanted anything else. "We're all set," Fallon replied.

Tony tapped his fingers on the table. "Look, folks, it's nice talking about the election with you, but my son's being watched by my neighbor. It's getting close to his supper time so can you let me know what I can do for you?"

Two and Out

"Do you recollect where you were on Friday afternoon, September 15, and on Monday morning, October 2, Mr. Amonti?" Nelson asked.

Tony lowered his cup. "Why?"

"On September 15 a Brinks truck was robbed of over two million dollars at Northeastern University by three men wearing rubber masks depicting Gore, Lieberman, and Cheney. Two weeks later, the same group—four this time—stole a similar amount from a Mafia boss outside South Station, only this time someone was murdered. You hear about them?"

"Of course. Who hasn't?" Tony replied.

"We have reason to believe you may have been involved," Mike said.

"Is that right?" Tony replied indignantly.

"Your employer tells us you weren't at work either of those days, Mr. Amonti."

Tony leaned forward, placing his elbows on the table. "I don't know where I was then or on any other dates around those days for that matter. I'm a taxi driver, not a fuckin' lawyer with a detailed schedule. If I wasn't at work, then I was probably at my trailer, on the beach, at a movie, picking up my son from school. Any number of places. You people got a lot of balls checking on me with my employer or anyone else that could cost me my job. You..."

"We heard you're going to California," Nelson interrupted.

Tony grimaced, his eyes flashing anger. "Let me finish my thought, please! It's none of your business where I'm going. One place I'm goin' is to see my lawyer, I'll tell you that."

Mike shook his head. "There's no need for that, Mr. Amonti. We're not here to arrest you."

"On what basis do you determine I'm involved?" Tony asked.

"We can't divulge that," Mike replied.

"What is this now—a Communist state? You come down here, harass me, check with my employer, jeopardize my job, and you can't tell me what ties me to this shit?"

"You'll know what ties you if we proceed down this pathway," Nelson said.

Amonti snorted and pushed his chair away from the table. "You people are somethin' else. We done here?"

Fallon glanced over at Nelson. "For now, Mr. Amonti. If we need to talk with you again, we'll let you know."

Amonti glared at them. "You do that. Let me know, because the next time I want my lawyer present—see if he's hearing this the way I am. I'm a good citizen. I pay my taxes, take care of my boy, and never have had any problems with the law. Ever. My suggestion is you go down some other pathway 'cause you're on the wrong track right now."

He stood and threw two dollars on the table.

"I don't understand where you're coming from, Mike. What was the point?"

They were heading north on Route 3 somewhere in the area of Weymouth, the heater working overtime, the night wind whistling against the windows. Above them, a pale moon peeked between ribbons of scudding clouds.

"Marilyn, you know and I know we don't have shit. We need to force something to happen, a mistake. If Amonti is involved, maybe he'll panic, call one or more of the others. I just want to roust him a bit. If there's nothing there, then okay. I was wrong. But I can smell something. Call it instinct."

Nelson raised her fingers to her lips and blew some heat on them. "I don't know Mike. I'm not seeing it."

"Well, what did you think?"

"He reacted the same as any citizen would—surprised, indignant, upset, outraged. Because a guy calls people 'sport' he's a prime suspect?"

Mike shook his head vigorously. "A guy who's an ace driver, moving to California soon, not at work on the involved dates."

"And with no record, no heavy bank deposits, no unusual calls, dating a girl who's a teacher, taking care of a retarded son? My instinct tells me you're wrong."

"We'll see. We'll watch for a while. See where he goes, who he calls. He's not a saint, Marilyn. That broad he was shacking up with last go-round, the one that ran off, has a rap sheet as long as that hair running down your neck."

She laughed. "You noticed, huh?"

He smiled broadly, the laugh lines forming around his lips. "I did."

"Well how about stopping for some dinner and feeding your good looking partner?"

"You mind if I pass? Someone's with the girls now, but it's getting late now, and I..."

"Fine. No problem. Just remember you owe me a dinner."

"You're on," he replied.

"The guy's fuckin' dead?" Joe Sansone asked incredulously.

"That's what I fuckin' said," Sally Ayala replied.

"I know what you fuckin' said, Salvatore. I just don't get it is all. Why kill the guy?"

Sally Ayala pedaled his bicycle a little faster in exasperation. Every Thursday afternoon he and Joe Sansone spent an hour at the Boston YMCA on the bikes. Unfortunately. First of all, he hated the exercise and secondly, since the robbery, all Joe wanted to do was remind him of the loss and threaten him every ten minutes or so.

"Because I got what I wanted, Joe. I now know who was behind it and who killed Sonny."

"Fleming, you said. It figures a copper would be involved. But how do you know this stoolie told you the truth?"

"You see the papers this morning? The guy's real name was Phil Hanrahan. Our friend at District 3 tells me this guy knew Fleming. It's legit, and I got my $500,000 back."

Sansone stopped pedaling. "Yeah, but you don't yet have my money back."

Sally decided not to respond.

"If you didn't kill the guy, maybe followed him, captured the prick, hit him over the head with a Slugger a few belts, maybe he would have given us the names of all the crew. You ever think of that, Sal? That is, if you ever think?"

"He was one of them, and he was tryin' to steal from me, Joe. Fake I.D., y' know? Killin' him was the way to go."

"If you find Fleming."

"I'll fuckin' find him and our money."

"My money."

They pedaled in silence for a minute, the two of them alone in a corner of the huge room. Diagonally across from them a personal trainer was demonstrating the proper way to perform push-ups to an overweight male executive. He did ten one-hand push-ups a la Jack Palance at the Academy Award presentations a few years ago.

"That 300 pound fucker will die, he tries that," Joe Sansone said. "So where's Fleming, seein' as you fuckin' iced the guy who could have led you to him?"

Sally rolled his eyes toward the ceiling. "He left Revere couple of days ago. Moved to L.A. with no forwarding address. Paulie and I are goin' out there tonight on the red eye."

"What to kill him before he tells you where my money is?"

Sally let out a deep sigh. "Joey, let me try this one more time. This guy Hanrahan fucked with me. He was one of them for sure, turning on Fleming. One down, the leader identified, probably two more to go—which I will get out of him."

Sansone increased his pace. "How did Paulie get close to Hanrahan anyhow?"

Sally grinned at him. "Easy. The asshole left me a ticket at the pick-up booth, thinkin' I wouldn't be able to arrange somethin' in advance. We dressed Paulie in a Boston patrolman's uniform. He waltzes up to the booth, asks to look at

Two and Out

the ticket for Salvatore Ayala, identifies the location. A few minutes later, I pick up the ticket.

"Before the game Paulie stations himself on the walkway above the grandstand, waits for me to sit down, even stands next to the stoolie for a while, and when he sits down next to me, Paulie hangs around watchin' the whole deal. A cop looking at us all the time.

"The guy gets up, mixes in the crowd, and Paulie follows him out to the parking lot. Uses the silencer, picks up my money, and walks away."

Sansone jumped right in. "Picks up your money, huh? You know, Sal, it's a miracle you got your money back. So far, you lost me almost $3 million, I penalize you $1.5 million, and you are fuckin' lucky—that's what I believe, just lucky—you don't lose another $500,000 to this guy."

One more comment and Sally was ready to get one of those barbells over in the other corner and mash Sansone's brains. "I got the situation under control, Joe. You'll get your fuckin' money back and I'll take care of Fleming and you'll be givin' me back my dough."

Sansone waited a long beat. "You remember what the guy—who was it? Robert Duvall?—said to John Wayne in that closing scene in "True Grit"?

"No," said the Prince of Darkness.

"He said, 'That's big talk for a one-eyed fat man'."

"Fuck you, Joe," Sally muttered under his breath.

54

For three days the sun had floated bright and hot over the Los Angeles basin, pushing people to the beaches and into backyard pools just to escape its intensity. And for three days Vic Fleming toured his new city, acquainting himself with its different sectors.

On the first day, he had checked into a cheap motel on Wilshire near UCLA. He could, of course, have afforded an expensive room over in Century City, but he decided to pay the lower price for a few days before committing to something more upscale. Eventually, in a month or so, he would buy a condo in the Valley or near Beverly Hills or maybe over in Venice.

On that first day he also felt an urge for company so he had taken a bus to the downtown near the Parker Center, a big white building which houses the Police Department of the City of Los Angeles. On the surrounding streets he had a choice of fifteen to twenty small bars, all of them frequented by off-duty cops. He sat for hours in two of them, talking about the Job with both active and retired comrades. They accepted him right off, pleased to hear East Coast war stories that matched some of their own.

On the second day, he had picked up a rental at the Hertz place in Westwood and spent a good part of the day driving around Beverly Hills. He purchased one of those maps that highlighted the homes of film stars, both past and present. After touring most of the morning, he was slightly disappointed to see that the homes of legends such as Jimmy Stewart, Gary Cooper and Humphrey Bogart were so protected by winding hills, high fences, and long goose-necked driveways that they were hardly worth the visit. Yet, it was still a thrill to be on the streets where once they had lived.

On the third day, he visited Tyrone Power's grave at Hollywood Memorial Park. Nearby, on the rolling green acres, he observed the tombs of Douglas Fairbanks Jr., Rudolph Valentino, and Marion Davies. He stood for a while by Power's plot, which was marked by a white marble bench overlooking a nearby shimmering pool. It is inscribed with the famed couplet from Hamlet: "Good night, sweet prince, and flights of angels sing thee to thy rest."

Although she had passed away in the spring of 1998, to him, Alice Faye would always be alive, and so he never even considered visiting her place of rest.

In the early evening, in the still sweltering heat, he parked his rental over on Pico and strolled around the 20th Century Fox outer grounds, looking down at the movie sets from the bridge around the corner on the Avenue of the Stars. In a day or two he would wander the entire lot and fantasize of movies made decades before while, with any luck, he might catch a look at those now in production.

From the studio grounds he walked down to the Century City Mall where he meandered through the array of small shops, enjoying a drink at one of the open air restaurants, relishing the pastrami at the Stage Deli, the food just as good as that served at their flagship Manhattan location.

By nine o'clock he was back on Wilshire picking up a Boston paper from the grizzled old man at the out-of-town newstand. He knew it was important that he follow the news emanating from the Hub, at least for the next few weeks.

At the apartment, he poured some Jack and spread the newspaper across the kitchen table. He wished for his CD player so that he could hear Faye sing "You'll Never Know," now that he was actually here where she had made her name. But most of his possessions were now in storage over in Venice until he located a permanent place.

And then he saw it. Front and center on page one of the City section. He read the story, slowly and carefully, and when he was finished, he read it again.

Phil Hanrahan was dead. Murdered in a parking lot near Fenway Park, his wallet taken by unknown assailant (s). The police were unsure of the motivation. Was it the work of juiced-up teens, or a crazed maniac? People within the parking lot had not heard any gunfire and yet Hanrahan had been shot three times.

When he had finished reading the article for the third time, he poured himself another shot of the Jack, stood, and ran some tap water over the amber. He opened the refrigerator and threw ice cubes into the glass.

He switched on the cheap television set in time to hear the sportscaster lamenting the non-existence of professional football in the City of Angels. Vic stared at the guy but didn't really see him as he contemplated his situation.

Long ago, while a young man on the Job, he had learned to anticipate the worst. If Hanrahan were dead, then the Prince of Darkness was on to them. He didn't even consider that the death was a random hit or the work of some teeny bopper. He didn't believe in coincidence.

But how had Ayala found Hanrahan? Phil had not participated in the robberies themselves and had never even met Brian and Lieberman. The connection to Hanrahan was through Vic alone.

Had Hanrahan flashed the money around town, or gotten intoxicated and talked too much? No. He knew Hanrahan to be solid and stable. He wasn't the type to discuss his business or to show big money around.

Vic sipped the Jack and began to think of other possibilities. If Hanrahan were dead, had he spoken to Ayala before he was killed? And if he had, to what purpose? Could it be possible that Phil had gone to Ayala? He couldn't see it. But what if he had? Then Ayala had Vic's name for sure. And probably the kid's name, the driver, as well.

He had to plan as if Ayala were on to him. There was nothing in the papers about Brian or that friend of his—Lieberman. He would buy the papers each day, think about maybe even calling Frank Sheridan back in Boston to see what was going on.

Two and Out

He thought of his new found friends at the Parker Center. He would need to prevail on one of them to put him in touch with someone who could provide a weapon. Right now, he was unarmed. You couldn't cross the country on the airlines with a Glock.

Should he warn Brian? He didn't know how to contact Lieberman or Cheney. No. They had agreed on no contact. Besides, if Hanrahan had betrayed him, they would be coming for him and for Cheney, the only ones Phil could identify.

He had to prepare.

Earlier, sitting in his taxi, Tony Amonti had read the very same story regarding Phil Hanrahan. The name and the story would have meant nothing to him if a picture of Hanrahan had not accompanied the piece. But there he was, the gray man. He studied the picture carefully. There was no doubt it was the gray man, the one who had recruited him.

Tony parked the taxi at Glendon Beach and stared at the water, trying to think clearly, the fear knotting his stomach. Ayala must have found Hanrahan, but how? What mistake had the gray man made? He wasn't even a member of the crew. And if Ayala had found him, how far behind other members of the crew could he be? As far as he knew, Hanrahan was the only person who actually knew his real name. The leader, Bush, had prided himself on having protected their identities, even from each other.

Now suddenly, he was facing pressure from two different directions. For some reason, the FBI was watching him, armed with some potential tie to the crimes. Could the FBI have gotten to Hanrahan? Since his meeting with Fallon and Nelson, he had searched his memory, retraced each step through both robberies, and could not think of any connection they might have made. But he wasn't about to panic over the feds. If they really had something, they would have been all over his case by now. He was reasonably sure they were simply on a fishing expedition.

Bush had stressed they were not to attempt contact with one another. He had followed that instruction. Besides, at this point, who did he know to contact? Assuming the FBI had been monitoring his phone calls, even they would have their doubts regarding his involvement.

What the feds could find, if ever they conducted a search, was the unregistered Glock. And there lay a dilemma. He needed it to protect himself if Ayala or his men were ever to pay him a visit.

According to the newspaper, Hanrahan had been murdered last night. As Gore had warned, unlike the FBI, Ayala would not be concerned with due process and individual rights. If the Mafia was on to him, he could expect them within a day or two. FBI or no FBI, he would keep the weapon near him at all times. He reached under the seat and fished it from the floor. He checked the weapon and chambered a round.

He thought of his money. Mrs. Adams had been delighted to store his locked suitcase, understanding that he needed to clear room before he returned the rented trailer. Unless the feds were to search the entire trailer park, they would never find the money. Later, they had agreed, in a month she would forward it to him in California at his expense.

On Saturday he and Doug would leave for California. He would not deviate from the plan and raise further suspicion, and with each passing day he could assume he was safe.

He had to leave for Grace's sake as well. She was an innocent who potentially could get hurt. Maybe some day they could be together in California or even back here, but right now there were too many issues on the table. They needed distance between them for now.

For the next few days he would keep Doug away from the trailer as much as he could. Mrs. Adams would love the idea of her favorite sleeping overnight with her on his last three nights on the Cape. And he would sleep with Grace at her place, making love until they tired, and then, while she slept, lying awake with a protective arm around her, until Saturday morning dawned. Nobody knew anything about her so they should be safe.

Fuck them. If Ayala came, he would be ready. He stared into the rearview mirror, noting the calm in his brown eyes. He had made his choices, and now he had to make sure he and those he loved came through this unscathed.

55

"Thanks for not having us baby sat, Dad. That was really embarrassing." Jessica beamed her radiant smile at him from across the dinner table.

"Yeah, Dad, we don't need some geek baby-sitting us," Nicole chimed in. Some scrub tellin' us what to do."

"Excuse me, Nicole? Watch the language or I'll have a English instructor in here after school hours instead," Mike Fallon replied without much conviction.

"Pass me a chicken wing," Melissa said, "and some more duck sauce." For the moment food was more important to her than the conversation.

Once or twice a week he brought home take-out, especially when it was his turn to cook. Thanks to Rita, the two older girls had long ago learned to light a stove and prepare a table. But he insisted on taking his turn periodically and on other occasions bringing home a treat.

Just a night ago he had agreed to the elimination of an after school sitter. Against his better judgment. But Rita had always stressed the importance of offering the children challenges—chances to grow or fail and to learn through each.

"Remember we agreed it was to be an experiment," he said, spreading some hot mustard over his pork strips. "I don't really feel comfortable leaving you alone after school."

"Judith says we're all latchkey kids," Melissa volunteered.

Mike nodded in agreement. "Judith's right. And that's what I don't like. Having you come home to an empty house. When I was a kid..."

"In the olden days?" Melissa interrupted.

He decided to get back on safer ground. "I'll be home by six o'clock every night, but if I mess up too much or you guys can't handle being alone, then Mrs. North is coming back."

"If you mess up, like don't get home in time, we have to have a sitter? That's gross and not fair," Nicole said.

"There's a lot that's not fair in life, young lady. You'll find that out fast enough."

"I already have," she pouted.

"Michael swore in school today," Melissa interjected.

"What did he say?" Nicole asked gleefully.

"Should I say what he said, Daddy?" Melissa asked.

"That's not necessary, Melissa. We get the point that Michael swore."

The fifteen going-on-forty-year-old diplomat intervened. "Did you catch the Candidates yet, Dad?"

She knew and he knew that a part of his ritual with Rita had been some discussion of the events of his workday. Jessica playing Rita.

"Not yet," he replied. Rita had treated young teens as adults. Answer their questions as seriously and as fully as you would those of a forty-year old, she often said. "But we're following up on some leads."

"From squealers?" Nicole asked.

"From informants," he corrected.

"Judith wants to know if you have a girl friend," Melissa chimed in from another planet.

There was a momentary lull in the conversation as the two older girls waited for the answer.

"Judith's stupid," Nicole finally said.

Treat them like adults, Mike said to himself. "Melissa, you tell Judith I do not have a girl friend, and when I do, she'll be the first to know."

Wrong answer. He knew it as soon as he had uttered it.

"You lookin?" Nicole asked, reaching for the last chicken finger.

"No, I'm not looking," Mike replied, shaking his head vigorously. "I'm very content with you girls."

"Judith's mom is looking," Melissa replied.

"Eck! Judith's mother is a freak," Nicole said.

He noted Jessica stayed above the fray. She smiled confidently at him across the table.

"What?" he asked.

"Maybe you should begin to think about meeting someone," she suggested shyly.

Enough was enough.

"Don't you girls have any homework to do?"

"Billy Flanagan wants to trade up," Nelson was saying.

He looked at the clock next to the bed. Midnight.

"For what?"

"He says he has some more information on the Ayala heist."

"He's a regular Victor McLaglen, isn't he?"

"Who's he?" Marilyn asked.

"Never mind."

"Says what he's got should protect him for a lifetime."

"Sounds good. Did you set the meet?"

"Noon tomorrow. Marblehead. On the Neck. Chandler Hovey Park."

Mike laughed heartily. "What's he going, upscale?"

"He says nobody knows him there. It's right on the Atlantic. Sightseers go there to look out at the ocean. Not too many crooks there."

"That we know of. I'll see you in the morning, Marilyn."

"Sleep tight, Mikey."

The silver bird glided above the Pacific allowing its passengers a clear view of LAX. The Los Angeles International Airport loomed to the right, and as they descended, Paulie Ayala could see the planes below taking off, veering left to turn back over the States or proceeding straight ahead across the Pacific.

"You arranged for some equipment, huh?" Paulie asked.

Sally nodded without responding. He flipped through the People magazine and pointed to a quarter page photo of Jamie Lee Curtis kneeling beside two young children. "That broad's got sex appeal," he said.

"Speakin' of which, how's Carol doin'?"

"Wearin' a bandage makes her look like one of them Indians with turbans, y' know? She's feelin' better."

Paulie tried again. "What equipment did you get?"

Sally let the flight attendant pass before answering. "I asked them for a sawed-off shotgun, a Glock, a .38, and a baseball bat."

"They find Fleming?"

"Not yet, and I don't know how hard they're looking. He could be out here under another name or maybe movin' around, staying with a friend. Wherever he is, we'll find the prick. And the bastard will suffer for Sonny, Paulie."

Paulie nodded. "Sonny was good people."

Sally gave him a long look. "Now you say so."

"Will they give us much help out here?"

"They'll inquire around a bit is my guess. Not much. We're not too close to the West Coast families. We'll probably have to find him ourselves."

"It's a big fuckin' city," Paulie replied.

"If he's using his own name, which he probably is, it's not," Sally said.

56

Should he break his own rules and contact the crew? Brian sat in a corner of the faculty center over on the edge of the Fenway. He sipped his late afternoon cocktail and thought about it carefully. He nodded to two colleagues from the business college as they walked into the lounge and sat on a couch on the other side of the room.

Why was he even considering it? First of all, he didn't even know Cheney's real name. Secondly, Vic Fleming would be someplace in California by now. He would see Johnny on and off anyway.

He smiled to himself and sipped some more of the whiskey sour. Why contact them anyway? Because he wanted to brag a bit, breach his own no contact rule just to demonstrate how sharp he was, review his triumph with them. Did they all understand he had made them rich and not one shred of evidence tied any of them to either crime? They were all home free with no sign of either the FBI, the Boston Police, the Mafia, or any other nitwits in pursuit.

He picked up the copy of today's <u>Globe</u> and turned the pages one by one. What was two weeks ago a front page story was now relegated to brief updates in the middle of the City section. Today, that FBI spokesman—that dead looking guy who had been on TV repeatedly—reported "progress' was being made. Yeah, right.

Did his crew really appreciate his skill? He swallowed the last of his drink and signaled the waiter for a refill.

In the end, history would record his achievement. The error that the Brinks crew had made back in the middle of the century was utilizing individuals who all knew each other. He had been much smarter. Even he did not know the identity of each crew member. Who could ever find him or any member of the

Two and Out

Candidates? No motivation, no opportunity, no case. And no sense breaking his own no-contact rule. At least not for now.

———

Billy Flanagan and Martin O'Shea sat huddled on a bench under a green pavilion at Chandler Hovey Park. They faced the rolling sea and a spectacular view of the Atlantic. To their left and right majestic old-world mansions hovered high along a coastline of jagged rock. On a windy October afternoon only a half-dozen others, probably neighbors venturing from the winding roads and set back homes proximous to the park, wandered the rocky terrain.

Fallon parked the Taurus on the street outside the entrance and walked toward the pavilion accompanied by Marilyn Nelson and Frank Sheridan. They each turned up the collars of their outer coats to break the bite of the wind.

As they approached, O'Shea turned and stood. "Thank you for coming, Mr. Fallon, Frank."

"This is Marilyn Nelson from the Bureau," Fallon said.

O'Shea flashed his lawyerly smile. "Pleased to meet you, Marilyn," he said.

Billy Flanagan remained seated, not bothering to either turn toward them or greet them.

"Good afternoon, Billy," Fallon offered. He had guessed that whereas for this trip Flanagan really didn't need a favor, they would encounter a hard-ass attitude, but, on the other hand, Flanagan had asked for the meet.

"So before we all freeze to death, what brings us together?" Fallon asked.

"My client has come upon certain information pertaining to the robbery-murder at South Station, that may be useful to your case," O'Shea said.

"We're listening," Mike replied.

O'Shea took a long look at him and finally showed a small smile. "We would like you to do more than listen, Mr. Fallon.

We would like you and Detective Sheridan to remember my client's assistance in the event that some future allegations are made against his good name."

Sheridan almost choked at the mention of Billy's 'good name'. "Can we cut the bullshit, Martin, and come to the point?" he asked.

"Short of murder is what I want," Billy pronounced as he stood and faced them for the first time.

"Run that by me again, Billy," Fallon said wryly.

"What I got is right from the Mafia itself, Fallon. It'll put you on track to catch the Candidates crew," Flanagan said.

"What's that mean?" Nelson snapped. "You either have something concrete or not. We don't need "on track" stuff."

O'Shea raised a hand. "What Mr. Flanagan can tell you is the name of one of the crew. In addition, he can tell you where Ayala's search for the other members is taking him. He can also tell you the occupation of the leader of the crew. Is that good enough for you?" He stared belligerently at Nelson. "You're going to find his information solid. We need to know whether in exchange..."

Flanagan cut him off in mid-sentence.

"I need a pass should I have a problem with the law down the pike."

Fallon cast a quick glance at Sheridan. "Both the FBI and Boston will consider Mr. Flanagan a friend should he need our help in the future. Provided there aren't any embarrassing, unfortunate circumstances associated with his conduct that would make our involvement impossible." Billy probably said it better—short of murder.

O'Shea nodded. "Then we're in agreement. I hope I don't have to remind any of you of this meeting in open court in the future. And one other thing—the source of this information stays hidden except for those here today, or there's no deal."

Fallon looked out at the Atlantic and waited a moment before replying. "Mr. O'Shea, I don't need your threats. If you and I and Frank here have a deal, then I'll honor it, and we'll protect the source."

"Tell them what you have, Billy."

Flanagan lifted the collar of his bomber jacket and hunched his shoulders. "A few nights ago, a guy was killed over near Fenway Park. You aware of that?" he asked Sheridan.

"Not my district, but I'm aware. So?"

"Guy killed was Phil Hanrahan. He tried to collect the $1,000,000 reward Ayala is offerin' around. My source within Sansone's family says the dead fuck was trying to trade in the Candidates crew for the reward."

"We know this Hanrahan?" Fallon asked Sheridan.

"No. Not off the top."

"Go ahead, Billy," Mike said.

"Before the guy croaked, he claimed some retired cop shot Sonny Rossetti and led the crew. They know the guy's out in California somewhere."

"So this Hanrahan was a crew member?" Mike asked.

Flanagan rolled his eyes. "I didn't have time for twenty questions, Fallon. I appear too nosy, I end up where this Hanrahan did. I was havin' a drink or two with my friend. Yeah, I think he probably is—or was."

"He say what kind of cop the guy was?" Frank Sheridan asked.

"Just said a retired cop."

A retired cop. A guy named Hanrahan whose name didn't mean anything to them right away. It made some sense, Mike felt. And it was directly in line with his own recent theories. A new crew. A cop involved. They were getting closer.

"Anything else?" he asked.

Flanagan shook his head. "That's it."

"One question, Billy. You ever hear anything about a race car driver from Loudon being involved in this?" Fallon asked.

"Never heard of that," Flanagan replied.

"Ask around. See if you can pick up anything about it. We'll be forever grateful."

Flanagan grinned broadly. "I bet you will be. Got a name?"

Alarmed, Nelson caught her boss's eye, engaging him, expressing her concern about where he was going.

"No," he finally responded. "Just a rumor out on the streets."

"We done here?" O'Shea asked.

"We are, Mr. O'Shea," Mike replied. "That we are."

As she walked out of the park alongside Mike, Nelson leaned into his ear. "If you had given him, Tony Amonti's name, he would have been a dead man, you know that, don't you? Innocent or guilty, dead."

"I know," Mike grunted.

"He's very probably not involved," Nelson persisted.

Mike stopped for a moment and locked in on her. "Marilyn, I do have a conscience, okay? I wouldn't put his name out to them."

"I hope not," she responded huffily, as she lengthened her stride and walked ahead of him.

Jesus, he thought, it wasn't easy working with someone who personally interested you.

Johnny climbed the hill on Route 1, the A-frame of the Kowloon Restaurant looming directly ahead. He parked in the lot of the Chinese eatery and followed the long lines through the carpeted lobby toward the main dining room. From the entrance, he spotted Laura, with her back to him, as Donna and Steve waved to him from a booth halfway back.

Their table was adjacent to a rock garden and a small body of water. Down the line of booths, youngsters pitched pennies into the pool for good luck.

Today, "almost thirteen" became officially thirteen, and for her birthday Laura had asked for dinner with just the adult set. At least for today. Johnny couldn't understand the new configuration for birthdays celebrated by the young. They usually had two different parties, one with family, one with friends, sometimes one, two, or three weeks removed from the actual day. Lucky he had just Laura to worry about, otherwise, with a good-sized family, one could lose control of the birthday dates or spend half the year celebrating.

"Hi, Dad!" Laura greeted him as he approached the booth.

"Happy birthday, princess!" he bellowed, moving to embrace her as he slid next to her.

Sitting across from them, Steve and Donna greeted him effusively. "So what do you think of our birthday girl, Johnny?" Steve asked.

"I'll tell you what," Johnny replied in a serious tone. "As of today, she's going to tell us all she's almost fourteen. Now you watch."

Laura came to full blush as she studied the large menu. "That's not true," she replied. "Dad exaggerates."

"How's teaching going?" Donna asked, excitement in her voice.

"I'm at Saugus High as a sub, probably for the balance of the year. I think if I'm steady enough, you know—if there are no incidents—I have a good chance at a full job in the fall."

Steve grinned broadly. "Great, Johnny. I'm happy for you." And he meant it, Johnny knew.

Donna reached for her mai tai. "I'm very happy you decided not to go to Florida," she said quietly.

He noticed Laura scanning the menu, averting his gaze, waiting for his answer, attempting to appear disinterested. "I have no intention of going," he finally said.

Laura breathed outward and exuberantly said, "Let's get the pu pu platter! It's got shrimp, chicken wings, teriyaki, egg roll and some other stuff."

"You want a club soda, Johnny?" Steve asked.

"Just Coke when the waiter brings the birthday girl here half of China for her appetizers," Johnny replied.

John A. Curry

They followed the platter with a chicken dish and fried rice, and afterward Steve signaled the waiter to bring on the white cake, small in width but still two tiers high.

He had never seen Laura so happy, so content, and when he presented the two tickets to New York City to her, tickets dated for June and her graduation from Sacred Heart, she just beamed.

"New York! Awesome!" she said, using the tired adjective common to all teens these days. "You and I are going?"

"That's right," Johnny replied. "We'll stay at the St. Moritz near Central Park, take in some shows, go bike riding in the park..."

"Awesome!" She interjected.

He had to agree.

57

Vic had to thank the Boston Police Department for allowing him to keep his detective's badge on retirement. It was proving absolutely essential as he pursued his plan of action. First of all, he had moved out of the place on Wilshire over to a similar roach coach on Sunset. When he registered, he had flashed the badge, coupled with a phony ID which he had acquired over in Hollywood, and told the creepy looking desk clerk he was in from Boston on official business, would pay cash in advance for three days, and wanted no one, absolutely no one, to know he was here. Or else the criminals might get away, he had confided to the clerk, who bore an uncanny resemblance to Elisha Cook, Jr., the guy who had played Wilmer the gunsel in "The Maltese Falcon".

Then once he had planned his next step, he visited the five to ten hotels he knew Ayala might select. By reputation, Ayala would choose a first-class establishment, something like the Beverly Hills Hotel or the Beverly Wilshire or the Hilton.

He had decided to find Ayala before he found him. In addition, he decided not to contact anyone, including Sheridan, back in Boston. If Ayala were out here, that would speak for itself. Why call attention to himself?

And he now had a weapon, a Glock nine found for him by one of his chatty policeman friends at the bar just up the street from the Parker Center. The retired cop had no trouble understanding why another retired cop would want a weapon. Not if you'd served in Los Angeles yourself for years, you didn't. He had pointed Vic to a dealer over in Venice who took care of friends.

Vic strolled on Rodeo Drive near Sunset, window shopping a bit late in the afternoon of his fourth day in LA. He wasn't convinced that the $150.00 white dress shirt in the window was worth five times his $30.00 shirt. He'd much rather have five like the one he was wearing. But to each his own.

He nodded to the doorman outside the Beverly Hills Hotel and proceeded straight to the main desk. He waggled a finger at one of the older clerks and pointed to an open window just off center from the two long lines.

The tall man with the pencil thin mustache walked as erect as he could toward the window. "What may I do for you, sir?" he asked in a self-important tone.

Vic flashed the detective badge and withdrew it quickly before the clerk could really scan it. "I'm in from Boston on official business. We have reason to believe that one of your guests may be involved in a situation back home. I repeat, may be involved." He was deliberately vague and downplayed his comments, trying to elicit a response strictly through his authority.

"Yes, sir. What is it exactly you require of me?" the clerk asked, preening.

"Thank you for your cooperation, Mr.?"

"Artis."

"Mr. Artis," Vic asked, "do you have a Salvatore Ayala of Boston registered with the hotel?"

"One moment, Detective," Artis responded, as he turned and accessed a computer. He tapped the key and scrolled what appeared to be a list of names and studied them. Within a half minute he was back to Vic.

"Excuse my delay. There are two Ayalas registered here, hence the confusion. And they're both from Boston. Salvatore is in room 620 and Paul in 624."

"When did they arrive, Mr. Artis?"

He turned to the computer and hit the key a few more times. "Both on the same day, yesterday."

"Are they here now?" Vic asked.

"You mean right this moment?"

Vic nodded. "Call their rooms. See if there's any response."

Artis scanned the huge slot bank behind him. "All of their keys are missing." He then phoned both rooms but received no response. He shook his head vigorously toward Vic. "No one there," he said.

"When are you on duty, Mr. Artis?" Vic asked.

"I'm the head desk clerk, Detective," he announced solemnly as if he were declaring sainthood. "I'm on duty noon to eight, six days a week, every day but Sunday."

Vic looked him straight in the eye. "I know I can count on your discretion, Mr. Artis. I may check back with you tomorrow. We're going to be observing Mr. Salvatore Ayala for a day or two. When this is all over, I want you to give me the name of your superior so that I can inform him of your great help."

Artis blushed a shade. "Thank you, Detective...I didn't catch your name."

"Detective Quinn."

"Of course, sir. I hope to see you again soon."

They congregated in one of the large conference rooms at Boston Police Headquarters just across the street from Ruggles Station. Fallon and Sheridan sat on one side of the coffee cup strewn new table, Nelson and Harper on the other.

Sheridan addressed the group. "What we have on Hanrahan is very light. No felonies, no misdemeanors, no record at all. He used to run a liquor store over in the Fenway. In later years he sold the business, made a big-time profit."

"When was that?" Fallon asked.

"1998. Seems he's been inactive, retired since then."

"Go through our stuff, Paul," Mike said.

"Graduate of South Boston High School. Boxed professionally for a couple of years. Went to Korea in the early 50's. Came back and married a Dorothy Rafferty. She had a little money. Father was a mid-level Boston banker, one of the up and coming Irish when the Yankees were dominating the banking business."

"Before Terry Murray?" Sheridan laughed.

"Long before him," Harper replied. "With her help, he bought the liquor store over on Queensberry Street."

"Investments? Debts?" Fallon asked.

"Plenty of investments, very few debts," Paul replied. "Looks like a straight citizen all the way."

"Any connection to the Amonti kid?" Mike asked.

Harper shrugged his shoulders. "No calls from Amonti to Hanrahan, and none from Hanrahan's house to the kid, either. Far as we can tell, there's no connection. He has very few friends. People describe him as a loner."

"There's something here we're just not seeing," Nelson said.

Fallon sat back in the conference chair and lifted a hand to his brow. He rubbed the bridge of his nose and pinched it with his thumb and forefinger. "Let's forget Amonti for a minute. The evidence's too light on him anyway. Let's stay with Hanrahan," he said.

"Stay where? He's clean as a new born baby's ass," Harper said.

Mike shook his head. "Flanagan says he wasn't, and something's telling me he was right." He pointed an index finger at Sheridan. "Frank, your records and ours show no criminal activity on Hanrahan's past. But do your people have any records of crimes committed against his business or person?"

"Depends on how far back you want to go, Mike, but yeah, we're pretty well computerized now," Sheridan replied.

"If you can't find anything under his place—what's it called, Paul?"

"Hanrahan Liquors, Queensberry Street."

"If you can't find it on your files, try the <u>Globe</u> and <u>Herald</u>. They show anything concerning robberies, extortion, connections with criminals—anything at all? How long will a search take, Frank?

"Depends. I'll get a top priority on it here, and we'll get to the papers right away. I'll beep you if we find anything."

Mike and Nelson took a lunch break at Brasserie Jo's over at the Colonnade Hotel. Over fresh French bread and grilled chicken Caesar salad they discussed the case, trying to gauge where they were.

"You really think Harper will find any connection he didn't find the first time?" Nelson asked.

"It's worth a second look," he answered, probably too defensively.

In reality, he was pleased to be alone with Marilyn, and he knew there was little chance that Harper would come up with anything a second time around. What he really wanted was the companionship of a woman, an appealing woman. Just the two of them. He felt both guilty and pleased. "I'm sorry I jumped on you about the Amonti kid over in Marblehead. I just wouldn't trust Flanagan not to run to Sansone or Ayala with his name, y'know? They'd kill him anyway, proof or no," Marilyn said.

"Forget it," Mike replied teasely.

Nelson tried a new approach "You were right about the involvement of a cop, I'll give that, but these connections between one suspect and another aren't falling into place."

"You mean Hanrahan to Amonti?"

"I mean anyone to anyone."

"That's because their leader is one clever bastard. A real smart cop."

She broke a small piece off the roll of French bread and daintily placed an eighth of a slab of butter on it.

For the first time, Mike smiled so that the laugh lines around his eyes spread and his nose wrinkled. "You sure you need all that butter?" he asked.

"Wise guy! A girl has to watch her figure, you know."

"I guess," he said, smiling once again.

She looked across at him. "It's good to see you laughing again, Mikey. It really is."

He felt like a young guy on his first date, not wishing to do anything or say anything that might negate the opportunity for a second date.

Maybe she sensed his discomfort or wasn't comfortable with the direction of their conversation because she suddenly was back to the business. "What makes you think the leader is a cop? Why couldn't one of the other guys—the ones in the Bush or Lieberman masks for instance—be the leader?"

"Good question," Mike responded. "I figure at the university the one in the Gore mask took charge, barked the orders, stripped the guards of their weapons. He did the same at South Station. He's the one that skulled Ayala, the guy they really had to neutralize quickly. He also shot Sonny Rossetti. Bush wasn't even at the Brinks job, and Lieberman froze at South Station, according to the wits, and Cheney's the driver. The guy in the Gore mask is a cop and he's more than likely the leader."

Marilyn pushed the remnants of her salad toward the center of the table. "How many are you thinking make up this crew?"

"I figure four totally. At the Brinks site you had three—Gore, Lieberman, and Cheney. Add Bush in at South Station. And we're on to two—Hanrahan and the cop—with Amonti as a weak but possible third. There's one, maybe two, we don't know about."

"You're probably right," Nelson agreed. "but what if the planner, the real mastermind didn't participate? Maybe there's more than four."

Mike nodded. "That's possible. Anything's possible. But I figure the insider, the one who knew when the truck would be at the university, and when Ayala would be at South Station, is the cop. He's the planner."

"How are things at home?" she surprised him by the quick change to a new topic. Maybe she was as unsure as he was.

Two and Out

"Fine, the girls have me wrapped around their little fingers, all thirty of them," he laughed.

Go full speed ahead now or forget the whole idea, he thought. "Marilyn, would you like to go to a play a week from Saturday? I've got tickets to "Dead End" over at the Huntington. Maybe afterward we could have some dinner and drinks somewhere downtown? But if it's not something you'd be comfortable with, if I'm bothering you..."

She raised a hand. "Whoa! Slow down, horsey! The answer is yes. To the first question," she added. "To the second, I'd love to. As for the third, I won't dignify it with an answer."

"Well, that's great! I just thought where we work together, you might think..."

She placed her hand on top of his. "Let's just go where it takes us, Mike. And I'm really glad you asked me. I am," she added tenderly.

His cell phone rang, breaking into their interlude. "It's Sheridan," he whispered to Marilyn. He punched in Sheridan's private number quickly.

"Yeah, Frank?"

"Can you meet me here right away? We have something."

"We're on the way."

58

Sheridan waited until they all were seated. "The cross check shows Hanrahan Liquors was the victim of a major robbery back in 1982—a $25,000 heist by two Black pros who whacked Hanrahan over the head. Other than that robbery, there's been no other involvement with criminals we can find."

"What about the Black pros?" Fallon asked.

Sheridan scanned the sheaf of papers in front of him. "One Wallace Smith of Mattapan and Reggie Logan of Roxbury, two thieves both of whom have records back to the cradle. Smith received a twenty-year sentence, actually served twelve. Before he caught too many rays of sunshine, he was back at Walpole for another robbery, this time a jewelry store over on Washington Street. He's still there. Logan got fifteen years for the Hanrahan heist and was out in ten. No trouble from him since."

"They're pros, but they're not major league pros. You know what I mean?" Nelson said.

"It's a dead end in all probability," Fallon said. "Can we check on Logan anyway? See who he might be seeing these days?"

"Will do," Sheridan said.

"What about the papers?" Fallon asked.

"The Globe guy—Jerry Bernstein—said he'd be back to me by two o'clock."

The wall phone screamed just as he finished the sentence. Sheridan picked it up on the second ring.

"Jerry? Yeah, thanks for getting back to me. I'm putting you on the speaker. I'm with Mike Fallon and Marilyn Nelson of the FBI. Okay, go ahead."

The distinctive voice of the Globe's primary crime reporter resonated throughout the room. "Good afternoon, all. I've got the articles in which you expressed interest. What do you want to know?"

Two and Out

"You said articles, Jerry. This is Mike Fallon. Start with that. How many articles?"

"Just three. The first one concerns the robbery itself on April 17, 1982. The second, a day later, covers the arrest of Wallace Smith and Reggie Logan, and the third their day in court."

"Can you fax copies to us?" Sheridan asked.

"No problem."

"Jerry, Fallon again. Out of curiosity, anything unusual that strikes your eye?"

"Just the trouble at the trial is all."

Fallon frowned. "What trouble? Didn't they get convicted?"

"Just a minute," Jerry responded. "Here it is. The lawyer for Smith claimed that the individual robbed, Philip Hanrahan, was running another business—fake I.D.'s and passports—out of Queensberry Street. Our reporter at the time writes he gave the arresting officer a hard time, inferring a police cover-up.

"They jury didn't buy it. Hanrahan was robbed, pistol-whipped, was hurt badly. And these two guys had a history. They believed the cop."

Fallon pushed his chair back and stood at the table. He saw the look of shock register on Sheridan's face as he scanned the file in front of him once again.

"Who was the arresting officer?" Fallon asked.

"Victor Fleming," Jerry responded.

Sheridan shook his head in disbelief.

"Can you fax that material to us right away care of Detective Sheridan?" Mike asked.

"Consider it done."

"You've been of great help, Jerry," Fallon said.

"Wasn't Hanrahan the guy shot outside Fenway Park the other night?" Jerry asked. "What can you guys tell me?"

"We'll get back to you, Jerry," Sheridan said. "We're just checking any past trouble he may have had."

"Well get back to me, Frank. Let's scratch each other's back, huh?"

"Will do, and thanks again, Jerry."

Mike paced around the table. "Fleming's the connection. He must have pulled Hanrahan out of some deep shit back in '82."

Sheridan continued shaking his head. "It could fit. Flanagan says a retired cop in California. That's where Vic always wanted to be—in Los Angeles. But I don't believe it, Mike. I just don't believe it!"

"Wouldn't Boston have investigated allegations against one of their own that came up at trial?" Nelson asked, curiosity strong in her voice.

"Not necessarily," Sheridan responded. "In those days, the long records of the Black pros, Fleming's reputation, the injuries inflicted on Hanrahan probably would have lead to a conclusion the lawyer was introducing a red herring."

"We need to find him and fast," Mike said. "If he's still in Revere, let's get him in and talk to him. If he's not around, we need to show pictures of Hanrahan to Fleming's neighbors, see if anyone recognizes him."

"I've known him for over thirty years," Sheridan said. "I've never heard of any charges being brought against him. He was a cop's cop."

Fallon ignored the comment. "Marilyn, get a picture of Fleming and go see Hanrahan's wife. See if there's been contact after 1982. Maybe there's a forwarding address known to her or the neighbors. And, people, did Hanrahan show any new money in recent months?

"I've got a feeling we won't find Fleming in Revere. If not, we'll alert agents in LA. And we'll go out there tonight. What Fleming probably doesn't know is that Ayala's either in California right behind him or has someone else out there tracking him down. We better find him first."

Two and Out

Joey Sansone stirred his coffee while he listened to his long-time friend. He said nothing until Vincent Vega had finished, just occasionally glancing about the social club which was half filled at 1 P.M.

When his accomplice was done, Sansone sat forward and held his coffee cup in both hands. As he drank from it, he raised it only slightly and sipped by moving his head down to it. "How well do you know Flanagan?"

Vincent Vega shrugged. "I goes over to Charlestown occasionally for a drink or two, y'know?"

"Keep the fuck out of there," Sansone snapped. "You can't trust those Irishers. You believe what he says?"

Vincent shrugged his shoulders once again. "I got no reason not to."

"Flanagan's a fuckin' woman beater. A drunk. I've known him for years and I don't trust him."

"So what you want me to do?"

"What have you been tellin' him?"

"What do you mean, Joey?"

"What I mean is a dog that carries a bone very frequently takes one away with him. You tellin' him anything about our business?"

Vincent felt the beads of perspiration forming on his upper lip. "I swear to God, Joey..."

Sansone waved him off. "You fuckin' better not, and keep the fuck out of their neighborhood."

"This might be good information," Vincent suggested.

Sansone looked into the coffee cup. "You go up to New Hampshire. Check around the racetrack. See what you can learn about any driver up there who could be involved."

———

Once Artis had told him the Ayalas were still in their rooms at six o'clock, Vic parked his rental up a few yards from the main entrance and waited. He lay the Glock under the newspaper at his side and adjusted the rearview mirror. Behind him, as night slowly descended, he observed scores of pedestrians hovering around the window displays along Rodeo Drive, most of them young and full of life, some walking well-groomed dogs on leashes that looked like they were bejeweled.

At exactly 7:55 P.M., a long, sleek, black limo coasted to a halt directly in front of the hotel. The doorman, dressed in a flowing green cape, approached the vehicle, said something, saluted, and stepped back to the entrance.

Suddenly, through the revolving door walked the Prince of Darkness himself, followed by a shorter, plump man. The other Ayala. Abbott and Costello, Vic thought. The Prince surveyed the area for a brief moment, but didn't appear to be on any special kind of alert. He wore jeans with an open-necked black linen shirt, while the fat one was dressed in a pale gray Italian suit complete with tie. Jesus, Vic thought, between them they were dressed for all occasions.

Slowly, the limo left the curb. If they were out here to find him, they were in no particular hurry, their night on the town obviously of more importance, Vic thought. He fell in behind them. He could have been a half-mile in the rear and still have spotted the lumbering limo so he relaxed, enjoying the music—Jerry Vale singing "You're Breaking My Heart."

They cruised into West Hollywood and stopped at what looked like a trendy restaurant—Dan Tana's. At its entrance, the beautiful people congregated on the sidewalk. Was that Alec Baldwin signing autographs for an elderly couple?

The Ayalas stepped out of the limo, moved around the commotion, probably not knowing Baldwin from Haile Salaisse, Vic thought. They moved into the restaurant while the limo driver eased across the street into a parking lot.

Vic passed by the restaurant and, at the next intersection, made a U-turn back toward the parking lot. About fifty yards from the lot, he pulled to the curb and cut his lights. At close to nine o'clock, the street traffic was considerably reduced and few strollers passed him by. He could observe the limo driver reading by the overhead light, facing the restaurant.

He figured them for two hours at least. Close to 11 P.M before they came out. The way Salvatore was dressed, he couldn't be carrying, although the plump one probably was. Would the limo driver cross the street to accommodate them, or would they walk across to him? The latter, he felt. Or else the driver would disrupt traffic in both directions.

After an hour or so, he noted the light in the limo was out. Nap time for the driver? Probably. Stop it, he corrected himself. Think of the driver as a potential problem as well. He could represent a private limo service, or he could be mob affiliated. It could be three against one, or maybe worse if Ayala were to exit in the company of some Los Angeles family members. Then he would have to abort.

Think alertly but positively, he willed himself. Chances are the two Ayalas were just out enjoying Tinseltown. Chances are they would drink too much, their guard would be down, and the driver was strictly a citizen.

He would soon find out.

59

The good-looking blond agent in the blue poplin suit greeted them at the gate and escorted them toward the baggage area practically on the run.

"Glen Storey," he introduced himself as they moved toward the down escalator. "We've got a car waiting out at the curb. We'll be at the Bureau within fifteen minutes."

"Any news at all?" Mike asked.

"Not much," the agent answered, a note of self-importance in his voice. "There's no Vic Fleming registered at the majors, and we've got agents and the LA police hitting the motels in the city right now. It's going to take some time."

"How about the movie buff lead?" Nelson added.

"We've got his photo out already at the major theaters, but it's a long shot. The dizzy kids that sell the tickets can barely make change let alone notice who they're selling to," Storey replied.

They stood at the carousel waiting for the luggage. "I read about how you caught Jonathan Ordway, the Photographer," Storey enthused. "Pretty impressive."

Fallon stared him down. "That was then; this is now, Agent."

Storey decided to change the topic. "The guy stayed out at Century City last time he was in town, a couple of years ago. We found that out, but he's not there now or at any of the hotels in that area."

"Did anyone think of trying the cop spots around the Parker Center?" Marilyn asked. "He could have been around the downtown looking for company."

Fallon nodded in agreement. "Get copies of the photos around Parker and the vicinity," he directed.

Two and Out

Storey's cell phone rang shrilly. "Yeah?" he responded. He listened for a moment. "Good work, Jim," he said, before punching it off.

"Good news," he said to Fallon and Nelson. Salvatore Ayala's registered at the Beverly Hills. There's a clerk there with a story about a Boston cop inquiring about him yesterday and earlier today."

"Jesus! That's Fleming!" Marilyn said.

"The clever bastard found Ayala before he found him," Mike said admiringly. "Something's going to go down quickly. Do they know where Ayala is now?"

"No," Storey replied. "A limo picked him up around at eight o'clock, but the hotel says it was a private arrangement so they have no record of the livery service. He's out on the town somewhere."

"My guess is Fleming's not far behind," Mike replied.

He turned to Nelson. "And we're always one step behind him." Then he grinned. "But we're closing fast."

Sally Ayala tossed down his third vodka martini of the young night. Enjoy, he said to himself. Tomorrow he and Paulie would get back to more serious business.

Paulie cast his shit eatin' grin at the young waitress two tables over. "You feel like gettin' laid tonight?" he asked Sally.

To Paulie, the Prince of Darkness looked more relaxed than he had for the last two days, or else he never would have asked him the question.

"We'll see. Maybe later," Sally finally answered.

"I already looked into one of them escort services," Paulie announced as if he should have been awarded a gold star or something.

He relaxed a bit more himself, seeing as where his coiled spring cousin appeared to be halfway friendly tonight. "Maybe Joey will give you back our $1.5 million, y' know?"

Sally sobered considerably. "What the fuck you talkin' about?"

Paulie shrugged his shoulders and looked down at his hands. Why was it that Sally made him feel as dumb as a fuckin' stump? "What I mean is we found out about this Fleming guy and aced Hanrahan. Maybe he'll show some gratitude y' know. Show his regard."

Sally pointed to Paulie's scotch. "How many of them you had, Paulie?"

"Why?" Paulie asked defensively.

"Why? Because I think your brains are fried enough as is, that's why. You fuckin' tellin' me that Joey Sansone is gonna return $1.5 million to us? In your dreams. Not until we get all his money back. And what do you think the chances of that are? Huh, Paulie? These fuckin' guys dressed up like the candidates, we got one so far. One. And zero money. Any of this registerin', Paulie?"

Paulie decided to act confident, or rather show some confidence in Sally. Anything rather than sit here and be insulted the rest of the night.

"You'll find Fleming, Sally. No one busts your balls," he said.

Sally started bouncing on his toes, a bad sign. "And when we find him, what do we do then, Paulie?"

How the fuck should I know? Paulie thought to himself. Whatever he said, Sally would have a better answer. But maybe the question was the softball it looked to be. "We beat the fucker's brains out," Paulie replied adamantly.

Sally looked to the heavens for guidance or deliverance from the fools on earth that surrounded him. "Wrong answer, Paulie." He signaled the pretty brunette for another vodka martini. One or two more of them, Paulie thought, and I'll be in the ground with Hanrahan.

"We have to capture him alive, Paulie. That thought ever enter that vacuum you call a mind? 'Cause if we don't get him alive, we're back to nowhere with no more suspects and no

Two and Out

money. If we do, we'll torture the fuckin' thief, find out who the others are, and get our money back. Maybe then Joey gives us back our money. So we got to get the drop on him. Cabeesh?"

"I'm with you," Paulie replied too quickly.

"That's what worries me," Sally said sarcastically.

For a moment the Prince of Darkness was quiet, his eyes following the pretty brunette back to their table. She smiled the smile the waitresses saved for those they perceived to be big spenders, one of those "you can fuck me for a price" looks.

That seemed to uncoil him for the moment. "Paulie, go call that escort service now. No, wait, never mind. Let's do it back at the hotel. And when you call, set me up with a brunette, a pretty one."

Paulie came alive again now that the conversation was back to more pleasant topics. "Well, then, let's go, Salvatore."

"Here's the bill," Sally said, passing it across to him.

As they stopped at the men's room, and paused at the urinals, Sally surprised him again.

"You carryin' that extra price?" he asked.

Paulie moved to the mirror and threw some cold water on his face. "Yeah, I'm wearin' the shoulder holster, and I've got a back-up on my hip."

Sally looked around the elegant wash room to be sure they were alone. "Let me have the back-up. I walked out undressed tonight."

"Yeah, sure," Paulie replied. What you gonna do? Shoot one of the whores?"

Sally didn't reply. He just stared at him through the mirror with that Richard Wildmark, don't-fuck-with-me look on his face.

60

"Doug Amonti, meet Mickey Mouse." Tony laughed as he joined their hands. His little boy tried to move behind him, but Mickey would have none of it.

"Hey, Doug! Where you from?" the animated figure asked, bopping him off the head with a soft touch.

"The Cape," Doug shyly offered, his gaze shifting from Mickey to his father and back again.

"Which Cape?" Mickey countered. "Good Hope? Kennedy? Cape Fear? Cape Cod?"

"That's it!" Doug replied. The last one!"

"Actually we're moving out here to San Diego," Tony said. "This is a promised stopover on the way."

"You want a hug?" Mickey asked, and before Doug could respond he raced around them in a circle three times, fell backward onto the asphalt, and urged Doug to pounce on him. Doug yelled with glee as from the sidelines Minnie Mouse and Donald Duck scampered to join the party.

Five hours ago they had arrived at John Wayne Airport in Orange County, just a couple of hours south of Los Angeles. They had checked into a motel outside the airport and rented a car for the short ride to Disneyland. They would stay here for two days and then complete the two-hour drive down to San Diego. On Monday, he would enroll Doug in that special school for the learning disabled in San Diego that Grace had arranged through her friend. And then he would seek a job, wait for the suitcase to arrive from Mrs. Adams.

How safe was he out here? He didn't know, for sure. He no longer had the Glock. That was one thing you couldn't transport on the cross-country flight. He would look into finding a weapon down around the border.

Two and Out

It was now five days since the report of Hanrahan's death had appeared, and as each day went by, he felt a bit safer. Maybe the gray man's death had nothing to do with Ayala.

As Doug jumped up and raced after a fleeing Mickey Mouse, Tony thought of Grace. Only one day and he missed her already.

One, two, three. Do it in three steps just as he had contemplated for the last two hours. Vic Fleming glanced at his watch. They should be coming out of the restaurant at any moment.

He thought through the approach once again. When they exited, go for the short, plump guy first. If anyone was carrying, it would be him. Second, take out the limo driver. Chances are he was provided by the local Mafioso. Thirdly, go for the Prince of Darkness himself. Dressed in jeans and linen shirt, there was no chance he was carrying. One, two, three and done.

It would be much easier if the limo stayed right where it was. If the driver moved across the boulevard, so be it. But that could be a problem right outside the restaurant and all.

And there they were, striding out of the eatery, the doorman speaking to them, the Prince shaking his head, and pointing across the street to the darkened limo. He walked to the edge of the sidewalk, his hands at his side, and then for an instant his right hand was at his back. Just a gesture? Hitching up the jeans? Vic thought so.

As they started across the boulevard the lights appeared on the limo. Vic quietly stepped out of his vehicle, his hands out of sight. To any observer, he was crossing to the restaurant.

He deliberately waited until Ayala and the plump man were more than halfway across the street, the illumination of the lights on the limo certain to cut down on their visibility. When he was within ten yards of them and halfway across the street himself, he turned as if he had forgotten something and advanced quickly from behind them.

Say nothing. Just do it. One, two, three. He tried to stay in the shadows on the edge of the illumination to give the driver less of a target. He had the advantage of surprise on his side anyway, unless the driver had something in his hand to begin with.

Paulie Ayala turned at the sound of approaching footsteps, not in any way concerned at the noise. So he never knew what hit him. A burst from the Glock sent him reeling backward to the pavement, his head bouncing hard off the concrete, like a fighter having taken a hard blow, and then an even harder blow when his head met the canvas.

Without hesitation, Vic knelt on the pavement and fired a second burst from the automatic toward the windshield of the limo. Although he couldn't tell for sure, the driver must have pitched forward onto the wheel because suddenly the horn screamed in a constant shrill.

Within a second he turned to Ayala, whose right hand was coming forward from behind his back, fast and rhythmically. Later, he would remember that it all happened at once. The searing pain tore into his stomach just as Ayala tumbled backward from the force of the headshot.

Vic stumbled to his feet and walked the few steps to the prone Ayala. From behind him he heard the screams of two or three people near the restaurant. He stood over Ayala and fired another burst into his head. Without looking back, he staggered the short distance to his car, started the ignition, and then kept the lights off as he drove right by the restaurant.

"Ayala's down in the street over in West Hollywood. Across from a restaurant—Dan Tana's," Nelson yelled from her position across the street from the Beverly Hills Hotel. Mike nodded and gestured for her to join them.

"I know where it is. We can be there in ten minutes," Storey said.

"As soon as she's in the car, go!"

Vic pressed his right hand as tight as he could across his stomach. He drove down Wilshire toward his motel, his left hand doing all the work.

One bad thing about being a cop was that you knew too much. And he knew there were few wounds as bad as a stomach wound. The red flow was cakey with a small amount of black mixed in. The pain had not yet overwhelmed him, but he also knew that was only momentary, as he was still in shock from the wound itself.

He pulled into the motel lot and sat for a moment waiting both to orient himself to his surroundings and to be sure he could lift himself out of the seat when the right time came. In the dark he studied the hole, a much smaller one than he had anticipated, given the large amount of blood saturating his shirt.

God bless motels, he thought. With luck he would be at his front door in just five steps and with minimal exposure. Looking around one more time, he opened the car door with his left hand and planted his left foot. He leaned against the open door for support before he stepped completely out. As he advanced toward the door, the pain level rose. He pressed his right hand more firmly against the wound and with his left hand inserted the key into the door.

On entering, he snapped on the light and stumbled toward the bathroom. Tentatively, he slipped out of his linen shirt and began washing around his wound. As soon as he wiped away the blood, new clusters of red erupted from the hole. He held the towel tight to the stomach and dragged himself to the bed.

He needed medical attention and quickly. If history was any precursor of events to follow, then he estimated he had less than an hour to live without that assistance.

He elevated the pillow against the headboard and lay down, his right hand on the Glock set on the table next to the bed. He needed to think.

They were halfway to West Hollywood when the call came to Storey. A Los Angeles motorcycle cop had discovered the rental provided to Vic Fleming over at the Blue Penguin Coach on Wilshire.

"Forget Ayala. How far are we from the Blue Coach?" Fallon asked.

"Three minutes," Storey replied.

"Then go!" Fallon said.

Storey applied the brakes and reversed direction, cutting across the divided highway, almost causing an ongoing truck to jackknife in the process.

"No sirens, just hit it," Mike ordered.

In the back seat, Nelson pulled out her P7 9mm and looked it over. While Storey tore down Wilshire, Mike grabbed the phone and asked to be patched through to the motorcycle cop.

"Officer Fielding here," the youthful voice replied confidently.

"Officer, this is Special Agent Fallon of the FBI. Listen to me carefully. Do you know which room Fleming is in?"

"I've kept out of sight after talking with the manager. Fleming's in 6A, ground floor under the name of James Quinn. The manager identified the photo."

"Good work, Officer. Stay back. We're a minute away."

61

Vic lay there, concentrating. It was easy enough to calculate his options. Zero and none. He was slowly dying, and even if he were to summon medical help, he faced a lifetime in prison if not the gas chamber itself. And even assuming he could beat the charges against him both here and in Boston, Sansone would send others to kill him. The Mafia would now be more determined than ever to bring him down.

If he were gone, then Brian and Lieberman would be protected and in the clear as best he could determine. He was the lone connection back to them. And if Amonti had been betrayed by Hanrahan as well, then he was already dead. If not, then with his demise, the Amonti kid might be home free as well.

Better that he not survive. Better all around. He would just lie here and think pleasant thoughts until the pain knocked him unconscious, until the blood stopped flowing.

He yearned for his video and his CD, to both see and hear her for the final time. But that was not going to happen. So he improvised, drifted a bit and thought of her old movies. He smiled wistfully through the hurt, remembering how well Faye had blended with up and coming Betty Grable in "Tin Pan Alley." He wished he could see them together one more time doing that number. What was it? The Sheik of Araby.

He wasn't going to be able to take that full tour of the Fox Studios, but he wasn't really disappointed. Every movie buff had his imagination, and in his mind he had toured New York Avenue, the western sets, the Brooklyn of Betty Smith's novel, and countless other places where he had lived vicariously.

He looked at the Glock at his side and thought about putting it in his mouth, eating the thing, ending it all. If Ayala's henchmen were around, if they were to come upon him, he would, rather than divulge what he knew. But otherwise, he was no coward. He wouldn't commit the cardinal sin against his religion.

He heard the noise for the first time. Maybe the shuffling of feet from outside. He tried to concentrate, to shut out other sounds, to lay perfectly quiet. He picked up the Glock and kept it at his side.

Nothing. Maybe it was his imagination. He felt woozy now, the pain also increasing. He studied the towel, now virtually saturated.

Then he heard a very slight noise at the door, as if someone were readying a quick open-and-kick. Either Ayala's people or the police. The technique was simple enough. Slip the key quickly into the lock, turn it, and push the door. When and if the door hit the chain, then the second man would kick it in. With the technique you were usually in the room before the target had a chance to react.

In one quick motion, Vic set the Glock against the side of his head. Suddenly, the knob turned and someone kicked in the door, and Mike Fallon exploded into the room screaming, "FBI! Freeze!"

Fallon. All the way out here in L.A. So it was over. How had he gotten this close? Somehow, it had to connect to Hanrahan. No matter. There was no way out.

He wasn't going to be taken alive, and he wasn't going to exchange gunfire with a fellow cop. He had some element of pride. Ayala was one thing, Fallon another.

What would be the last thing he would see, the last thought he would think? Something pleasant so he would not feel more pain.

That part was easy. He saw her cavorting in that harem sarong, then standing by the telephone dialing up John Payne, letting him know that "You'll Never Know."

And then his theater went completely dark.

62

"Congratulations, Mikey. To you and the whole team." Sam Morris wore his best suit and his $80.00 Stephano Ricci tie in anticipation of the impending press conference. "I want you all downstairs at 11 A.M. We'll introduce Harper and Nelson, and I'll want you to say a few words Mike."

"Christ, Sam, what are we doing?" Mike asked, agitated. "We caught two of them as far as we know. There's at least two more, maybe three still loose on the streets."

Sam struck his bureaucratic pose, the father-knows-best one. He sat behind his desk, ensuring that Mike understood that distance meant authority. Still, he tried a soft approach. "Mikey, this is a big win for the Bureau," he said calmly.

"Says who?" Mike interrupted.

"Says the Director and me," Sam replied. We—you—that is—chased down the leader of a brilliant crime crew, causing him to avoid capture by killing himself. We were right there, outside his motel, you and Nelson tracking him down. And you made the connection between Fleming and Hanrahan, solving Hanrahan's murder along the way. In the process two vicious criminals—the Ayalas—got washed away as well."

Mike scowled at his boss. "Jesus, Sam. You're losing it. You ought to go write for Hollywood."

Sam waggled his index finger across the desk. "The Bureau has triumphed, Mickey. We recovered close to a million dollars of the stolen money from Fleming. We hope to recover the balance up ahead..."

"That's bullshit and you know it Sam. With Fleming and Hanrahan dead, we don't have a clue as to who or where..."

"Stop interrupting me, Mikey," Morris ordered. "We're declaring a victory, whether you like it or not. We need a goddamn victory with all this shit about Bulger and our people. Can't you see that? If we catch the others, great. And we probably will in time. If not, we're not going to worry about it. Because today we announce our great success."

"I'm getting a headache," Mike said.

"My sense is you'll be getting a promotion soon," Sam replied. "So be there and enjoy the limelight. And make sure your guys are there."

"What about Boston? Especially Sheridan. They sharing in this?"

Sam looked indignant. "Of course."

"Well be sure to give them credit before our relationship with them goes down the tube altogether."

"I'll do that."

"We done?" Mike asked.

"You really think we're stuck on the others?" Sam asked.

Mike ran his hand through his hair. "We've run through all known associates of Fleming's and Hanrahan's. Nothing."

"What about that Amonti kid?"

"A blank wall," Mike replied. "He doesn't connect at all to Fleming, and we can't find anyone who saw him with Hanrahan. On his trip out to California we ran through his luggage without him knowing it. Nothing. He's working out in San Diego as a mechanic, not spending beyond his means. He's a dead end. Like I said, Sam, right now we're dead in the water. So we shouldn't..."

Sam put up a hand. "Enough. The FBI needs an improved image. We need heroes. The man who caught the Photographer has now caught the Candidates' leaders. In time, he'll catch the others. Let me handle the press, and you handle the street. And today, for God's sake, smile and say the right things."

"Whatever you say, William Randolph Hearst," Mike replied, standing and smiling. "Long as we can keep after them."

"Get the fuck out of here," Sam laughed. "And be back at 11:00."

Two and Out

Vic Fleming and the Ayalas dead in Tinseltown. Brian Hughes stared hard at the headlines in the Globe and at the accompanying pictures. He sat in his faculty office and occasionally glanced out the window to the street below. Students dashed through the swirling rain as the wind cupped the red and orange leaves from the surrounding trees and tossed them in all directions.

It was in moments like these that the rigorous discipline required of the academic was of assistance. Logic was now important, to reason correctly and not let his emotions overwhelm him. Fleming had been careless, trusting whoever this Hanrahan was.

He folded the newspaper and placed it on his desk. Standing, he peered out the window and smiled broadly to himself. Whatever, it appeared he had overestimated Fleming. But he personally had made no mistakes. Nor would he.

Vincent Vega hadn't enjoyed his last conversation with Joey Sansone. So this time, he decided he would lie. He drove up to New Hampshire, circled the Portsmouth rotary, and drove right back to the North End.

"So what did you find out?" Joey asked him.

"The Irisher didn't know shit. I asked a lot of people up there about drivers who mighta' been involved at South Station. Nobody knew nuttin'."

Joey Sansone threw down the straight whiskey and followed it with the large drink of water. "Well forget about it then. That drunk Irisher didn't figure to know anything. You keep the fuck away from the micks. You talk with them too much."

He poured himself a double and looked around the club. "With Sally and Paulie dead out on the coast, we don't need any more trouble right now. I told that dumb fucker Sally, he was too smart for his own britches. He's huntin' them, and they gun him down. It figures."

"You want me to do anything else, Joe?" Vincent asked.

"Just keep your eyes and ears open. Maybe we'll get a real lead from someone other than those drunks in Charlestown."

Vincent Vega stood and walked toward the door. Billy Flanagan was a loose cannon who sooner or later would open his mouth once too often and have him in deep trouble with Joey. On his own, in the week or so, he would shut down that motor permanently.

Johnny Casey watched the last part of the 6:00 P.M. newscast the night before the election and then shut off the television set. For some reason he felt like a long walk, even though the early November night was cool and dank. He put on his mixed cashmere and wool overcoat, locked the apartment, and descended the three flights to Lewis Street.

Weeks had gone by now since he had read of Fleming's death along with the Ayalas. Initially, he had been petrified that either the FBI or the Mafia were now on to him. But he held his composure and with his new found confidence, decided to do exactly what Brian had demanded—no contact with him. And the days had passed. He had to believe that however Ayala and the FBI had been lead to Fleming, he was not involved. He was in the clear.

He walked west on Green Street, passing his old elementary school, now utilized as a home for the elderly. The long spiral fire escape still ran along its side, extending from the ground to the third floor against the old red brick wall. Across the street, St. Joseph's Rectory stood, and from his position, he could see the huge spires of the church itself at the next corner. On countless occasions he had marched out of the school to the beat of a piano and a drum as he and his classmates paraded in lines of two on their way to the church to confess their sins every Friday morning.

And that was exactly what he intended this evening. He would try to make his peace with God, see if He could forgive him or at least pass him a sign of understanding. He headed directly for the church itself.

The Gothic cathedral, like the old school and the rectory, was built of red brick, its steeple hovering like a sentinel high in to the skyline. He crossed Union Street, deciding to enter the less ornate first floor of the church, rather than the second floor with its magnificent beauty.

He opened the door just as he and his classmates had done back in the 70's. On entering, he touched the holy water and made the Sign of the Cross. He surveyed the rows of wooden benches before him and in the distance, the altar itself. He was alone in the church with his God, and suddenly the moment overwhelmed him. He willed himself toward one of the two confessionals along the rear of the church and sat in the last row just outside them. Again, he thought back to his youth, sitting in this very pew in this very seat, awaiting his turn to speak to the priest and through him, to God. Woe to the one who spoke in church or laughed or even grinned, especially with Sister Drucilla parading back and forth along the aisle seeking sinners and transgressors.

Although there was no priest in the confessional tonight, he hoped God would hear him. He stood and entered the confessional on his right, knelt on the pad, now alone in the dark with only his Maker.

"Bless me Father, for I have sinned. It has been four months since my last confession. But for years I had been confused, Father, and had lost my way. I have failed you in the past whenever you called on me to serve, and I have allowed that failure to follow me always, Father. In turn, I have failed myself and my family, not being there for them when they needed me. I am so like the lost shepherd, Father, and it is my hope that you can see, despite my crimes, that because of you I have found the way.

"I have stolen from others, Father, but in the process I believe I've become a better man. I have reconnected with my family. I can see the love for me in my daughter's eyes, and I now live for her, my God, to redeem myself, to make my life worth living. I no longer drink or gamble, and the money I have stolen—evil money—I have given back anonymously to charities, keeping only enough to provide for Laura's education.

"Help me to lead a good life, Father. Help me to be a better person. Please forgive me for my weaknesses, and help me to serve you by serving others, through my teaching and my good works."

He bowed his head and thought for a moment. He peered through the wire mesh of the confessional and made the Sign of the Cross before standing. He stepped into the dim light of the church itself, his eyes adjusting. Slowly he walked down the main aisle to the altar itself. He knelt directly in front of the statue of Jesus and began his Act of Contrition.

When he had finished, he remained kneeling, studying the visage of his Lord and Master. What was there in that beautiful face? Ambiguity. That element of religion that allows us to see a kind or an angry Father. He knelt there for the longest time, repeating the Act of Contrition every few minutes. And he saw a forgiving God, full of love and understanding, looking back at him, urging goodness upon him.

After an hour he stood and retreated to the rear of the church and then looked back to the altar once more. And then he walked out to the cold night, remembering his return to the school with his classmates years ago, all of them temporarily cleansed of sin, once again pure in heart with at least, then and now, the chance of remaining that way in the future.

Two and Out

On Election Day itself, Tony Amonti pulled the lever for Bush and Cheney, wishing he could vote for Cheney for president. After voting, he worked the full day at the track, loving the grease, the smell of the fumes, the car talk. He took pride in his good work and in compliments tossed his way by the chief mechanic and the wealthy customers.

At four o'clock, he crossed over to Coronado, to the private school where Doug awaited him at the day care center adjacent to the facility. From the enclosed knoll, Doug saw him park the used Toyota at the curb and waved to him frantically, two or three of the other boys joining him in a race to the fence.

"Hello, Mr. Amonti!" a tousled-hair Mexican boy greeted him enthusiastically.

"How are all you boys doing?" Tony asked.

Next door a tall, middle-aged woman descended the school steps and waved a friendly arm toward him.

"One minute, Doug," he said as the boys clamored around the fence.

Tony raised a single finger, asking for a minute or her time. She walked casually toward him and waited at the edge of the fence.

"How are you, Mrs. Morgan?" he asked.

"It's a beautiful day in Coronado, Mr. Amonti, so all's right in my world," she replied. And how are you?"

"I was just curious about how Doug's been progressing."

She paid him and all parents the kind of attention that most private schools provided. For $8,000 annually, the faculty was available, friendly, and concerned. Grace's friend had recommended the Courtney School, and he had been very pleased with the first month.

She answered his question with a question. "Are you working with him on those phonics exercises I gave you?"

"Every night," he replied.

"Well, it's working, Mr. Amonti. Indeed it is." She smiled at him over her glasses. "Doug's behind, mind you, but he's both trying and improving. He's interested in helping himself and that's a big part of any improvement. And he seems to like the other children."

"He's happy here. I can tell," Tony replied.

"You know, Mr. Amonti, almost every child can eventually learn where there is parental interest and involvement. You're a role model for him. Just keep it up. And once he's on a solid learning curve, he'll be happy here or anywhere."

Later that night, they were reading a story—the one with a great number of long "e" sounds when the phone rang.

"Hi, you," Grace began.

"Hi, yourself."

"I'm looking forward to seeing you at Thanksgiving. Got my ticket. I'll be there the day before."

"I can't wait," Tony replied. "Doug and I are planning to kidnap you and keep you here."

Grace laughed into the phone. "That might not be necessary. You and I need to settle on a place. I can't afford these long distance phone calls much longer. You're coming here for Christmas, right?" Grace asked.

"Yuck! Christmas on the Cape!" he teased.

"Hey! You want me for Turkey Day in San Diego, with its blistering heat, when I could be in New England at the best time of the year, then get here in December, bub!"

"Maybe I can do better than that," he said. "Doug needs this year out here. I'll try to keep an open mind about coming back there, maybe finding a job as a mechanic on the South Shore and commute from the Cape. All I ask is you keep an open mind about coming out here. Let's spend the time between now and June—you know—the vacation weeks—coming to some agreement. He wants to be near you, you know. He misses you too."

Grace let a moment go by. "All I know is I miss you, and I want to be where you are," she said.

"We'll be together somewhere, Grace."

"Mrs. Adams wanted to know whether you received the suitcase."

"A few days ago," he replied calmly, "and everything was fine."

For most of the last month, he had remained decidedly on edge. When he first read of Vic Fleming's death and of the shooting of the Ayalas, complete with pictures or otherwise Fleming's name would have meant nothing to him, he had nearly panicked. The chase had led the Ayalas to California. If they were on to Gore, then they were probably on to him.

But then time had passed. Stories from Boston featured the FBI agent—Fallon—who had braced him. It had came out that Hanrahan had betrayed Fleming to the Ayalas. He began to relax a bit. There was no way the Mafia would have waited this long if they knew of his involvement.

With each passing day, he felt more secure. He had arranged for most of the money to be placed under a fictitious name down in the Cayman Islands, and he had been spending sensibly as well. He had begun to think that if everything continued to go well, he could return to Massachusetts at the end of the school year or Grace might yet be convinced to come here.

"Doug says to tell you he loves you," Tony said.

"And I him, Tony. See you both soon!"

"I love you."

"A girl can tell."

"Can a girl tell what I'm thinking about right now?"

"Take a cold shower every day between now and Thanksgiving."

"And on Thanksgiving?"

"We'll talk about that when I get there."

John A. Curry

63

On January 20, 2001, Brian Hughes sat alone on the beach in Aruba, directly facing the sun, its rays baking his body bronze. He lay on his back on the lounge chair, his arms stretching to hold on to the upper frame of the chair.

The CBS reporter described the events of Inauguration Day in great detail. Brian could picture the new president stepping to the podium through the cold rain, confident and humbled. Following a tumultuous year, a year of ups and downs, he had emerged victorious. The year 2000 had been a good year for George W. Bush. A very good year, and now he had the right to glow in the limelight, to accept the adoration of a public ready to accept him.

Brian smiled as he considered the irony. Bush had won. And he had won. Cheney had become vice president and the kid, the driver whose name he did not know, had come through as well. Gore had come close to winning, but in the end as with Fleming, was dead in the water. And Lieberman? Like Johnny, he was still there, still a U.S. senator, his future to be determined.

And the FBI and the Mafia were nowhere in sight. He had used his superior intellect to outfox them all. Idiots.

As the reporter enthused about the changing of the guard, Brian reached into his duffel bag to find some protection against the sun's increasingly strong rays. He looked around the nearly deserted beach, most people having left for lunch in order to escape the noon high sky or to view the Inauguration on television.

He placed the Bush mask directly over his face and began to listen to what he hoped would be a brief Inaugural address.

———

"You don't know how to cook much?" Melissa asked.

Two and Out

"Our mother could cook," Nicole announced proudly.

"Girls! Girls! Please! Marilyn is our guest," Mike chided.

"That's all right, Mike. I can do more than boil water, girls, but not much more. I've been too busy out there capturing criminals."

"Did you ever shoot anyone?" Melissa asked.

Mike threw up his hands. "Okay. That's it. Jessica would you organize the inquisitors and see if they can wash and dry the dishes as well as they can talk."

Jessica smiled across at Marilyn. "They're really happy to meet you," she said.

"Are you going to marry Daddy?" Melissa asked as she started toward the sink.

"Come on, Melissa. Help us out," Jessica said, steering her little sister toward the sink.

Later that night they sat alone in the living room looking out the window to a clear night. In the distance, the Prudential Center covered the skyline and along St. Botolph Street college students walked hand in hand on their way to the shopping centers at the Pru or up in Copley Square.

"So what did you think of my three girls?" Mike asked.

"Well, I'm no expert in bringing up kids, but they seem well adjusted."

"I can tell they like you," he said, placing his arm around her shoulders and drawing her close.

"Well, they better," she replied, feigning anger, "because I sure as hell like their father."

"They just need a little time to get used to you," he replied.

"I'm in no hurry, Mikey. We'll do it right."

They stood staring out the window without speaking for a moment. "A penny for your thoughts," Marilyn whispered into his ear.

"I was just thinking of the Candidates. Where the hell are the other two or three?"

John A. Curry

Marilyn touched his lips with her index finger. "We may never know. It's been four months now, and not a word, not a sign, from anyone."

"It's not over yet, Marilyn. Something will happen. Someone else could turn."

She raised her lips in search of his. And he drew her toward him, pressing his mouth to hers, the excitement and discovery of new love encompassing them.

—The End—

About the Author

John A. Curry is President Emeritus of Northeastern University. He is a graduate of that university and earned his doctorate from Boston University. From 1989-96 he served as president of Northeastern University, elevating its status to that of a research institution.

His first novel *Loyalty*, available through 1st Books, was rated "a four-star novel" by critic David Brudnoy's Bookshelf and labeled "a truly successful first novel."

Two and Out is Curry's second novel. He lives in Saugus, Massachusetts, where he is currently at work on a third crime fiction novel, the sequel to *Loyalty*.

Printed in the United States
713300001B